THE BEARING STONE

THE BEARING STONE

Margaret Williams-Coker

Strategic Book Publishing and Rights Co.

Strategic Book Publishing & Rights Co., LLC
USA | Singapore
www.sbpra.net

Cover design by bob@newenglandstandard.com

For information about special discounts for bulk purchases, please contact Strategic Book Publishing and Rights Co., Special Sales at bookorder@sbpra.net.

ISBN: 978-1-952269-85-1

Dedication

To my sons:
James, Robert, Michael, and Andrew

Acknowledgements

I am deeply grateful to those who have served to inspire this novel: my family of origin, my sons and their partners, my colleagues, and my dearest friends. In particular, Kim Hostig and Sharon Bova, who during the most difficult of times walked beside me. I am also thankful to Laurie Smith-Teal, who with her spiritual gifts helped me work through the events of my past, and to James V. Miller and the late Sarah Morgan for their many years of support. I much appreciate the honest feedback from my friend, Hadia Stephanou. And finally, to Dana Goettler and Rebecca Copp for their edits, time, and hard work. Thank you.

PART I

LIMESTONE

Chapter 1

It was Saturday, a beautiful day in early April. Beautiful, that is, if one looked up. The last snowfall in late March had dumped another eight inches on the ground. As it melted, all the muck underneath rose to the surface; wet gray leaves smashed into the mud, windblown newspapers all wet and turning to paste, sticks, branches and dead weeds together painted a backdrop of misery. It was the ugly part of the year. People had had enough. Even though they knew it could snow again, the day beckoned them to clean up the mess. They didn't mind that. Any reason to be outside was good enough.

Nate Bearing longed to be out there too, but for him it was just another day in the shop with his father, Alexander. He was hopeful, though. It was supposed to reach seventy degrees today. Maybe they would quit early. He and his father had been working six, sometimes seven days a week. With the ground thawing, graves could now be dug, and the backlog of monuments could be set into place. They were essentially caught up on their orders, and many headstones awaited their final destinations to the cemeteries.

Nate was working on a special project. He was carving a stone, roughing out the form of a lamb. It was for a child. The parents had chosen the lamb to honor their child's innocence. It wasn't often that he and his father sculpted the monuments themselves; it was simpler and far less expensive to choose from the inventory of pre-carved stones that they engraved. His father was just finishing the engraving on a gray granite monument, one of the last orders from early March. He yelled over across the shop.

"Nate, could you give me a hand over here?"

Nate put down his chisel and walked across the floor to the sandblasting room, kicking up stone chips along the way. His boots crunched with each step, reminding him that today was cleanup day.

"Whew, this one must have taken you a while," Nate remarked as he examined the detailed border around the lettering. It was a vine that twisted its way to the upper right-hand corner, a circuitous route leading to deeply carved rose blossoms. The many leaves and curls were more elaborate than their usual engraving jobs.

"Yeah, it did," his father replied. "At least eight hours. Thank God, they picked a design that I could order. I can't imagine having to cut out all the stencils myself, considering how busy we've been. This one had eight depth levels."

Most of the time, the lettering in the stone was engraved at the same depth, unlike that of the piece his father had just finished. What made this job even more challenging was that it required an accurate and keen eye. The blasting machine didn't know when to stop.

"I want to get this over to the cemetery on Monday. I have another one to set there too. That one is already in the truck. Let's move this one over there."

The monument was already on the pallet mule ready to roll. Nate knew that his father didn't really need his help to do it. This stone was smaller than many. Nate liked working with his father. Sometimes though, has father annoyed him, especially when he assumed that Nate didn't know how to do something, when in fact he did.

"Dad?"

"Yeah," his father said without looking at him as they guided the mule.

"How'd we get so good at this?"

His father laughed. "Good at what, rolling stones?"

"No, you know what I mean. Stonework … cutting, sculpting. All that."

"I don't know," Alexander mused. "I guess it's in the blood. Your grandfather, Manuel, was a master at it all. I mean, a *master*."

"I thought all he did was build walls."

His father stopped pushing. After an uncomfortable silence, he chose his words carefully as he looked at Nate.

"Build walls, you say? As if that is nothing. Son, your grandfather didn't just build walls, he was an architect and an artist. His Mayan ancestors especially, your ancestors and mine, excelled in mathematics and geometry. As far as I'm concerned, they wrote the book on building with stone."

Nate felt embarrassed. He was not expecting this. "Dad, I didn't mean it that way. I'm sorry."

"No need to be sorry," his father replied as he started pushing again, "I just want you to remember your roots. That's all. Now let's get this thing moving."

The truck was equipped with a crane and a hoist. It also carried the materials and tools needed for setting the headstone on its base, and even a portable compressor that allowed them to engrave on-site if needed. They pulled the straps through the spaces between the stone and the pallet and carefully lifted it up and into the bed of the truck. They laid it on a pallet next to a larger but simpler stone. The base stones were there as well.

Nate went back to work on the lamb. His father went back to the sandblaster and turned the compressor on. Nate appreciated the sound that rattled the corrugated steel walls. Better than having his nerves rattled by his father. His father was a man of few words, much like his grandfather, Manuel. Maybe that was a Mayan thing too. Yes, he thought, his grandfather was a master. No one knew stone like he did. He deeply admired them and was grateful to be a part of a family business that was so well respected in the community. Started by Manuel over forty years ago, it had seen many changes. His grandfather was an artisan who eventually expanded into contracting and distribution. However, when he retired his son downsized the company to specialize in making and selling monuments. The Bearing Stone Co. was quite successful.

The compressor finally stopped. Nate was hopeful. Maybe they would also stop working. He longed to be with Haley today but didn't want to ask his father for time off. He struggled to focus on his work but found his mind wandering, thinking about the last time he was with Haley. He was so preoccupied, chisel hitting stone, that he didn't hear his father coming up behind him.

"I was just outside," his father said. "It's a nice day."

"So I've noticed," said Nate.

"Why don't we take a break?"

Nate thought he meant a coffee break. "Nah, I'm good. I'll wait till lunchtime."

Nate's father laughed. "No, I don't mean a coffee break, I mean, why don't we take the rest of the day off?"

Nate wanted to turn around and hug his father. It was exactly what he had hoped for.

"Really? Does that mean you want some help cleaning up outside, or does that mean I can take the rest of the day off?"

"Take off," his father said. "We'll clean up tomorrow afternoon."

"Maybe I'll go spend some time with Haley. Between her work and mine, we haven't been able to get together much lately. I'm thinking I may spend the night."

His father smiled. "How could I have guessed? I could do without you around for a while too."

"Good one, Dad. I'll get myself together and be on my way. Anything you need in town?"

"If I do, I can get it myself."

Nate crossed the lot, went right to the house that he shared with his father, and called Haley. He was hoping she hadn't already booked herself up for the day. She answered on the second ring.

"Hello?" It was more of a question than a greeting.

"Haley ..."

"Nate! Aren't you working today?"

"I did work—all morning. My father decided we would quit early today. I've even got tomorrow morning off. Do you have plans today?"

Haley hesitated. Nate felt his heart sink a little. "Well," she said, "I'm supposed to go see my cousin today, but I can go do that now. When will you be here?"

"As soon as I can. How much time do you need?"

"Give me a couple of hours, OK? I need to pick up some groceries for her and the kids and then spend a little time with her. I shouldn't be too long."

"OK," said Nate. "Take your time. I'll be there in an hour. If you're not there, I'll just let myself in."

"Help yourself to the refrigerator. Then again, you usually do," she laughed.

"Yeah, yeah, yeah. Promise I won't eat you out of house and home."

"Well, if you do, you're just going to have to take me out to dinner tonight."

"Way ahead of you. Think about where you'd like to go."

Haley couldn't wait to see him but didn't say so. Instead, she said, "Look, Nate, dear honey, let me get going so I can get back."

Nate didn't know if he could wait an hour. He got busy, taking time to shower and shave. He packed a few things in his shoulder bag and would wear the faded jeans he reserved for going out. He was planning to bring Haley to a decent restaurant.

Chapter 2

Haley. What a beautiful woman, Nate thought as he drove to her apartment. He remembered their first meeting, almost three years before. He had been at work in the shop sandblasting when he noticed that the red light was blinking on the wall, a signal that someone had just come into the store. His father wasn't around, so it was up to him to go see who it was. He was brushing the dust off his clothes as he neared the back entrance to the storefront. The steel door had a window. Through it he saw a young black woman sitting in one of the brown vinyl chairs, her head down, fingering a hole in the seat cover. She looked up as Nate opened the door.

Under any other circumstance, it would have been love at first sight, but this was neither the time nor the place to be drawn in. Instead, he calmly walked out from behind the counter and introduced himself. Reaching out for her hand, he quietly said, "Hi, I'm Nate. Nate Bearing. Sorry for my appearance. I was just working out back. How can I help you?" Nate could tell that she had been crying. She took his hand and rose from the seat.

"It's good to meet you, Mr. Bearing."

"Please, just Nate is fine."

"Thank you, Nate. My name is Haley Jackson." Fingering a used tissue, she looked down at the cracked linoleum floor, buying time before she could speak. The lump in her throat was making it difficult. Nate didn't hurry her. She finally managed to say, "Well … my mother passed away last week, and I …" Her voice started to crack.

"I'm so sorry for your loss, Ms. Jackson."

"Haley, please," she said as she dabbed her eyes with the tissue, mascara loosening from the lashes that shadowed her deep black eyes.

"Haley," Nate responded as he encouraged her to take a seat. She stared ahead at the pine-paneled wall behind the counter. "I can't imagine how you feel right now. It must have taken a lot for you to come here."

She didn't look at him, but haltingly said, "Yes … I never thought it would be this hard." She swallowed. "But … my mother, well … it was just so sudden. She wasn't even sick."

"What happened to her?" he asked, as the light from the window behind them revealed her beauty.

She dared a glance at him and caught the sincerity and compassion in his deep brown eyes. Looking ahead again, "It was a heart attack. She was in the kitchen, cooking up something with my aunt, and she just grabbed at her chest and crumbled to the floor. It was so sudden … my poor aunt. She did what she could, but it was over even before the paramedics got there. I was at work."

Haley had to stop again. She was struggling, quiet tears pooling in the wells of her eyes. "I wish I could have been there. Maybe I could have …"

Nate interrupted again, steering her away from her guilt. "Do you have any brothers or sisters?"

"No. Just me. I'm an only child … now a lonely one." She managed a brief laugh.

"Well," Nate said sympathetically, "I'll help you all I can. It's difficult enough, even when there are other family members here. Let me tell you about what we do here. I'll help you make some decisions."

"Thank you. You're already making this a little easier for me."

"I hope so."

Nate picked out a couple of catalogs from the rack on the wall and invited her to look through them to get some ideas. He offered her a cup of coffee.

"No, thank you," she said, and started browsing through the pages. He walked behind the counter and flipped through some files, looking for pictures of some of the work that he and his father had done. He occasionally looked over. Nate felt her sadness and saw it didn't mar her beauty. He was struck by her high cheekbones, full, sensuous lips, and long black hair that was pulled back behind her jeweled ears. He came out from behind the counter again.

"Haley," he said, "here are a few pictures of some of the work we've done here. If you'd like, we could go out back and I can show you some of the different stones we use."

Getting up, she said, "I would like that very much. Can I look at these later?"

"Yes, of course. You don't have to make any decisions today. Take it easy on yourself. There is no hurry now. You can take the material home with you. Take your time, you know."

Nate led her out to the yard to look at the variety of headstones. He watched her carry her lean, tall stature with grace and dignity. In their conversation, he found that her outer appearance only magnified her inner beauty and goodness. When they finished looking at the stones, he had answered her many questions. He gave her the catalogs, photos, and a business card to take home with her. Thanking him, she then left with her emptiness.

A few days later, Haley returned and met with Nate to discuss her decision, a monument that was simple but elegant. It was a red granite arch with the inscription, 'Harriot Jackson. Mother to Haley and to all who met her.' Nate promised to be in touch with her when it was finished so that she could appraise the work and arrange for delivery to the cemetery where her mother had been laid to rest. He knew that he would have a special connection with this stone, and he did. When it was finished and finally put in place, Nate's work was completed, and he was pleased with it.

Weeks went by. Nate gave Haley time to grieve. He very much wanted to see her and eventually summoned the courage to call her. Little did he know that she had wanted to see him as well. He was different from men she had met before. She had experienced him as a man of sensitivity, compassion, and character in her greatest hour of need. She agreed to meet him for dinner at a quiet restaurant. He had arrived first that night, his heart skipping a beat when he saw her walking to the entrance.

"Hi, Haley," Nate said as he reached out to take her hand.

"Hi, Nate," she said. "It's good to see you again."

"How are you?" he asked with concern.

"I'm OK, I guess. Life has been keeping me busy. I guess that's a good thing."

"It is," Nate replied. "It helps you move through it." She didn't need him to explain that.

Nate remembered that she had ordered a light fish dinner with rice and roasted vegetables that night. She ate her food at a delicate pace, allowing them time to get to know each other. He normally ate rapidly, but this time he ate the steak and baked potato deliberately, not wanting to rush the evening.

"You know," she said as she sipped her wine, "you would have loved my mother."

Nate looked at her knowingly and said, "Well, if she was anything like you, I'm sure I would have."

"You flatter me, Nate. But no, my mother was special. She had a joyful spirit, a certain charisma that was infectious. She was able to draw people out of themselves with ease, much like you did for me when we first met."

"Now you flatter me," said Nate.

"No, really. She was a great listener, not a talker. People knew that she cared about them. And boy, could she cook. She cooked all the time. At least I can say that she died doing something she loved. She used to make so much food, and then she would bring meals to people who lived alone. She stayed with them while they ate too, a quiet companionship."

"She sounds like a saint to me," said Nate.

"I guess in a way she was. So many people came to her funeral, most I had never met. They told me so many stories about how she affected their lives. It was so touching, and so consoling. She made such a difference. Many of them told me that her death was like losing their own mother."

"So that's why you chose that inscription," Nate said.

"Yes, exactly. I wasn't the only one who lost her."

Nate's mind meandered in these fond memories as he turned down Haley's street. Trees shaded the sidewalks on both sides. Once a run-down section of the city, over the years this neighborhood had become more gentrified, catering to young working professionals.

Nate crept down the street looking for a parking spot. He was lucky today. Someone was pulling out on the right-hand side two cars down. It was a tight fit, but anyone who lived on the street had to be a parallel parking specialist. He looked up and down the street for Haley's yellow VW bug. It wasn't anywhere in sight. Not home yet, Nate surmised. He sauntered down the sidewalk, his bag slung from his shoulder, and climbed the steps into her brownstone building.

Haley's apartment was on the second floor. Nate put the key in the ornately embossed bronze plate and turned the polished glass doorknob to let himself in. He headed straight for the refrigerator and pulled out a soda and a handful of cold cuts. Slurping down the soda, he was in the middle of making a sandwich when he heard Haley come into the apartment. He was as surprised as she was.

"Nate?"

"Yeah," he shouted out. "In the kitchen. What are you doing home so early?"

She came into the kitchen.

"What am *I* doing here so early? What are *you* doing here so early?"

"I was hungry," he said in a deadpan voice. He turned around and smiled at her. "I couldn't wait to see you."

Haley put her packages down and walked over to Nate to hug him. They held their embrace, kissed each other, and rocked in place for a few moments.

He whispered in her ear. "I really do miss you."

"I miss you too. We don't see enough of each other." She hugged him harder. "I'm so happy you're here."

Nate responded, "I'm happy I'm here too."

Haley extracted herself. "You go sit down at the table. I'll finish making your sandwich."

"You don't have to do that. I'm a big boy, you know."

"I know I don't *have* to do it. I want to. Go sit down."

Haley put the plate down in front of him and added potato chips. Nate always had to have chips with his sandwich. She went to the refrigerator and pulled out some low-fat yogurt, a V8, and an apple, the same lunch she had every day of the week. She never needed a big lunch and generally didn't have time for it anyway. But Haley never missed breakfast. Fetching another spoon and soda for Nate, she came over to the table and sat down across from him.

"So why are you home so early?" Nate asked. "I thought you were going over to your cousin's."

"I did, but she wasn't home. It's such a nice day. Maybe she brought the boys over to the park. I left her a few groceries and a note to give me a call. Maybe I can get over there tomorrow afternoon."

"Works for me," Nate quipped.

"I thought it might. So, what do you want to do this afternoon?"

"Well, I don't know. Did you have anything in mind?" He knew she did.

"As a matter of fact," she said coyly, "there's somewhere I've wanted to go for some time now. I was waiting for a nice day. This is one of the first ones we've had in a while."

"So?" Nate pursued.

"I want to go for a hike. There's this place off the road I saw a couple of months ago when I was driving to the mall. I passed this sign. I thought it might be a park, so I turned around out of curiosity, and voila, it was a nature trail. I heard there's a waterfall in there. I want to see it."

"It's pretty muddy for that, isn't it?"

"I have boots, and you're wearing yours, like always. Let's do it."

"I'm coming," he shouted. "Right behind you."

Chapter 3

Hand in hand, they made their way back to the jeep. They were a mess but laughing about it.

"I told you it was too muddy. You just don't trust me," said Nate as he tramped out of the woods laughing.

She looked incredulous. "Trust you? Why should I trust you? You let me fall. Look at me! I look like I've been in a mud wrestling match!"

"I'd love to see that. Besides, I wasn't expecting you to fly off your feet and take me down with you! I didn't bring any other jeans with me. I guess I'll just have to go out to dinner looking like this."

"Maybe I'll let you. Maybe we should both go like this." Haley looked down at her jogging pants and pulled them out to full width. "God, what a mess I am."

They laughed, grabbed each other's hands, and carried on all the way back to the apartment. Once in the door, Haley stopped and wouldn't let Nate pass.

"We're not going to drag this mud all over the place. Take all your wet and filthy clothes off and drop them right here."

She scooped the clothes and brought them into the kitchen. The washer and dryer were behind doors in what used to be the pantry. Haley suggested that they watch a movie.

She picked one out and put it in the DVD player. As Nate expected, it was a 'girl flick.' He loved her too much to protest.

Haley then went into the kitchen. Soon Nate smelled popcorn. He should have guessed. Haley could never watch a movie without popcorn. She came out with the blue plastic bowl overflowing, went back to the kitchen, and brought out two glasses and some soda.

Nate set the glasses down near the popcorn. "Where's the remote?" he asked.

"I think the couch ate it. I haven't been able to find it."

He sighed and went over to push the play button. Haley cuddled right up to him. She just loved to cuddle. During the sad parts, she sniffed. Nate pulled her even closer to him. That was the good thing about watching 'chick flicks.' He wasn't paying too much attention to the movie. He was more intent on watching Haley. He loved to look at her.

Then Haley noticed the time.

"Nate, it's almost six o'clock. Do you still want to go out?"

"Sure, honey, don't you?"

Nate put on the clean clothes and went out to the living room while Haley went into the bathroom to dry her hair and do her makeup. Nate waited—and waited. He was watching the news, tapping his fingers on the armrest of the couch. In his mind, he was saying to himself, 'Let's go! Let's go! Let's go!' Then he smiled. He would wait forever for Haley. He was going to take her out to the best steak and seafood restaurant in town. He loved her so much. He loved steak too.

After a leisurely dinner, they lingered over coffee and dessert, Haley's dessert. She always ordered cheesecake, and the same kind of cheesecake, graham cracker crust with strawberries on top, but she could never finish it. She encouraged Nate to pick at it too, and, as always, he did. After leaving the tip, Nate escorted Haley out the door. She was wearing a black, scoop neck blouse trimmed with lace, showing just a hint of cleavage. The buttons were small and sewn closely together, hugging her upper torso and ending just above her pierced navel. A simple gold ring adorned it. She drew her black flowing pants to her hips with a drawstring. Nate noticed that she turned a few heads on the way out, and he felt even prouder to be with her.

The day had been warm, but the evening brought more of a chill to the air. Haley shivered. Nate took off his blazer and put it around her shoulders. He had his arm around her and pulled her closer. When they got to the jeep, Nate opened the door for her, went around to the driver's side, and started the car.

"Heat, please," whimpered Haley as she hugged herself, trying to get warm.

"It's coming. Just a couple of minutes," Nate said encouragingly.

Late the next morning, after a home-cooked breakfast of sausage and French toast, Nate said goodbye to Haley. Neither of them wanted to part.

"I'll call you tonight," Nate promised.

"I'll be here," she replied.

Nate opened the door, gave Haley a peck on the cheek, and made his way out. There was a bounce in his step as he walked back to his jeep.

Even though he was expecting to work that afternoon, his thoughts of Haley would help him breeze through it. As he drove home, he found himself whistling. He didn't recognize the tune, just random notes wandering around in his mind. It was another nice day. Two in a row. He felt optimistic. As he approached his house, he flipped on the right turn signal and pulled into the lot. He picked up his bag and went inside the house.

"Dad, I'm home!" he said with a leap in his voice. No answer.

"Dad?" Nate walked around the house. His father must be out in the shop, he thought. His truck was out there, so Nate knew he was somewhere around. He went out to the kitchen to see if there was any coffee left. He poured himself a cup and heated it in the microwave. He then opened the back door and stepped out to the gravel lot. He headed toward the shop. Entering the building, an eerie feeling came over him. It was way too quiet.

"Dad? Where are you? It figures you'd start without me." Then his eyes focused on the hoist at the far end of the building. "Dad?" No answer.

Nate walked slowly and fearfully toward the monument that lay on the floor. Looking down, he saw his father lying underneath the granite, motionless, with dried blood around his mouth. He frantically punched 911 into his cell phone, but he knew it was a futile request for help. He fell to his knees and stayed there.

Chapter 4

Nate sat in one of the metal folding chairs in the front row, staring at the coffin. Bouquets and wreaths of flowers surrounded it. He was alone. The wake was not scheduled to begin for another hour. He was grateful for that. The funeral director, John Walker, a friend of the family, had led Nate and his grandfather through the process of choosing a coffin, choosing the hours for the wake, the arrangements for the church and cemetery, and all of the other details that make for a proper burial. Nate thought his grandfather to be a much stronger man than he under the best of circumstances and let him make most of the decisions. Thank God. Haley and Jack were there for him too. Jack O'Leary, his best friend, had been uncharacteristically quiet last night as they all sat together in Nate's kitchen drinking coffee. The conversation had been light and avoidant.

At the funeral home, sitting by himself, Nate finally let the tears flow. He wanted to finish crying before anyone else showed up. The room that he sat in seemed so much smaller than he remembered. The last time he was here was when his mother died when he was only twelve. At that time, he had not understood cancer. He hadn't understood death. He hadn't understood why his mother had to die. He wished to God that she could be here with him now.

No one ever knew him better. When he was a boy, she had understood his propensity for mischief and procrastination, especially when it came to doing homework. She never yelled at him, and her quiet and humble way made him want to please her. His father tended to be more introspective but not shy. With a down-to-earth view of things, he had his opinions but didn't get distracted by them.

His mother spent much of her time gardening and landscaping around the house and storefront. She also brought Nate to church regularly. Although both of his parents were Catholic, it was his mother who took the religion seriously. After she died, his father brought him to church only on big occasions, more for the sake of his mother than the sake of grace.

He searched the room and spotted the prayer cards. The picture of clouds with rays of sunlight shooting out was nice, he thought. He picked one up and turned it over. 'In memory of Alexander Bearing. June 14, 1945–April 9th, 2008.' A prayer to the angels followed. Nate tucked it in the pocket inside his jacket, remembering how much he had been loved.

Once again, losing himself in his memories, Nate remembered he was told when his parents were married, they wanted a child. Several years passed before Nate came along. They were elated when he entered their lives and christened him Nathaniel, a gift from God. As a boy, it seemed that they were always around, and he didn't always want it that way. As gentle as his parents were, they were also strict. He sometimes envied the other kids whose parents gave them the latest video games. He was only allowed to watch a certain amount of TV, then he had to spend time reading with his parents or talking with them. Because of that time together, he learned about and came to revere his heritage. It was his mother who told him the stories.

* * *

"Mom?" he would ask as he sat at the kitchen table doing his arithmetic.

"Why do I look so different?"

"What do you mean, honey?"

"My eyes. Something's wrong with my eyes. The kids at school say I have slanty eyes." He started to cry. She turned off the stove, pulled a chair up next to him, and pulled him close. He was seven years old.

"Daddy's got slanty eyes too, worse than mine. No one makes fun of him," he whimpered.

"Kids can be cruel, honey, especially when they don't understand something."

"Well, I don't understand it either."

"You will soon," she said. "Go get your globe, and I'll tell you all about it."

"Now, first I want you to show me where we live." Nate turned the globe on its stand to show North America and then pointed to New York State. "Good," she said with great encouragement. "You're a smart kid. Now I want to show you where Grandfather Bearing came from."

She let her finger glide to the middle part of the globe, turning it only slightly. "See here? That's called the Yucatan Peninsula. You see? It sticks right out into the water. That's why it's called a peninsula. It's sort of between North America and South America."

"I see it," he said excitedly. "And that's the Gulf of Mexico. And that," he looked more closely, "is the Cara-bean Sea."

"Exactly," his mother said without correcting him.

"Now your grandfather used to live there, and so did your father until he was sixteen years old." She was pointing to Belize. "That's the country that they came from."

"Oh," Nate said as if he understood. "That's far away." He hesitated and then asked, "Mom, do they have slanty eyes there?"

She laughed a little, but not enough to make him feel stupid. "Some do, and some don't," she said. "People from all over the world came to live in Belize. Some were already there, like the Mayan natives, for example."

"You mean like the Mohawk Indians?" he asked, trying to get the concept.

"Yes," she said matter-of-factly, "much like that. And other people came there too. It used to be called British Honduras when the English were in charge."

"They were in charge here too!" Nate said, his interest more intent.

"You are so smart! Yes, like that. But when the English left, the people named their country Belize, and your grandfather and father lived in Belize City, the capital."

"But grandfather doesn't have slanty eyes, Mom. He looks more like an Indian to me."

"Be patient, I'm getting to that. Now, your grandfather, when he was a young man, fell in love with a Chinese woman named Hua. She sold fruits at the open market. Your grandfather loved fruit. Soon enough they got married. Do you know what Chinese people look like?"

"I don't know for sure," Nate said.

She left the room. When she returned, she held an older framed picture in her hand and showed it to Nate.

"See here? Who's that?"

"Well, the man looks a little like Grandfather. And, well, I don't know her, but *she* has slanty eyes!"

"OK. So, let's agree not to call them slanty eyes anymore, OK?"

"OK. So, what do I call them?"

"Oriental eyes, they're almond-shaped, you know, like the nut."

"So, I have nut eyes?"

She laughed at his little joke. "No, Nate, dear, you have your grandmother's eyes, like your dad."

"So, what happened to Grandmother? Why did Grandfather and Daddy come here?"

"Well, that part is kind of sad. There was a bad storm, a hurricane. Your grandfather and father were far away from their house that day getting some stones."

Nate knew that the family was in the stone business. "So, what happened?"

"Your grandmother died in the storm. There was a terrible flood. Everyone else in the family died, and all the buildings were destroyed. Your grandfather had built a lot of them. When your grandfather and father got home, there was nothing left. Eventually, your grandfather decided to move north to the United States. He learned to speak English. In Yucatan, he primarily spoke Yucatec and Spanish. He eventually came to New York. We don't get many hurricanes here in upstate New York, only whatever's left over from them."

Nate's mother taught him about his ancestors, his culture. She taught him to be proud of who he was, even if kids made fun of him for looking different. They just didn't know. She told him he could tell the other kids about his grandfather and grandmother and then they would understand. They would think he was cool. She was right, Nate thought. Other kids did think he was cool after a while. As Nate got older, he became more curious, looking up Mayan history, Belize, the immigrations into the Yucatan, and especially the hurricanes. It was Hurricane Hattie that hit Belize in October of 1961, the one that killed most of his grandfather's family.

Nate jumped when he felt a hand on his shoulder. He turned to see his grandfather, who simply sat down next to him in silence.

Soon Haley appeared. Nate stood up and gave her a hug. She turned to his grandfather and took his hand into both of hers. Nothing was said. Then Jack came in. He solemnly approached the coffin and knelt in front of it. After a few moments, he crossed himself and went over to Nate and gave him a side hug, saying quietly, "So, buddy, are you ready for this?" Nate nodded.

John Walker came into the room and told the family that it was time, making sure that everyone was OK. They all gathered to the left of the coffin as the doors opened. A din of conversation seeped into the silence and with it a testimony to the life of Alexander Bearing. After signing the guest book, one by one people filed in, first kneeling at the coffin, some praying, some touching the cold hands, some standing silently. The 'family,' which included Haley and Jack, stood in line waiting, watching, and accepting the condolences from the guests. Some of them were acquaintances, some were friends. Many people were in the business, and some people Nate had never met.

The litany of 'I'm sorry' droned on. Nate shook many hands, thanking each person for coming, making small talk. Now and then, he would look out the door into the foyer—so many people.

Then something caught his eye. He tried to focus into the crowd. He could swear he saw his grandparents out there, his mother's parents. He had not seen them in years. After his mother died, they had tried, but it was just too painful for everyone to keep the relationship going. However, there they were, coming into the room. He just stood there, his anxiety rising as they came closer to the front.

They knelt together in front of the casket. She was holding her rosary, fumbling with the beads, murmuring her prayers. Nate couldn't help but notice how much they had aged. They got up and approached him, fighting back their tears.

"Nate, we're so sorry. Your grandfather called us," his grandmother said.

"You're a grown man now, Nate. You look so much like your father. God, it has been so long. I'm sorry we haven't been in touch …"

Nate put them at ease. "No need to apologize. I could have called you too."

Nate was much like his father. One could tell that the apple didn't fall far from the tree, both in manner and in appearance. Both were hard workers and never took shortcuts with their stonework. Both were exceptional in their craft. Both were well-liked by many people. They did look alike too, but at six foot two, Nate was taller than his father. They had dark brown, almond eyes, light brown skin, and straight black hair. Their physical labor kept them in good shape, strong and lean. Nate's features were more distinctive, as if he had been carved and sculpted. Haley knew other women were attracted to him. He looked like a Greek god. So handsome, she thought, but never arrogant about it. She was proud to be standing with him. She tried to be strong for him.

Chapter 5

It was a high Mass, the rite of Christian burial. The organist played and sang hymns vaguely familiar to Nate. After communion, he almost lost it when the refrain from "On Eagles Wings" was sung. Its melody set to the words, 'and He will raise you up,' incrementally soared above the mourners. Nate felt his heart fill up, and maybe his soul as well. Many people quietly wept as they sat and listened. Nate managed not to. Crying alone was one thing, crying in public another. He felt vulnerable enough already. Nate, already exhausted, just wanted the interminable Mass to end.

"It was a nice ceremony," Haley offered, anything to lighten things up. They all agreed with her without saying so. Jack was fidgeting with his tie. He had a hard time dealing with silence. It started to rain again.

"Look at this," Haley commented as she looked out the window. "I didn't know it was going to rain most of the day."

"You know what the Irish say?" Jack asked as he looked across at Nate.

"No, tell me," Nate said, knowing that Jack would anyway.

"The Irish say that if it rains on the day of the funeral, it's a good thing. I never quite got that, but that's what they say."

Haley said, "Maybe they think it is an indication that the person is in heaven."

"Yeah, maybe," Jack said without further comment.

They buried his father next to his mother. Nate tried to console himself. Maybe they're in a better place, he thought. He felt like an orphan, though, and wondered if other adults felt that way when their parents died. He made a mental note to ask Haley. She would know.

At the reception following the funeral, the atmosphere was livelier. Jack made the arrangements at O'Reilly's pub. Nate didn't mind the Irish atmosphere. The back room was set up with a brunch buffet. Some people were sitting, and some were wandering from table to table. Some were drinking coffee, some Bloody Marys, and some, beer. There were many toasts and off-the-cuff eulogies. Jack raised his glass many times, adding more humor to each pint. Nate appreciated his friend, who took the center of attention away from him. Shortly before two o'clock, people began to leave. Nate and his grandfather sat off in a corner, drinking their coffee and watching.

"Jack's a great guy," Nate said in trying to engage his grandfather. He felt awkward. He was rarely with his grandfather without his father also being there.

"Yes, a good friend to you," his grandfather replied. "We all need friends. Not too many, though."

Nate agreed. None of the Bearing men liked crowds and small talk. In some way they were introverts, replenishing their energy from time spent alone. Jack, in contrast, loved to be around people. It pumped him up.

"Nate," his grandfather offered, "if you would like to come up to the cabin for a few days, you know you are welcome."

"Thank you, Grandfather. I'll keep that in mind. I'm not sure what I need now. I think I would like to take some time to assess things. You know, see where I go from here."

"Well, if you need my help, you know where to find me."

"I appreciate that. Don't be surprised if I show up."

His grandfather got up from the chair. Nate followed him out. In the parking lot, his grandfather patted Nate on the back and reached out to shake his hand.

"Take care of yourself, Nate. Don't be afraid to ask for help."

"Don't worry about me. I'll be fine. Thanks for everything."

When Nate arrived home, he was about to announce his arrival when he caught himself. His father was not there. The reality that he never would be again had not yet sunk in. He made himself some coffee and sat down at the kitchen table. He was alone for the first time since the accident. He focused on the dripping faucet in the sink. I'll have to fix that, he thought. Then he noticed the dirty dishes on the counter. I'll have to wash them, he thought. One by one, thoughts entered his mind of all the things he would have to do, all without his father. He began to cry. He didn't do much of anything for the rest of the day. He fell asleep on the couch, only to be awakened by a knock on the back door. He looked at the time on the cable box. He was surprised to see that he had slept for two hours.

He let Haley in. She put her bag down on the kitchen table and turned to hug him. He didn't cry, but simply stared at the wall behind her. She suggested that they go sit on the couch together. He followed her in silence and sat down next to her. She pulled him into where he allowed himself to listen to the beat of her heart. He felt so small, and he sobbed. She cried with him, for him. He felt some comfort then, if only for a few minutes. Then he heard another knock at the back door. "Jack," he said as he wiped his face and pulled away from Haley. Nate got up to let him in.

"Hey, buddy," Jack said as he gave Nate a slight punch to the shoulder. "How're you doin'?"

"OK, I guess. It's all kind of strange, you know. Haley's in the other room. Come on in."

"I'm not interfering with anything, am I?"

"Would it matter?" Nate said, busting on his friend a bit.

"Of course not," Jack said flippantly.

Jack greeted Haley and sat back on the chair nearest the couch, sipping his beer. He saw she had been crying, and immediately started talking about the business.

"Nate, I want you to know that if you need any help in the shop, I'm there for you. I can come over after work if you'd like, or even part of the weekends for a while, that is, until you can get things back up and running again."

"Thanks, Jack. You have already been a big help. The guy from the Occupational Safety and Health Administration will be here tomorrow. It's part of the routine at work site accidents. He sounds like a decent guy."

"So, you don't know what happened?" Jack asked, a little surprised.

"Not exactly … I mean … I know the rock fell. But to tell you the truth, it was all I needed to know."

"Understood," said Jack.

"Tomorrow I'll know exactly what happened. I probably could figure it out myself, but this guy needs to be here anyway, so I'll let him do his thing."

"Why not?" Jack said. "He makes a living at it."

"It might be good to have someone else with you, Nate," Haley added. She couldn't imagine having to do something like that by herself.

"You're probably right, honey," Nate said. "Bill Thompson is coming over too. He's known our family for years."

She was right, he thought. Going back into the shop for the first time since the accident was not something Nate wanted to do at all, let alone all by himself. He felt a shiver go up his spine.

Though none was very hungry, Jack went to pick up some take-out Chinese food for them. It was a way to pass the time. Around eleven, Haley announced, apologetically, that she needed to go home. She needed to get up early for work. Jack said the same. Neither of them wanted to leave their friend, but at the same time, both knew that Nate needed time to himself.

When they left, Nate picked up the half-eaten containers of food and put them in the refrigerator. He noticed that there was one beer left. He hadn't had one all day, and normally he didn't drink much anyway. Now seemed like a good time. He took it in the living room, flipped on the TV, and popped the top to the beer. He sipped it slowly. It tasted good. For some reason, he wished he had a cigarette to go with it. The one he had at the funeral home tasted great. Reminding himself that he had quit, he pushed the thought away. He focused on the news of the day, insignificant to him, but something to distract him. He wasn't looking forward to tomorrow.

Chapter 6

The next morning, Nate was up before five. He hadn't slept well, tossing, and turning, thinking about the events of the past couple of days. He was worried about how he was going to manage things without his father, how he would manage anything. He went to the kitchen and made some coffee. He noticed that he was running out. He would have to get to the store to get some groceries, something his father routinely did. It was just the way it was with them. They'd had a good division of duties around the house, much like a married couple. Nate was mostly in charge of laundry, picking up, and cleaning the main rooms. His father shopped for groceries, cooked, and cleaned the bathroom. The house was always neat and clean. That's just the way it was with them. They had been a team in nearly all aspects of life. Now it was all on him.

On his way outside Nate went down the hall and stopped at his father's bedroom door. It was closed. Part of him wanted to open it and find his father sitting and reading in the chair near the window. He started to tear up. His father was dead. That's it. Before going out the back door from the kitchen, he took a deep breath, as if he were going to take a dive. He let the air out audibly so he wouldn't have to hear himself think. He saw the vehicle from the Office of Safety and Health Administration pull into the lot and park near the shop. He opened the door, pulled himself together, and put on his business persona.

Nate walked slowly toward the SUV with the official OSHA emblem on the side. He picked up the pace when the man got out of the car and closed the door. Nate was dressed in his usual work attire of jeans and a denim shirt. This man wore a suit. Nate felt a bit intimidated by that. He greeted the man, who with his thinning gray hair, seemed older than his father.

"Hi, I'm Nate Bearing." He reached out to shake hands.

"Tom Crieghton," the man said in a perfunctory fashion. "Are we still waiting for Bill?"

"Yeah," said Nate, quietly disliking this man. "He should be here anytime now. Can I get you a cup of coffee?"

"No, just had some," Tom curtly replied. "Why don't we go ahead and take a look."

Nate didn't want to. He wanted to wait for Bill, whom he had known for a long time. Bill was the contractor who installed the overhead rails. He made frequent visits to the shop to check out the installations and sometimes just to shoot the breeze. Not a good day for him to be late. Sucking it up, Nate said, "OK then, right this way." Nate pushed the button to open the overhead doors. He needed as much air as he could get. They went into the shop.

"Where's the scene of the accident?" Tom inquired. Nate pointed to the far end of the building. "Right back there," he said. Reluctantly, he followed him.

Tom walked around the area slowly, looking up at the rails, down at the stone, up at the straps. Nate saw dried blood on the floor. He averted his eyes. He thought he was going to throw up.

"Didn't you tell me it was your father?"

"Yes," said Nate without offering any other information. He didn't trust this guy.

"Sorry to hear it," Tom said insincerely.

Just then, Nate heard footsteps. It was Bill Thompson. Thank God, he thought. Nate walked toward him as he entered the opening to the shop and shook his hand.

"Thanks for coming, Bill."

"Nate, I'm so sorry this happened. I couldn't believe it when you called. It's gotta' be tough. Your father was a good man."

"Thank you, Bill," Nate said graciously. "The guy from OSHA is back there." Nate pointed over his back.

"Let's do this thing, Nate. I'm here for you."

Nate followed Bill to the back. Tom saw them coming and took a step forward.

"Tom Creighton," he said, reaching to shake hands.

"Bill. Bill Thompson. Good to meet you."

"Right," Tom quipped. "This is a real mess here."

So sensitive, Nate thought. He wanted to punch him. Bill started to inspect the equipment. Both men took notes as Nate looked back and forth from them to the back wall. He wanted them both, especially Tom, to get the hell out of here. Tom spoke first.

"The mechanisms all look fine to me. What do you think, Bill?"

"Well, I'm not seeing anything obvious. The rails are clean and oiled. It doesn't look like anything got jammed up."

They had unhooked the hoist from the straps. "The remote is fine too," Tom said as he pushed the buttons, causing the hoist to move backward, forward, and up and down.

Nate was silent. The two men were examining every detail.

"You know," Tom said to Nate. "No one should be operating this equipment alone. I know it's done all the time. But it's foolish. We tell people that for a reason."

Nate could feel every muscle in his body tighten up. He could not believe the audacity of this man, implying that his father was foolish. He was ready for a fight but said nothing.

Tom continued his inspection. Looking at the straps, he said coldly, "Here it is." Bill came over and looked at it. He looked over at Nate to catch his eye. It was as if he was apologizing to him for what was about to be said.

"You see it? The strap's torn---right there."

Bill said, "Yes, you're right."

Tom looked at Nate and asked accusingly, "When's the last time you inspected this?"

Containing his fury, Nate responded, "I inspect the straps every day. We do, did, everything by the book here."

"Yeah, right. So, when's the last time you inspected it?" Tom pushed.

"Saturday morning."

Nate was scrambling to remember. It was something he did every day. He must have done it. He always did it. *Did I do it Saturday? Did I? I don't remember if I did or did not. God, what if I didn't? Of course. I did ...*

Bill broke into Nate's mind. "Nate, it looks like there might have been a tear in the strap. It had to be small. Maybe you missed it. This kind of thing happens. That's why they're called accidents."

"But I inspected it Saturday, like I do every day. That was my job."

"Well," said Tom cryptically, "you missed it. That is why it's so important to be thorough. A rock like this, or even a smaller one, could rip through a strap that has the slightest fault."

Nate snapped, "So, are we finished here?" daring Tom to say another word.

"Just have to write it up and send it in. Probably won't be any fines or lawsuits to deal with. At least that's the way it is for most family-run businesses. We're just here to help."

"Right," said Nate coldly.

Tom finished writing on his clipboard in silence. Bill was hanging back, eyeing Nate, watching him unravel. He came up and stood by his side in alliance. Tom then handed Bill the clipboard. "You need to sign here." Bill did and handed the clipboard to Nate, pointing to where he needed to sign. Then Bill said, "I'll see you out." Nate followed behind the two of them and stopped at the opening as Bill walked Tom to his car. After Tom left, Bill came back to Nate and put his hand on his shoulder.

"Got a cup of coffee?"

"Sure, Bill. Yeah, in the house." Bill followed Nate into the kitchen. Nate poured them each a cup of coffee and they sat down at the table.

"Look, Nate. I know what you're thinking. First, that guy was an asshole. A real asshole. The world is full of them. It's unfortunate for the likes of us that we must put up with their bullshit."

Nate was silently drinking his coffee. He couldn't look up at Bill. His mind wasn't functioning. It just seemed to have shut down. Bill kept talking, trying to bring him around.

"Nate, I know you. You are one of the most responsible people I know. You take your job seriously. If you said you inspected that strap on Saturday, then you did. If there's a weak spot in the strap, it's not always apparent. You know that. We do the best we can. That's all we can do."

Nate just stared ahead. He still couldn't remember if he had inspected the strap on Saturday. He just couldn't remember. The day began just like any other day. Bill interrupted his silence again. "Nate." Bill reached over and put his hand on Nate's shoulder. "Nate look at me." Nate looked up and then over to meet Bill's eyes. "Now, listen to me. Are you listening?" Bill waited until

Nate made some acknowledgment. He continued with a sense of urgency.

"Nate, you listen to me. Listen hard. This is *not* your fault! Do you hear me? *Not* your fault!" Nate nodded unconvincingly. "Look, I'm telling you. If you let that guy get to you, he wins. You're better than that. You're Nate Bearing. Your father was incredibly proud of you. Don't let him down. He would never want you to blame yourself for this. Shit happens. You got it?"

Nate nodded again and managed to say, "Got it."

He wanted to be alone. He appreciated what Bill was saying, what he was trying to do for him, but he wanted him to leave. So, he pulled it together enough for Bill to leave believing that he would be OK.

"Thanks so much, Bill, for everything," Nate said sincerely. "My father respected you. He liked you. You have a lot of integrity. And you're not an asshole."

"Thanks, Nate. I'll be seeing you. You know that. Take care of yourself. I mean it. Let me know if I can do anything for you. I'm here for you. Don't you forget it."

Nate let him out the back door, waving him off as he drove out of the yard. He sat back down in front of his now cold cup of coffee. He couldn't move.

Chapter 7

It was early September but felt no better than August. The summer had been hotter than Nate could remember, and the air conditioner in the living room hadn't worked all season. Even though the sweat was pouring off him, he wouldn't open the windows. He couldn't stand the noise of the traffic coming in from the street. The sound of the eighteen-wheelers that rumbled by was bad enough, even with the windows closed. He kept the TV on low, not enough to really hear it, but more to let it just drone on over the intrusions outside. Nate didn't move much. He hadn't for the past four months.

The weeks right after the funeral, Nate somehow managed to finish what he and his father had been working on. He finished the lamb sculpture, but nowhere near the quality of his usual work. He didn't have the concentration to carve detail. But it was good enough, he had told himself, and the family was not unhappy with the job. Jack, a mason himself, had helped Nate deliver the lamb and the monuments that were still in the truck to the cemeteries. The last time he had seen Jack was in June. Jack had some time off from work and stopped by to see if Nate wanted some extra help.

Nate jumped when he heard the loud knock on the back door. He got up from the kitchen table that was strewn with paperwork and saw the back of Jack through the window. When Nate opened the door, Jack turned around. Nate let him in.

"Hey, man," Jack said when he saw Nate. "Don't look too thrilled to see me." He crossed over to the counter. He opened the cupboard to grab a mug, but there were none. He fished one out of the sink, rinsed it out, and poured himself a cup of coffee. He brought it over to the table, sat down, and took a sip.

"This tastes like shit," he said as he shoved some paper away and put the mug down on the table.

"Sorry," Nate said as he sat across from Jack. "Want me to make a new pot?"

"Shit no," said Jack. "You suck at it."

Jack looked at the table. "What's all this shit?"

Sighing, Nate replied, "This is my life, man."

"It's a mess."

"Guess so," said Nate. "My father always took care of all this, but he was so damned disorganized. I can't find half the shit I need. I don't know who owes me or who I owe. As far as I can figure, no one owes anything, but I can't be sure." Nate shoved some of the paper aside and said, "Fuck it."

Jack was quiet for a moment, and then asked, "So, what's with the sign in the window?"

At first, Nate didn't know what he was talking about. "What sign?" he asked vacantly.

"The one in the storefront window, closed for remodeling."

"Oh, that," Nate replied. He had forgotten that he changed it in June. "I'm going to gut the storefront and modernize it."

"When?" Jack gently challenged.

"Pretty soon," Nate said. Jack was unconvinced.

"You know, I told you I would help you. I've got some time off now. Want me to help you get it started?"

"Ah, not now," Nate said. "I've got to get all this stuff settled first," as he waved his hand over the table.

Jack was silent, mulling things over. Then he said, "Nate, man, you know I care about you, but Jesus, every time I call, you put me off. Why don't we leave this shit here and go down to the pub? You need to get out, man. You're becoming a goddamn hermit. You can't work all the time."

"I'm not working all the time," Nate said defensively.

"OK, so you're not. So, let's go out."

"Maybe this weekend," Nate said. "I don't feel like it now."

Jack couldn't stand anymore. "OK, do what you gotta' do." Jack stood up to leave. "Give me a call this weekend if you want to get together."

"Sure," Nate placated. "I will."

"See you later, then."

"Later," Nate replied. Later never came. Jack stopped calling.

* * *

The day had been sweltering, and as tired as she was, Haley stopped by to see Nate as she usually did on her way home from work. This visit would be different. Her heart was heavy as she thought about what she had to do. It was going to be a difficult evening.

Arriving at Nate's house, Haley let herself in with her key. Nate had stopped answering the phone and the door as well. She tried to ignore the mess in the kitchen as she passed through to the living room, where Nate was lying on the couch. She sat down at his feet.

"So … how are you feeling today?" she asked him.

No response. Nate just stared at her, not knowing what to say. He had said it all. Nothing had changed since yesterday, the day before, or the week before that. As much as he cared about Haley, he was tired of the constant questions. After a long silence, Haley spoke.

"Nate, I wish it didn't have to be this way, but I can't keep doing this. Look at you. You are unshaven, uncombed, you smell like you haven't even showered this week. The place smells like urine. You've been wearing the same clothes for weeks, even though I've done your laundry. I've even helped you keep up with your bills. God, Nate, you wouldn't even have your jeep if I didn't remind you to pay the bill, or the insurance, for that matter. You only eat if I bring you something or cook you something. Look at this place."

Nate looked around. Empty beer cans and bottles all over the room, cigarette butts overflowing in the ashtrays, a dirty path worn in the carpet leading from the couch and forking one way to the bathroom and the other to the kitchen.

Haley continued. "There're dirty dishes in the sink and on the counters, and you haven't taken the garbage out in weeks. The bathroom is so filthy I don't even want to use it."

Staring at the ceiling, Nate tried to sound apologetic. "I'm sorry, Haley. I'll clean the place up as soon as I can. I do appreciate your help, you know that."

"Nate, you've been saying that for months, but you haven't moved. The only time you go out is when you go to the store to buy booze and cigarettes. That's all you do is smoke, drink, and watch TV, even when I'm here. You're not doing anything with *me*."

"Haley," he said, his voice halting, barely audible, "I can't help the way I feel. I don't know what to do. It feels like I can't move, like I have this huge weight bearing down on me." Nate saw tears streaming down her face.

"Nate, I've tried so hard to help you. I've asked you to get help and you haven't. Your father died in early April, and here it's September. It's as if you died with him. I've been trying to give you the time and space you needed. Now I feel like you don't care about me, Jack, anyone else, or anything else. You've given up, and there seems to be nothing I can do to make any difference. I've been going down with you." She looked away, choking on her words. "I just can't do this anymore."

Nate dreaded what was coming, but there was no defense. Trying to come up with something to say, he looked at her. *Think of something to say, you idiot,* he thought. *Anything. Say something.* He couldn't.

"Nate, honey, I know you love me. I can't tell you how hard this is for me. I have loved you for so long." Sobbing, she looked at him, and then looked away, not wanting to meet his eyes. "I can't live like this anymore! You don't want to live! You are *not* the person I fell in love with. You left me, Nate. And now …" She stopped, stared ahead at the TV, wiping her face, not wanting to say it. She forced herself to look at him. He avoided her eyes, his darting around the room looking for somewhere to land. The walls seemed to be closing in on him.

"Nate … I have to leave."

He stared past her, unresponsive. He fixed his eyes on a web in the corner of the ceiling. In it lay a spider, resting quietly.

After a heavy silence, she asked, "What are you thinking, Nate?"

"Nothing," he lied. "Nothing you haven't already heard. If you must leave, then go. I understand. I don't blame you." Forcing calmness in his voice, "I want you to be happy, and you haven't been … I've been dragging you down. I don't want to hurt you any more than I already have."

Haley, still crying, got up from the worn couch where Nate had been lying for months. There were cigarette burns on the cushions, and the armrests were frayed. The back cushion near his head bore the stain of his oily hair. She started to leave. She stopped to look at him one more time.

"Nate, I'm so sorry I have to do this. I will miss you so much. You can't imagine. Maybe if you get some help. Maybe if you get back to work before you lose everything. I don't know. All I know is that I have to go. I will pray that you can find your way. I'll never stop loving you. Please, take care of yourself."

She started to leave the room. Turning back, she said, "Goodbye, Nate." He heard her crying as she opened the back door and gently closed it behind her.

Nate lay on the couch, stunned. He couldn't think. After a long while, he got up, dragged himself into the kitchen and opened the refrigerator. It was empty save for some old ketchup and mustard, some apples that Haley had given him, now rotting, a stale loaf of bread, and the beer. He had plenty of beer. He grabbed two, popped the lid on one and started to drink it on his way back to the couch. He noticed the bottle on the floor next to the couch. He used to drink the best single malt Scotch, and then only in social settings. Then it was Johnny Walker Red. Now, at less than ten bucks a bottle, it was Old Crow Kentucky Straight Bourbon. It wasn't like he couldn't afford the good stuff. There was still money in the bank. He just didn't give a shit what he drank and preferred doing it alone. He drank the beer and used the cheap whiskey as the chaser. He lay back down and lit a cigarette.

He replayed the plan he had pictured in his mind over and over again for weeks. He was in his truck. He had been driving all night on the expressway, drinking, thinking, and trying to muster up the courage to take his own life. He planned to pull off at a rest stop, run the hose in the window, and drink until he fell asleep. But Haley always kept coming to his mind. She would be devastated if he killed himself. He never wanted to hurt anyone, especially Haley, so he would never end up doing it. But now she had left his life, and the thought of ending it became more powerful. The more he thought about it, the more possible it became.

He kept drinking, smoking, mulling over his miserable life and what he had become. The only family left was Grandfather. Nate didn't think his grandfather would miss him all that much. He hadn't seen him since the funeral. He took another couple of long swigs from the bottle, downed the beer, and got up to get more. Sitting back down, crying, he decided that this would be the night. He lit another cigarette and started to feel some relief. Soon it would all be over.

Chapter 8

Nate tried to open his eyes. He had to use the bathroom, but he didn't want to get up. Many times, he'd awakened, only to find that he'd wet himself. But now he was awake enough to know he had to go. "Damn it," he said to himself, not wanting to move. Now he remembered that he had planned to kill himself, but instead he had passed out. Forcing himself up, he unzipped his pants and stumbled to the bathroom in the dark to relieve himself. As he was leaving the bathroom, he caught sight of himself in the mirror over the sink.

He didn't stop to wash his hands anymore, but now he stopped, supporting himself with his hands on the sink. He looked through the smoky film and just stared. *Look at you*, he thought. *You're a fucking mess. What the hell are you doing to yourself? No wonder she left. You wouldn't want to be around you either. You are no good for anybody.* Tears emerged in his reflection. *What the fuck happened to me? I've screwed up my life. Wouldn't Dad be so proud of me now?* Remembering his family history, Nate said aloud, "I'm the weakest goddamn link in the chain ... yeah." He laughed bitterly. "The black sheep of my lineage." He looked down at the sink, tears dripping onto the porcelain.

He blew his nose on some toilet paper. His eyes stung. Squinting, he made out the path back to the couch. He hit his knee on the corner of the coffee table, the pain sharp, then throbbing. He bent over to rub it out, and said to himself, "Shit, you can't even walk right." He then threw himself back on the couch. He couldn't go back to sleep, so he felt for the bottle on the floor. Empty. "God damn it!" he said out loud as he slammed the bottle on the floor. "Shit!"

Nate had to get up again. It wasn't like he had a choice. He had just gotten up to go to the bathroom, and now he had to get up again to get something to drink. Drink and piss. He sat up and turned on the light that sat on the end table. The shade was originally an olive green. Now it was cracked and yellowed. The 25-watt bulb that Nate had chosen to put in took advantage of the rips in the shade, the dim light breaking through. Nate got up in the shadows and made his way into the kitchen. The only thing left to drink was a couple of six-packs. He grabbed the plastic grips that held the cans together and brought one of them back into the living room.

He ripped a can away from the rest of the pack, opened it, and guzzled it down in one swig. Then he grabbed another, and another, and another. Each gulp mixed with a few drags. He couldn't think straight. His mind was racing, but only against itself. One thought ran over another. Nate was flooded and drowning in memories and emotions. Sobbing, as he did every day, he begged his father for forgiveness. "Dad ... I'm so sorry, please forgive me," he said out loud, as his chest heaved out the burning flashback as if it were yesterday. "I should have been there!" He crunched over, grabbing his gut, his mind trapped in another place and time.

He should have been there. He checked the belts and equipment every day. Maybe he had been in too much of a hurry to leave that day and didn't take enough time to inspect the straps. He was sure that if he had been there, that somehow it wouldn't have happened, that maybe he could have done something to prevent it.

The eruption subsided, and the cycle turned again. Nate lifted his head, wiped his face, cleared his throat, and in his fog, got up to use the bathroom again. The beer just ran through him. Upon leaving, once again he stopped in front of the mirror. He looked even worse now. He felt nothing. He could never forgive himself. He wanted to kill himself. He stood there looking at himself and what he had become. After a long while, weighing all the pros and cons, he decided to give himself one more chance.

There was only one person left who might be able to help him. Someone who had known his father better than he did. Someone whose loss was just as great. Even though they had barely spoken since the funeral, Nate decided he needed to see his grandfather, his only living relative. He decided he would go see him today.

Lying on his back he stared at the ceiling, his mind going back and forth, trying to talk himself out of the decision he'd made. Facing his grandfather would be humiliating. His thoughts floated into an unconscious stream. He drifted off.

Nate woke up and tried to orient himself. He didn't know what day it was. He didn't know how long he'd been sleeping. He looked at the clock. Six. The last time he looked, it was around four. He didn't remember if it was day or night. Then he came to. The sun was peeking through the clouds. He was going to go see his grandfather today.

His brain was spinning, trying to think of what he would say to his grandfather, trying to imagine what his grandfather would say to him. One thing he knew for sure. He couldn't visit his grandfather looking the way he did, so he climbed into the shower, which he hadn't done in nearly two weeks. He let the hot water run and thought of how good it felt on his body, soothing him, comforting him, relaxing him. He stayed there until the water started turning lukewarm. Getting out, he grabbed a towel, feeling grateful to Haley for the clean laundry that had sat in a folded pile in the laundry basket.

Drying himself, he pulled on clean underwear, his best jeans, and a gray short-sleeved shirt. His clothes were wrinkled from sitting in the pile for so long, but at least they smelled fresh. He then looked at himself in the mirror. The stubble on his face was thick, and he knew it would take a while for him to shave, especially since the blade in his razor hadn't been replaced in months. He took his time, careful to avoid nicking himself. The aftershave stung his face, but it helped to wake him up. It wasn't a close shave, but he looked better than he did before. While he liked his hair long, to the nape of his neck, he was now badly in need of a cut. He put some gel on it and combed it back behind his ears. It would do for now.

Examining himself, he noticed how drawn and pale he looked. There were dark circles under his eyes. He had lost weight, and it showed in his face. Brushing his teeth twice, he rinsed with mouthwash, the last bit of it. He looked at the bathroom and understood why Haley didn't want to use it. It was filthy. There was mold in the shower and toilet, and the wastebasket was overflowing. He left the bathroom to find his boots. He hadn't been outside for a while and couldn't remember where he'd left them. Finding them under the kitchen table, he forced his feet inside and laced them up. Though he was still hungover and tired, he felt better than he had in quite some time.

He went outside, hoping his truck would start. The jeep he saved for special occasions was parked beside it. Since the convenience store was just a block away, it had been weeks since he had used either vehicle. He was hoping that the battery in the truck still had some juice in it. He loved his truck, a red Dodge Ram that he'd bought a couple of months before the accident. He was proud of it, still looking like new. On the driver and passenger side doors, 'Bearing and Son, Inc.' was inscribed. Nate got in the truck. After a few cranks of the ignition, the engine turned over. He was relieved that he didn't have to call anyone to jump it. He set out to his grandfather's house, anxious about how he would be received. He was hungry and planned on stopping along the way to get something to eat.

His grandfather's house was about an hour away. Not that the city he lived in was that big, but his grandfather had always wanted to live closer to nature, away from the noise and asphalt. When the business generated enough money to do so, he moved to an area of forest located in the foothills of an old mountain range where a large creek had cut its path. His grandfather had always loved the sound of water running over the rocks. He found it to be peaceful and life-giving. There he built his house, a log cabin that blended in with the trees surrounding it. It wasn't a big place, but it was perfect for his simple needs.

Nate didn't leave his house until just after eight, when the liquor store down the street opened. He bought two bottles and stowed them under the driver's seat, thinking one would be enough for one day at his grandfather's place, the other as a backup just in case. After stopping at a local diner for a breakfast sandwich to go and a cup of coffee, he set out on the highway that led to his grandfather's home in the woods. He was on autopilot, having traveled there many times with his father. He too loved the woods and the water. When at his grandfather's he always felt like he was on vacation, even if there for only a few hours.

Despite his anxiety and trembling hands, he was looking forward to being there. He felt a sense of security knowing that the bottles of whiskey were under him. He'd wait until he got there to slug some down, just to calm his nerves. He had heard too many tragic stories about drunken driving and swore a long time ago he would never drink and drive, unless of course, he was intending to commit suicide. As his mind wandered, Nate almost missed the turn off to his grandfather's place. He had to stop suddenly to make the right hand turn down the unpaved road that led into the woods. His heart pounded like the tires on the rough road.

Chapter 9

The one-lane road into the woods was dry. He watched the dust kick up in his rear-view mirror. Since it was Grandfather's private road, it was well rutted. Whoever needed to travel it, would do so regardless. Nate pulled over. Reaching under his seat, he pulled out a bottle, opened it, and took a few slugs as he took in his surroundings. The area was heavily forested, shadowing wildflowers and birds of all kinds; chickadees, bluebirds, red-winged black birds and more. He could hear the birds that he didn't hear at his house. Having been here so many times over the years, Nate was familiar with many of their calls. As a young boy, whenever Nate would ask what kind of bird he was hearing, his parents and grandfather knew and taught him. They cared about that kind of thing and taught Nate to care too.

Nate's favorite bird was the hummingbird, even though it could rarely be seen or heard. Of all the birds, he was most fascinated with it and the way it could almost stand in flight and then dart from one blossom to another. His grandfather told him that the hummingbird was naturally drawn to the more tropical climate of Belize and that it held special honor in the Mayan culture. Beauty is drawn to beauty. He said that the hummingbird opens the heart to experience the goodness in life and in others. The memories came flooding in and he could feel his heart melting in the sadness of missing his parents and the times they were all here together.

Inhaling deeply, Nate started up his truck and continued along the narrow road. Pulling up slowly, he parked the truck next to his grandfather's black Chevy pickup. It was probably fifteen years old, pockmarked with rust. Nate remembered when his grandfather bought it because it was not long after his mother died. His grandfather often took him out on weekend day trips to go fishing or hiking while his father worked at the shop and caught up with the housework. Grandfather knew that Nate's father also needed time to be alone to deal with the recent loss of his wife.

Nate stopped the engine and sat in the truck for a few minutes, still trying to decide what to tell his grandfather, how to explain why he was here. He was wondering why he had waited so long. As he was trying to summon up the courage to get out of the truck, his grandfather came around the corner from the back of the cabin. Axe in hand, he stopped and just stood there waiting. Waiting for Nate to get out of the truck. Nate opened the door slowly. He put his feet on the ground, closed the door, and leaned on the truck, looking at his grandfather. He knew his grandfather would not come to him. He had to make the first move. As he stepped forward, his grandfather said, "I could use some help chopping up the wood. I've been at it all morning, and I'm running out of steam. Come over here and give me a hand."

Relieved that he didn't have to sit down and start talking, Nate ambled over to his grandfather and took the axe. He wasn't sure how helpful he could be, not having done any strenuous work in some time. But he wanted to help and was willing to do what his grandfather asked of him. He followed his grandfather around to the back of the cabin. Seeing the enormous pile of wood, he felt his weakness, but he knew what was expected. He lifted a slab, set it on the block, and heaved the axe up to start splitting it.

It was less than an hour before he knew he had to stop. His arms were sore. He couldn't do any more. His grandfather just sat on a downed tree trunk, smoked his pipe, and watched. He could tell that Nate was struggling but sat there anyway, just waiting and watching. Nate didn't want to disappoint him, but when he put the axe down, he turned to look at his grandfather, who was shaking his head. Getting up, his grandfather said, "Take a break, Nate. I could use a cup of coffee."

Nate followed him into the house, two steps up to the front porch onto the planked floor. The floorboards were a well-weathered gray and warped in many places. Nate felt it added a rustic charm to the place. Pushing open the door, his grandfather silently led the way into the kitchen. It was a typical log cabin, no sheetrock on the walls or ceilings, simple window frames, and rather small rooms, which made it easier to heat. Living alone, his grandfather had no need or want for anything more.

Inside the kitchen, on the left, was a single stainless-steel sink under a bare window. A propane gas stove with four burners and a small oven was on the other side of the counter. The refrigerator was near the back window. In the right-hand corner was the woodstove. The door opening to the living room allowed the warmth of the stove to move through the cabin with ease.

His grandfather motioned to Nate to have a seat at the table. It also had a weathered look about it. It was much like a picnic table that had been sitting out in the elements for years. Perhaps it had been. His grandfather took the percolator coffee pot from the propane stove and brought it over to the table along with two old, stained pottery mugs. Setting one in front of Nate, he poured the coffee. Then he straddled the bench across from Nate, slowly sipped, and waited.

Nate couldn't have been more uncomfortable. He fumbled around with his mug and sipped the hot coffee without looking up. He could feel his grandfather's eyes going through him. He didn't know what to say, but he had little tolerance for the silence. He knew his grandfather well enough to know that he could stay this way for hours and hours, not speaking, but being fully present to the moment. Nate wished that he could just start with small talk, but his grandfather was not big on that either. He didn't like to waste his words, especially if no one was listening to him. He knew when they were listening and not just hearing his voice. Nate cleared his throat, as if to start to say something, but it was his grandfather who finally spoke the first words.

"Nate," his grandfather looked straight at him until Nate looked up. "Do you know why you are here?" asked his grandfather.

Nate shrugged his shoulders and looked down and up again at his grandfather. His face always reminded Nate of some old Indian chief he had seen in the movies he watched as a kid. In fact, his grandfather wore his now gray hair long and pulled back in a kind of ponytail. He had deep lines in his forehead, dark, almost beady eyes that were always certain in their gaze, a long, noble-looking nose, and distinctive lines around his mouth showing his age and the wisdom that came with it. His face showed strength much like his body. Even though he was in his late seventies, he was still built like a rock. Nate had always admired his grandfather, and in some ways, he was also afraid of him.

Feeling that fear, he mumbled, "Well, I guess I wanted to see you."

His grandfather waited patiently. Nate looked down again at his coffee, took another sip, set it down, and heard his grandfather repeat the question.

"Nate, why are you here?"

Nate thought, *That's the same question I've been asking myself and never getting an answer.*

Looking up at his grandfather, he said, "Grandfather," having been taught to speak to him with respect, "I don't know. I just decided to come and visit you." He paused and looked down at his cup.

His grandfather then said, "Well, why now? I have not seen you in months, and then suddenly you arrive at my front door. What do you want?"

Taking the risk, Nate started to talk. "Grandfather," he hesitated, "I'm confused. I've been feeling so alone. I've lost my desire to do anything."

He felt that clog in his throat again. Vowing not to allow his voice to crack, he struggled to keep going. "Haley left me. I've been thinking about killing myself for months now." His eyes began to fill. "Last night I was going to do it."

His grandfather asked pointedly, "Why did you not?"

Nate didn't think he heard him right. Wiping his face with both hands, he said, "What?"

His grandfather said, "You heard me. Why did you not kill yourself last night?"

Nate examined the table, his mug, the walls, trying to stave off his shame. "Because I passed out before I could."

His grandfather simply looked at him, not with pity, not with anger, but with understanding and respect. He then said, "Nate, you did not kill yourself because you were not supposed to."

He hated it when his grandfather spoke in riddles. Nate was too tired to try to discern the meaning behind what was just said. With that, his grandfather got up and took the coffee cups to the sink. Turning back, he put his hand on Nate's shoulder and said, "I do need you to help me get more wood piled for the winter. I will get the other axe, and maybe the two of us can get half a cord cut by dinnertime." Exhausted, but too proud to admit it, Nate followed his grandfather out to the back of the cabin.

Chapter 10

Grandfather and grandson stood not far apart, splitting, and stacking wood all afternoon. Sweat soaking his shirt, Nate would take frequent breaks while his grandfather kept at it, seemingly without much effort. Nate was acutely aware of how weak he had allowed himself to become, not only physically, but in character as well. As he sat on the same trunk his grandfather had been sitting on earlier, he perused the area surrounding the clearing.

Some large boulders and rocks naturally enclosed the space, separating it from most of the woods. A path into the woods declined gradually to a creek below, deep enough to never run dry. Nate wanted to go down there but knew that this was not the time to take a leisurely walk. As the sun began to set, the shadows made it more difficult to see.

His grandfather stopped and said, "Well, I guess that is enough for now. Let's go in and put something together to eat."

Nate sheepishly followed his grandfather back inside. There was now a chill in the musty cabin.

"Nate, you start up the wood stove for us while I get dinner going." Nate, feeling relieved, and without looking at his grandfather, said, "Sure. I'll bring in some more wood too."

They ate in silence, unlike the dinnertimes with his parents, when conversation was always more abundant than the food. Most often Nate would ask unending questions of his parents, who patiently and thoughtfully answered them all. Now there seemed to be no questions, and subsequently no answers. After finishing the rice and beans and Cajun catfish, Nate cleared the table and washed the dishes while his grandfather stoked the fire, adding more wood to the stove. His grandfather then went into the living room, waiting for Nate to join him.

Sitting on an old blue-green plaid cushioned chair that Nate remembered having once been at the family house in town, his grandfather lit his pipe, scenting the room with hickory. Nate came out and sat across from him on the matching loveseat and lit up a cigarette. His grandfather never knew that he had ever smoked, but didn't seem to mind. Nate was dying for a drink. He knew that there was no booze in this house. He planned to sneak out and take a swig from one of the bottles in his truck, but only enough to take the edge off. He couldn't dare get himself drunk.

Nate offered to get up and make a pot of coffee. His grandfather, who normally didn't drink coffee after noontime, said that would be fine, knowing that Nate needed an excuse to get up and slip outside. He also knew, without asking, that Nate had been drinking a lot. He had lost weight for sure but had a small beer gut that was never there before. He would have to address this issue, among many others.

Nate eventually reentered the room with the same two mugs that had been used earlier in the day, the only two he could find. He crossed the room and handed his grandfather his coffee. Sitting back down, Nate looked around the small room, hoping to find a familiar friend. He should have known that his grandfather would have no TV, no radio, no computer, not even a phone. Nothing to communicate outside of his own world. Nate decided at that point that he wouldn't be able to stay there much longer. He couldn't drink, which was preoccupying him, and there was nothing else to distract him from it. His grandfather just sat back comfortably in his chair and waited. Nate was getting irritated with this ritual. He couldn't stand it any longer and awkwardly started to talk.

"So, Grandfather, what have you been doing these past few months?"

"Living," he simply replied. Pausing, he then said, "Which is more than what you have been doing."

Nate's jaw tightened as he looked around the room, up at the ceiling, down to the floor. He could feel his guilt and shame rise to his face, knowing he would not be able to hide his feelings once he raised his eyes and looked at his grandfather.

His grandfather then asked, "How much money do you have left in the bank?"

Nate couldn't lie. His grandfather knew he had closed the business. It was only supposed to be a temporary arrangement until he was able to get things reorganized to take it over after his father died. He just couldn't get himself motivated to do it. The pain of losing his father seemed to loom larger, knowing that it was now his heavy responsibility to carry on the family tradition.

When his grandfather founded the business, Bearing Stone Cutting, he started small, as most businesses do. His specialty was in building walls, and he went about looking for work soon after arriving in the States. Luckily, after a couple of months, he was hired by a church to build a wall for a courtyard. The church wanted to have a special place outdoors for prayer and celebrations. He was also asked to build an altar. The magnificent church was built of red sandstone, mortar and roughly cut rock.

His grandfather's work was unusual and expensive. Through his innate charm and integrity, he was able to convince the church building committee that it was worth the money and that his wall would never need any kind of maintenance. It would last for many generations to come.

He relied on the techniques of his ancient culture rather than on the more modern, faster ways of cutting and fitting stone. While his walls did not compare to the pyramids and fortresses of the ancient Mayan civilization, he nonetheless was as meticulous and exacting as his forefathers. After many centuries, their walls still stood.

The wall his grandfather built matched the red sandstone of the church perfectly. It was so precisely cut that even a knife could not fit in between the joints. He built it just high enough so that the shadows cast by the wall would never fall on the stone altar in the middle of the courtyard. It was post Vatican II, so it was common in the Catholic Church to place the altar among the people where they could gather around it. He constructed the altar free of ornament. It was in great contrast to the architecture inside and outside of the church itself, allowing the natural environment to adorn it. When word got around about the wall and altar his grandfather built for St. Michael's, Manuel never had to look for work again.

So, as it goes, Nate's father learned the art of stone cutting. But he sought modern technology so he could expand the business beyond building walls. Alex had great respect and admiration for his father. He learned the skills it took to build without mortar. But he wanted to explore further into different types of stone that required more advanced cutting tools. He would need to rely more on pneumatic hammers and diamond drills to work with granite. It was becoming necessary for the monuments he was commissioned to do.

Nate got caught up in his past. He remembered that his father loved marble. He loved to work with hand tools, especially when he sculpted, as did the old masters who had no choice. Nate grew to love sculpting and did so whenever he could in his precious spare time. He worked on his carvings in the studio his father had attached to the house. Nate was not allowed to go in there alone when he was young. But as he grew, so did his fascination with stone and the desire to create. Carving stone is a special challenge and only limited by what can be imagined.

Chapter 11

Fifteen minutes passed, and Nate had still not answered the question. He was caught in memories, sitting in what looked like a trance. His grandfather did not intrude or intervene. He had asked a simple question, 'How much money is left?' He knew that this question was too overwhelming for Nate to answer. He waited, allowing his grandson to struggle, lost in time and memories.

Nate agonized in his guilt as he weighed how he would answer the question. He had learned everything he knew about life and stone cutting and carving from his father. As a boy, he had watched his father cut and shape stone, carefully watching every stroke of the various chisels. Occasionally, his father would let him chisel off some rock on the first layer of a stone, but only because if Nate screwed it up, he could fix it.

Nate understood his grandfather knew how much money had been in the bank before his father died. Because of its location and commercial zoning, the property itself was probably worth well over a million dollars. The storefront, shop, and house were worth at least that. But because of the success of the business, his father owned it all outright, leaving only insurances and taxes to pay on it. Prior to his father's death, the total cash asset was significant. After he died however, many of the orders for new monuments were canceled, and no new orders were coming in. Nate couldn't commit to his customers, and referred them to other reputable monument companies.

Besides that, all the inventory of stones that his father had ordered still sat on the back of the property.

With Haley's help, Nate continued paying the insurance premiums on the property. They were exorbitant. His father had not bought any life insurance. Nate supposed his father felt that the business would be life enough for Nate if he died. With Haley's constant reminders, Nate spent most of the remaining money on bills, paying off the loan for his truck, taxes, utilities, and health insurance. His living expenses were minimal, consisting mostly of alcohol and cigarettes. The liquid assets continued to be depleted.

Embarrassed, Nate looked up briefly, and then downward and finally admitted the truth to his grandfather. "I guess it's somewhere around twenty-five thousand."

His grandfather shook his head ever so slightly, clearly disappointed. He simply asked, "So, what are you going to do about it? If you end up having to sell the business, you will be selling out yourself, your father, and me at the same time."

Nate got up and started pacing angrily around the room, like a caged animal. His shame had turned to rage. He was having a difficult time controlling himself with little alcohol in his system. His muscles were getting tighter and tighter. He had walked right into it and been caught. He wanted to blame someone, but he knew there was no one to blame but himself. That self-loathing was killing him. His anger turned on him. The thought of killing himself stabbed at his soul. Pacing, he could feel his anger sinking into remorse and guilt now that he was being asked to explain.

He stopped, turned, and faced his grandfather, who still sat back in silent observation. With his anger transforming into unwanted tears, he said, "Grandfather, I came here because I thought you could help me! I don't know what to do! I really don't! I have no energy. No motivation! No passion! No dreams! I thought that you would be willing to help! Obviously, you'd rather not be bothered with it!"

He bolted toward the front door. His grandfather shouted at him. "Nate! You come here and sit down! Right now!"

Nate stopped. Taking a deep, slow breath, he turned back into the living room, stood glaring at his grandfather, and then sat down. His grandfather spoke again.

"Now that you have taken one breath, I want you to take another one. This time, though, I want you to take it in slowly and let it out slowly."

Now Nate was even more agitated. This was ridiculous. He resisted, fidgeting, fingers tapping on his legs, looking around the room, rolling his eyes. He felt like an idiot and couldn't believe his grandfather was telling him to do such a stupid thing.

"Now," his grandfather said, "do it again, and I want you to simply breathe this way for the next five minutes. Then we will talk."

Nate struggled with this. It felt foolish and useless. But he did trust his grandfather for the most part. He finally settled into the rhythm of his breathing. He could feel his body loosen up, and he was beginning to feel more relaxed. It wasn't as good as drinking, but he admitted that it was helping him to chill out.

After the five minutes were up, his grandfather said, "Now Nate, you will sit back and close your eyes. Continue to focus on your breath."

Nate did as he was told. His grandfather started humming. It was no familiar song, nor did it even seem like a song. It sounded almost as if he were humming just one note with only slight changes here and there. It felt weird to Nate, but at the same time, the low pitch and slow rhythm was soothing to him, seeping further into him. Not only was his body relaxing, so was his brain. He felt like he was falling asleep, but he wasn't. He was in that half-sleep, half-awake place where dreams are remembered.

He found himself wandering back to childhood where dreams and wishes were most alive. He felt the energy of that time and the excitement of anticipation that children have. They expect their dreams to come true, finding only later in life that it is their job to make dreams happen. In time, the humming stopped, and Nate's mind returned to the living room. He didn't speak. He just felt like sitting there. His grandfather also did not speak.

After a few minutes, Nate looked up at his grandfather and quietly asked, "Grandfather, what did you do? I feel so different than I did fifteen minutes ago."

His grandfather responded with a question. "Did it help?"

Nate replied, hesitating to give his grandfather too much credit, "Yeah, some. At least I don't feel like I'm going to take your head off."

His grandfather waited a bit before speaking again. "Yes, Nate, you do need motivation ... and energy. Without those, your passion is dormant, and that dries up your dreams. You do need help, and I will help you get back on your feet."

Nate felt too tired to go home and too relaxed to go out and deal with the traffic. He was reexperiencing the fond memories of his childhood here and wanted the feeling to last through the night. He knew he would go out and grab the bottle from the truck so he could get through until morning, so he asked his grandfather if he could stay.

His grandfather already knew that he would ask. Nate had been drinking on and off all day. "Sure," replied his grandfather. "Take the front bedroom."

"Thanks, Grandfather, I appreciate it." Getting up, stretching, and yawning, Nate turned to his grandfather. "I'm just going to step out a bit for some fresh air. I'll be back in a few minutes. By the way, do you have an extra toothbrush? I didn't bring anything, as you know."

"Yes, Nate, in the bathroom cabinet. Go get your fresh air. "I'm turning in."

Chapter 12

Waking up the next day, Nate lay in bed, not knowing what day it was, where he was, or even what time it was since there was no clock in the room. He wanted to just stay there with the old quilt his grandmother had made pulled over his head and tight around his body. That quilt was one of the few things that his grandfather still possessed from his life in Belize. His father had told him about how enormously patient his grandmother was and couldn't even imagine sitting still for that long doing what seemed to be tedious and boring work. But Grandmother had worked at her quilting at every opportunity, making one for everyone she knew to give as a gift. She probably could have sold them for a good price, but they were labors of love.

His mind wandered here and there as he tried to avoid the haunting thoughts that always pushed him further down into hopelessness. What am I going to do? He asked himself again as if expecting an answer. The question was relentless. He wanted someone just to tell him. He had always known what he wanted. He always had goals to shoot for and would always reach them. He had dreams and faith in his future and felt like he had control of it. He had known what was expected of him and what he expected from himself. Now he knew nothing. And in that nothingness, he despaired of ever knowing again.

Nate could smell coffee and his grandfather's tobacco. In some sense he was relieved that he had woken up in a place other than the prison he had made for himself. However, he knew that he would have to face his grandfather again before he left. Remembering his angry and pathetic outburst of last evening and not knowing what his grandfather was thinking made it difficult to move. But to get out the front door he would have to go through his grandfather's space. He sucked up his courage, got up, and dressed in the clothes he came with.

As Nate passed into the living room, he heard his grandfather's truck pulling up to the house. He went into the kitchen and saw the clock on the wall. He was embarrassed to see that it was almost noontime. He knew that his grandfather had been up since six at least. This was no way to impress him, especially since he drank himself to sleep. Taking the mug that his grandfather had left out for him, he went over to the stove and poured himself some coffee. Taking a sip, he walked over to the screen door and let himself out. With coffee in hand, he was pleasantly surprised at how crisp the air was; the sun dappled through the trees overhead as the dust and insects floated in the rays.

He remembered the times of his childhood when his parents would go for Sunday rides out into the countryside. Now and then, the sky would be cloudy, but not so cloudy that the sun didn't have a chance. Driving along, his mother would get so excited and say "Look! Look at the sky. That's a God-sky!" Nate thought that the sky was always God's, but when he looked out of the car window, he could see why his mother would say that. Above them in the distance the sun would break through the clouds, its rays distinctively separate and spectacular. It was almost like seeing a vision, but truly more of a reminder that the sun can be seen without hurting your eyes, more of a reminder that there is power in the sky and that it belongs to God. Now, every time he noticed the sun's way of pulling apart the earth and sky, he fondly thought of his mother and father and those Sunday rides together.

His grandfather broke the trance with, "Well, are you still sleeping, or are you going to get over here and help me with these bags?" Nate smiled ever so slightly, something his face hadn't done in a while. He set the mug on the rail and stepped down to reach the groceries his grandfather had stacked in the passenger side of the truck. Between the two of them, it took only one trip inside. Laying the bags on the table, his grandfather started to empty them and put the food away.

Nate couldn't help himself and said, "So, you don't think you're going to shop again until spring?" By Nate's standard, there was enough food there to last for months.

As his grandfather started to stack the canned goods in the pantry cupboard, he said over his shoulder, "This is to feed two people."

Nate wondered who was coming. There weren't any other relatives to speak of, but his grandfather had made lots of friends over the years. Maybe one of them was going to stay there for a vacation visit.

Innocently, Nate asked, "Who's coming? They picked a nice time of year."

His grandfather said matter-of-factly, "No one is coming. You're not going."

Nate just stood there with a box of saltines in one hand and a can of tomato soup in the other, staring at his grandfather, who was essentially ignoring him. Nate had no intention of staying. As much as he loved the environment, and as much as he loved his grandfather, he could in no way live with him. They were completely different from one another. Normally, Nate liked to talk. His grandfather didn't. Nate liked to watch sports on TV.

Not only did his grandfather not have a TV, but he also wouldn't be into a football game. Nate liked to do housework when he felt like it, which wasn't often, especially lately. His grandfather was meticulous in his simplicity. No way could he stay here, especially if he couldn't manage to get out and buy some more whiskey. His brain was trying to come up with an excuse, any excuse. But that was a challenge.

Nate had no real reason to leave. The house would still be there, and the disastrous mess inside it. He had no pets, no work, and no one to take care of. There wasn't much left of the lawn anyway, so he didn't care for that either. There were too many weeds growing in the gravel, let alone in the small parking lot for customers. It looked like shit inside and out.

When he was little his parents created a couple of understated terraced gardens around the house. His father made the retaining walls and had soil dumped into the two-foot depth. His mother planted the garden. She found great joy in getting her hands into the dirt and then watching something beautiful happen. His father hired someone to keep up the gardens after his mother died. Nate felt bad. The weeds had gotten so thick that unless one looked closely, barely a single blossom could be seen. He made a promise to himself that he would recreate the gardens in the spring.

The silence was getting awkward as he passed the groceries to his grandfather to put away. He knew that he could walk out as planned today. But if his grandfather meant what he had said to him, that he would help Nate get back on his feet, then he should probably at least give it a try. If it wasn't working out, he could always leave. So instead of arguing with his grandfather, Nate managed to gather up some gratitude and said, "Thank you, Grandfather. I would appreciate that, but I'll need to get home and get some of my things first." Nate was more focused on getting enough liquor to last a few days.

His grandfather retorted, "Oh, believe me, this is not for you, it is for me. I need your help around here. I'm getting too old to be breaking my back trying to keep things up the way I want to. You may be a bit useless now, but it will not be long before you can actually do me some good."

Here he was thinking that his grandfather was going to help him, but instead the selfish old bastard was going to take advantage of the situation.

His grandfather knew exactly what he was thinking and said, "And by helping me, you will be helping yourself, and therefore I will be helping you."

Nate's mind had become too dull to keep up with his grandfather's witticisms, so he didn't respond. Once the groceries were put away, his grandfather made a couple of peanut butter sandwiches, gave one to Nate, poured his coffee, and went out to sit on the front porch. Standing there with sandwich in hand, Nate was puzzled, as if he didn't know what to do with the sandwich. Mechanically, he grabbed his coffee and went outside. His grandfather was sitting in an old Adirondack chair that was once painted white. He motioned to Nate to sit down in the matching one angled next to him. Nate sat down and munched on the sandwich. They sat there in silence eating their peanut butter sandwiches.

Trying not to be obvious, Nate regarded his grandfather as they sat there. His grandfather was a handsome man, despite his age, and always exuded confidence and strength. Yes, he was muscular and weathered, giving him that rugged outdoorsman appearance, but it was his sincerity and wisdom that drew people to him, that is, when he let them. His grandfather always dressed the same, not in the same clothes, which had become Nate's habit, but in the same denim shirt, faded jeans, brown belt, and tan construction boots, which in one sense was his life uniform.

His grandfather was always neat and clean-shaven. His gray hair was long, but always clean and combed out. His open neckline revealed his graying chest hair, which only added to his masculine physique. A widower when he arrived in the States, many women would have loved to have him as their life partner. But his grandfather had already had one at one time, and for him, that was all he needed or wanted.

When they had finished eating, they both sat still sipping the coffee that by now was lukewarm. Neither seemed to mind. Nate used to like a little cream in his coffee, but he had gotten to the point where he didn't want to bother getting anything that would expire less than two months, so he started drinking it black. Now he preferred it that way.

As they were sitting there, a commotion was brewing in the woods. There were several birds, chickadees, he thought, that were flying around looking like they were trying to get organized. He could hear the squawking of a blue jay nearby. It was late in the season. Nate knew there were no eggs or young birds to protect, and the migrations hadn't begun. It seemed to be more of a territorial issue. Most other birds didn't like blue jays, even though people seemed to. They had a way of intruding into the space of other birds, often wanting what the others had. A fight ensued, and eventually the jay knew he was outnumbered and flew off. The chickadees were not necessarily out to kill him, rather, they were just keeping themselves from being intimidated by him. As things grew quiet, his grandfather began to speak.

"Nate, you need to know something."

"What's that?"

"You need to know that I am not dead."

As usual, this was way too deep for Nate to get his head around. His grandfather continued.

"You used to always come and visit me with your father, but never alone. I would only see you if you came with him. Now that your father is not here, I never see you, as if you think I am dead too. In that sense, I have not only lost a son but a grandson as well. But I am not dead."

"And I understand how I have failed you and myself as well," Nate replied. "After my father died, I didn't want anything to do with anything or anybody that reminded me of him. I don't know why exactly, but maybe I thought it would prevent me from feeling the loss more than I already did. I guess I just wanted to be left alone with it. But now that you say it, I can understand that it didn't help me, or you."

"Then perhaps you are beginning to understand. In not dealing with your loss, your pain has only grown. It has grown out of proportion to life. You have disconnected yourself from me, and from most of life for that matter. And if anything, you are much worse off because of it."

"Grandfather, you're right, and now I understand what you're saying. Haley left me because I was killing her spirit. I was draining her. I have never wanted to look upon myself as a burden to others. But that's what I have become. I guess it would be different if some illness had been inflicted on me. But this I have inflicted upon myself." Nate started to choke up. "I haven't been able to get over the fact that if I had been there my father wouldn't have died. I haven't been able to get past it. I feel like I deserve to be punished for the rest of my life."

"Nate, you're the only one who feels that you need to be punished. Accidents happen, sometimes for a reason that we will never understand. But you must know, and you must believe, that your father, and your grandfather, and the father of us all have forgiven you. I never held it against you, ever."

After a pause, his grandfather continued, "You must forgive yourself. I have wanted you to come to me because you are all I have left, and I am all you have left in our family. We need each other, you more so than me. I have weathered many storms and have learned that certain things happen that I cannot do anything about. But you, you seem to think that you are the only one who has any control over anything. That is why you continue to blame yourself for the accident. One thing you need to learn, and I will teach you, is that you are not in control. None of us is, in the big picture. Our job is to make the most of what we have. You have not been doing that, and that is your shame, not your father's death."

Nate studied his fingernails as he pondered his grandfather's words.

After a long silence, his grandfather said, "Listen, I would like to sit around all day and talk to you, but there are things that need to get done. Help me out back. I need a lot more wood for the stove if I am to get through this winter."

There were still a few hours left of daylight. Nate knew that his grandfather would not stop working until the sun did.

Chapter 13

Nate went out to the truck, took a couple of gulps from the bottle, and went around to the back of the cabin to help his grandfather. They worked until they could barely see what they were doing. Nate hurt all over, his whole body aching from the strenuous labor. As soon as he got inside, he would see if there were some Advil or Tylenol, or anything that would alleviate some of his misery. He was hoping he could find something on his own. He didn't want to ask his grandfather because he didn't want to hear his comments. He was also starving. Normally he didn't eat much, preferring beer and hard liquor, but the peanut butter sandwich had worn out and so had he. Besides, he was ready for another drink. He was relieved when his grandfather finally said, "Well that's enough for today. Let us go in and get dinner going."

Inside the kitchen, Nate was expecting that his grandfather would be cooking the dinner while he sat down to rest. Instead, he was handed a bag of potatoes to peel, fresh green beans to wash and cut, and lettuce, tomato, and onion to chop up for a salad. His grandfather said, "Here, you get this going and I will start up the grill outside. I bought us a couple of steaks to throw on."

Nate, despite his disdain for making meals, was truly looking forward to a meat and potato dinner. With that, he told himself to stop complaining and do what was asked of him. As boring as it was to cut up vegetables, at least he didn't have to strain his muscles to do it. He was able to get to his room a couple of times to take a hit from one of the bottles that he had brought into the house. When dinner was ready, he sat down across from his grandfather and dug in. He ate like it was his last, or maybe first, meal. His grandfather watched in silence as Nate wolfed down his food so quickly that he wanted seconds. There were none. Disappointed, Nate should have predicted this. His grandfather cooked enough for only one serving. That's all he needed or wanted.

After dinner, his grandfather, without a word, simply left the kitchen and went into the living room, sat down, and lit his pipe. Nate was dying for a cigarette himself, which was particularly satisfying after a meal, but without asking, he knew his grandfather expected him to clean up the kitchen. Feeling that familiar resentment emerging, Nate did not react to it but tamed it into accepting this duty. When finished, he joined his grandfather in the living room, sat in his designated spot, and lit up.

His cigarette smoking had been slashed significantly in the short time he had been there. His grandfather kept him too busy to smoke much, though the craving was making him feel desperate. Taking in the first drag, he looked at his grandfather, half expecting him to start up a conversation. Instead, and as usual, his grandfather was silent.

Nate's discomfort with just sitting there had not diminished. Too antsy, Nate went into the kitchen to see if there was any more coffee left in the pot made earlier that day. He didn't care if it was fresh or not. At home, he was generally too lazy to make it. If there was some left from the day before he would just heat it in the microwave and drink it. He had stopped caring about a lot of things. Though he preferred it cold, he would drink warm or even flat beer if there was some left in a can.

Finding the pot empty, he looked in the refrigerator for something to drink. There was only milk and cranberry juice. He poured himself a glass of cranberry juice and walked back to his room, then out into the living room. Sitting down, he sipped the drink as if it were some fancy cocktail. It tasted better with the whiskey. He heard his grandfather pointedly say, "That is better for you anyway." He couldn't figure out how Nate thought he was getting away with something. After all, he reeked of alcohol.

"You know, I've been thinking about it. I don't think I can stay here for more than a couple of days. I'm happy to help you out," Nate lied, "but I need to get my life together, and I can't do that by sitting around here."

His grandfather said, "And how is that?"

"How's that what?" Nate asked with subtle defiance.

"How do you think you are going to get your life together when you came here yesterday saying 'I don't know what to do?' Have you figured that all out now?"

Nate, feeling even more challenged, said, "Yeah, I know what I need to do. I need to clean up the house, clean up the store, clean up my life, and get going again."

His grandfather said, "What makes you think it is that simple? You have not done anything in months. How is it that suddenly you have all the answers?"

"I've had time to think about it."

His grandfather chuckled a little. "Have you not been thinking about it all this time?"

His grandfather was right. How long had he been lying on the couch thinking? Not thinking about what he was going to do, but rather why he couldn't. He didn't have a clue, but he'd be damned if he were to let his grandfather make fun of him.

"Well, I guess I just needed to get out of the house for a while and get some fresh air to clear my head."

His grandfather then said, "You know what the problem is? You just cannot stand sitting still with yourself, or with me. What is that about? What are you afraid of? What is it that keeps you from moving or sitting? You cannot stand to move, and you cannot stand to sit. You have questions, but you do not want to hear the answers.

"You came here asking for help, and now you cannot sit still long enough to get it, or maybe you do not think you will. You do not trust me, and I doubt very much that you trust yourself. What is it that you are looking for from me that you do not think you're getting?"

This line of questioning flustered Nate. Pushing himself to respond he said, "I want to know how to get the business up and running again."

"You already know how to do that."

Nate knew he was right. Thinking of something else, he said, "I want to know how to handle the finances so I can keep all the records straight."

"You already know how to get that done."

Nate didn't think he did, but he had some ideas. Scrambling his brain, and hesitating to say it, he finally let it out, "I want to know how to get Haley back."

Once again, his grandfather said, "You already know what she wants and what you have to do."

Nate had had enough of this. His juice was gone. He knew his grandfather was counting how many cigarettes he had smoked in the last fifteen minutes.

Angrily he got up and said, "What is it that you want from me? You ask me what I want from you, and you tell me I have all the answers. Well, maybe I do. Maybe you're right. I guess since I know it all, I might as well leave! Were you this much of a pain in the ass to my father? If you were, he never let on. But let me tell you this, if you think I'm going to stay here and play your mind games, you're crazy, crazier than I thought. I'm leaving!"

Nate was headed to the door when his grandfather shouted, "Nate, sit down right now! You will stay here, and you will learn! You are asking me to help you with things you already know how to do. Sit down now and do what I taught you last night. Start breathing. Let yourself relax for a few minutes. Focus on your breath and close your eyes."

Nate, knowing this had helped him calm down last night, knew he had to do it, but he was fighting himself in his resistance to it and fighting his grandfather's authority. His grandfather knew this and waited while Nate paced around, trying to decide what he was going to do. His desire to leave was powerful, yet there was something inside of him that was preventing it. His pride was in the way for sure. He never wanted anyone to get the upper hand on him. But his grandfather did because nothing that he had said to him was false. Nothing that he asked Nate to do was without purpose, even if he didn't like it. His grandfather did have something to give to him. Nate just didn't know the right questions.

He decided to do what he was told and sat down. Initially he let out deep sighs, almost as if he were forcing the anger out. After a couple of minutes, he was able to slow it down into a rhythm that began to ease the tension. Then he heard his grandfather's humming, which again fell in harmony with his breathing. His mind was clearing and his body relaxing, but as that was happening, so was something else. He could feel his grief filling his gut, and his sadness trying to push its way out through his heart, like molten rock about to erupt.

Listening to his grandfather humming, feeling these emotions struggling to come out, tears started leaking down his face. He wanted to cry, and cry, and cry. He felt there would be no end to it if it started. He was not in control, and to be truthful, he didn't want to be. He wanted comfort and consolation. He wanted to know why he could not get beyond it. He wanted to know why he was here in this world.

He wanted to know why he had to suffer so. He wanted to know why others had to suffer. He wanted to know who he was and what his purpose was. What did God want from him? He wanted to know with certainty that God cared and that there was a reason for all of this. He had these feelings, but his pride kept him from saying anything. He'd be damned if he'd let his grandfather see him cry. He slapped his hands on his knees and matter-of-factly said, "I'm pretty tired. I think I'll go to bed." With that, he got up, said goodnight, and left the room.

Chapter 14

Nate lay on top of his bed thinking. His grandfather perplexed him. On the one hand, he was challenging him as if he were looking for a good fight, and Nate was angry at himself for letting it get to him. On the other hand, his grandfather seemed to know how to handle him, which Nate certainly didn't know about himself. After about half an hour, Nate decided to go back out into the living room. His grandfather was still there. Nate sat back down on the couch and looked at his grandfather, who was reading.

Eventually his grandfather looked up and said, "Well?"

Nate wasn't sure what to say, so he just said, "Sorry I got angry with you."

"OK. Is there something else you wanted to say?"

"Yeah," said Nate, trying to get his thoughts in order. "When I got here yesterday morning and told you that I wanted to kill myself, you said that the reason I didn't was because I wasn't supposed to, as if you knew that for a fact. You also hammered me earlier by telling me I already knew the answers to the questions I was asking you."

His grandfather said, "Well, admit it, you do know the answers to those questions."

"I guess so, even though I don't feel that way. But, uh, I guess what's bothering me is that you seem to know why I came here despite what I have told you. Do you?"

Without hesitating, his grandfather said, "Yes, I do," but didn't expand upon this.

Nate, frustrated, asked, "So why do you say that? Why do you think I ended up here?"

"It is because you were sent here." Nate tried to grasp this. His grandfather continued. "There is a reason for everything and a purpose. And the reason you are here is to find your purpose. It has nothing to do with the business, or the finances, or even Haley. It has to do with you and why you are here in the world. That is something I know that you don't already know. That is something I can help you with."

"Grandfather, how is it that you know me so well when we've not seen each other for months? How is it that you know why I am here, that you know what I need when I don't even know what to ask for? I don't get it."

"Nate, you do not need to know the answers to those questions. What questions do you really want to ask?"

Nate, not feeling put off, said to his grandfather, "I want to know why I cannot let go of my sadness over losing my father, and my mother for that matter. I want to know why they were taken from me. As old as I am, I feel like an orphaned child. I don't know how to be alone and to be OK with it. I want to know why I'm here. I want to know who I am. I don't know the answers to these things."

His grandfather listened and thought for a moment before he responded. "Most people do not know the answer to these questions. Many do not think to ask; many do not care to know. They just go about their lives doing just what is in front of them, never questioning, never examining why. They just settle for what they know, and that is enough for them. It is not enough for you. You have been questioning, and to your credit, you have been seeking."

Nate listened. And waited and listened. He found himself getting more comfortable in sitting with his grandfather. He knew that his grandfather knew what he was talking about. He recognized wisdom, something that he wanted but did not have. He recognized peace in his grandfather, something he wanted but did not have. He recognized truth but did not know his own. He no longer wanted to leave. He wanted to learn the things that his grandfather knew. And for that, he could sit still.

"Nate. Do you remember when you had the accident?"

Nate did remember what happened to him, but only because he was told about it. When he was about eight years old, he had been hit by a car. He was riding his bike along the highway near his house. He always made sure that he was way over to the shoulder of the road, and he always rode his bike with the traffic, as he had been taught. One afternoon after school, he took his bike up to the convenience store a couple of blocks from the house. He would spend a small part of his allowance on treats. It was the same store that he frequented lately to buy his beer and cigarettes. But when he was almost eight years old, it wasn't beer and cigarettes he was after. It was candy and soda.

For doing his chores his parents gave him two dollars a week, which was well worth it for him. They made him put a dollar in his box that looked like a safe, and the other dollar he could spend on what he wanted. On this afternoon, he had a craving for some Fritos and a Doctor Pepper, so he got on his bike to get them. On his way back, he carried the brown paper bag in one hand and was steering his bike with the other. He heard a siren coming up behind him and instinctively turned his head back to see what was going on. When he did this, his tire caught the edge of the shoulder and he lost control of his bike.

A car was trying to move over to let the ambulance by. Nate had swerved over toward the road trying to right himself and the car hit him, throwing him into the lane of traffic. By that time, many cars had already slowed to a stop and pulled over, but it was too late for Nate. He lay there in the middle of the road motionless and bleeding from his head.

Unknown to him or anyone else, the person in the ambulance was just a kid like Nate. A car had hit him too. But as the ambulance drove by, the kid inside came back to full consciousness. He was fully awake when he arrived at the hospital, and other than for a few bruises, he was fine and cleared for discharge. No one could understand how he survived the accident and then was able to leave the hospital.

His grandfather interrupted his thoughts. "Do you remember that?"

"Yes, grandfather, I do. I wasn't supposed to live."

"That is right. And I cannot tell you how hard it was for your parents, let alone me. We thought we were going to lose you. And in my opinion, there is no greater pain than losing a child. Your parents were grief-stricken.

"You were in a coma for three months. Every day your mother would go to the hospital and sit with you, praying endlessly, begging God not to take you away while your father and I tried to focus on the work. It was hell. But eventually you came out of it, and miraculously you recovered completely. Both a blessing and a curse," he laughed. Nate laughed too.

"There was no doubt in my mind, nor was there any doubt in your parents' minds, that you were supposed to be here. That there was a reason for you to be here, and that you were special in some way." He paused as Nate listened, wondering what he would say next. "You have a special gift, and you are here to use it."

Nate couldn't figure this one out. He did remember that something weird happened to him, but at that age he never gave it much thought, nor did he ever talk about it. It didn't seem to matter that much, especially when he finally did come out of the coma. His parents were so elated and thankful that they doted on him for months afterward. To say that they spoiled him would be an understatement. What he didn't tell them, or anybody, now that he remembered it, is that after the car hit him, he saw something that he could not describe or understand. He felt like he was floating in the clouds. The sun was so bright that he could barely see. Then he was on his feet, walking into this light when an image appeared before him, one that he could barely see because it was kind of in front of the light but nearly as bright.

He never talked about it because he felt no one would believe him anyway. But in that light, he saw an angel. Not the kind you see on 'cupid cards,' but an angel so big and so powerful that Nate stood in awe. His mother had talked about angels when he was little and how they were always there. He never saw them, so he just humored his mother. But here he was. The angel had a sword, and Nate knew that he was standing face-to-face with Michael the Archangel, who stood there like a sentry, not pushing Nate away, but not letting him pass either. In thinking back, Nate surmised that this could have been a near-death experience like he had read about in magazines. As his grandfather spoke, it took on more significance.

When his grandfather said he had a special gift, Nate assumed he meant that he had been given a creative talent for stone sculpting that was exceptional even to serious artists. Nate assumed that his grandfather meant that this was the gift that was given to him and that he needed to own it, get back to work, and use it.

Nate said to his grandfather; "I think I know what you mean. And I know I have been given a special gift. I know it's important that I use it and start sculpting again. I need to not take it for granted like I have. I can make beautiful things with stone. Sometimes I surprise myself. And I know that others greatly appreciate it, even though I need to charge them a lot. They do keep coming to me." Grandfather acknowledged all of this and let it be. Nate would learn in time. This was something his grandfather could not teach him.

Chapter 15

Nate finally went to bed that night exhausted, and not because he had been working in the yard most of the day. This exhaustion was more draining. Both his mind and his body were whipped. It was hard to fall asleep. He was tossing and turning, filled with worry and questions, still trying to figure out what he was going to do.

He was pacing himself with the alcohol, drinking only enough to stop shaking. The thoughts kept racing through his mind, and as tired as he was, he couldn't sleep. Since there was no clock in the room, he had no idea of the time, but the night seemed endless. He thought about going back to his house the next day to start cleaning it up. He tried to figure out where he would start but visiting each room in his head made him feel that he could never get things back to the way his mother had them, let alone his father. He wouldn't know where to start.

He thought about the shop. He hadn't been in there in months. He couldn't even imagine what it would look like, so he couldn't even imagine what he would have to do. He even questioned whether he should go back into the stone carving business at all. Maybe he wasn't up to it anymore. Maybe he didn't want the responsibility. Maybe he was afraid he would fail at it on his own. All these doubts kept him from holding onto the peace he had experienced earlier in the night with his grandfather.

After struggling to catch a break in the night's turmoil, he decided to get up. He pulled on his jeans and shirt, went to the bathroom, and then out through the living room toward the kitchen. Trying to be quiet, as he went by his grandfather's bedroom, he heard humming. It was the same kind of humming that his grandfather did with him the previous two evenings, though it had a different rhythm to it. It was faster and seemed to be more deliberate. Nate thought, *well, maybe he couldn't sleep either*. He went into the kitchen to put on a pot of coffee. He looked at the clock. Four thirty. His grandfather usually got up around six. Nate wondered why he was awake now. Nate decided to take care of himself and made the coffee.

He sat at the kitchen table drinking coffee and smoking one cigarette after another, as was his daily habit. He called it 'front-loading,' getting himself going with caffeine and nicotine to satisfy the cravings quickly. At home, the first thing he would do is flip on the TV and watch the news. Each broadcast lasted thirty minutes, and he would just sit there watching one after the other, the same news and weather report repeatedly. Each time a new segment started he would pick up something that he hadn't remembered from the previous one.

Even though he wasn't planning on going anywhere, he would always want to know the weather report. It used to be important, since much of the work he and his father did was outside. But he was still intent on getting the report, and then his mind would wander off. He would lose his concentration, and miss it altogether. He tried to catch it next time around but often missed that too. There were some mornings when he didn't get it at all. Frustrated, he would say to himself, "Who gives a shit anyway?" He sat there and drank the entire pot of coffee, feeling tired and now wired. Soon he would need a drink.

His grandfather came into the kitchen. "Well, you are up. That is a surprise."

"Yeah, I didn't sleep too well."

"That mattress is not the greatest thing. I did not spend a lot on it, figuring it wouldn't be used much. I never tried it out. But I suppose it beats sleeping on the floor."

"Beggars can't be choosers," Nate replied.

He wanted to question his grandfather's early rising but decided against it. Still guarded, he didn't want to intrude on his grandfather, nor did he want his grandfather to intrude on him.

He asked, "So, what's on today's agenda?"

"Well, I must go to the lumber store. There are some things I want to get done before winter that I did not get around to this summer. I don't know why. I guess I just got busy doing other things. I am missing a couple of cedar shakes on the back of the roof. And I want to caulk the windows. It was drafty in here last winter. I also need some new tarps to throw over the wood stacks. They are pretty beaten up."

"You want me to help you out with that?" asked Nate.

"No, not at all. I need you to split more wood. I went through so much last winter that I had to have some delivered. With you here, I'm hoping to have enough to make it until spring."

"Well, OK. I suppose I can do that, but if I'm going to be staying here for a while, I need to get back to the house and get some clothes and stuff. I don't think it will take that long, but it's an hour there and back, so I guess it depends on what time I get going."

His grandfather replied, "All right, you do that. Like I said, I would appreciate your help around here for a while, and it is easier if you just stay here instead of running back and forth from your place. The work will still be here, as they say. I think we both should eat some breakfast though. I have some sausage and eggs in the refrigerator. You get started with that while I go shave and get myself ready for the day."

Neither spoke about the night before. Nate was certainly relieved about that. He started cooking the sausage, got the eggs out, and found some bread for toast. Thankfully, his grandfather used real butter. He may be a health nut, but at least he ate food for real men. The breakfast was great. Nate usually skipped it at home, not wanting to put any effort into it, but he had to admit it was worth it. He cooked the eggs over easy so he could dip his sausage and toast in the yolk. His grandfather liked it this way too, which was at least one thing they had in common.

Afterward, Nate was all set to clean up the dishes when his grandfather surprised him by saying, "I will clean up here. You get ready to go. That way, you will be back with enough time to split a good amount of wood before dinner. The days are getting shorter and shorter now. We must take advantage of that."

Nate thought, *is he, or is the sunlight taking advantage of me?* He had his answer for that.

PART II

SANDSTONE

Chapter 16

Even though he had been there for only three days, riding down the dirt road to the highway made Nate feel like an adolescent again. He had escaped, if only for a while, from the constraints of living with a 'parent.' He revved up the engine of the truck and raced over the road. He hit and flew over potholes and mounds. It was exhilarating fun, challenging his ability to stay in control of the wheel. He just let loose. Turning onto the highway, he settled into the rules of the road.

He hit the radio and caught the refrain to Dobie Gray's 'Drift Away.' The words matched his mood: 'Give me the beat boys and free my soul, I wanna get lost in your rock and roll and drift away.' He had the window open, singing along louder than the radio. Even though the song came out before his time, he loved it. His father could get into it too. Maybe that's why he liked it so much. He never could get all the verses straight, but when the refrain came around, he was right there. He let himself become immersed in the music, not thinking. He just drove and sang. After about a half hour of this, he became aware that he hadn't felt this alive in a long time. It felt like party time, and he was pumped. Maybe that's what sleep deprivation does to people.

Arriving at the house, he walked in to see the mess he had left. He decided to pick up the dirty clothes, beer cans and bottles, and empty the ash trays into the garbage.

He then went into his bedroom to pack some clothes. He did so without much thought. He basically took the clean clothes Haley had washed for him, shoved them in a duffle bag, got his razor and toothbrush, and then zipped it up. He stopped to look around the room. It needed paint. It hadn't been painted in a few years, and his smoking had left things looking yellowed and brown. The room had been light blue, and the bedspread matched the curtains that were full of dust. He knew he would have to clean it up, but not today. He went into the kitchen.

Overhead the florescent light panels were yellow. The sink was still full of dishes. The white tiled floor had stuff stuck to it and needed a good scrubbing. He now saw what Haley was talking about. The stove had baked-on food. The oak cabinets had dust stuck on their grease. He didn't even bother looking in the oven. He went over to the refrigerator and opened it up. It too had spills of crap all over it, but there was still a six-pack of beer there. He popped one open.

He guzzled it, realizing how much he had missed it. It was around ten, but he wasn't living by any rules, so he didn't even think about what he was doing. He was feeling good for a change and he was ready to have a good time. He was about to grab another one but then decided to run down to the liquor store first. When he returned, he grabbed another beer, went into the living room, and turned on the TV. He was suddenly feeling quite comfortable in this familiar place.

He was starting to feel hungry and decided to take a brisk walk down to the store a couple blocks away. While there he picked himself up a sub and some chips, then walked around looking for something else. When he got to the coolers, he stopped and thought for about two seconds before he grabbed a twelve-pack of Bud. He paid for it, left the store, and walked back home. When he got there, he said to himself that he would just eat, watch a little TV, and get back to his grandfather's house. By two o'clock he had finished most of the beer, half the bottle of whiskey, and passed out. He didn't wake up until five hours later.

Chapter 17

Nate staggered to the bathroom. His head was throbbing. He felt like he was going to throw up. Flushing and holding himself up by the wall, he could feel his insides turning out. Slipping down to his knees, he bowed his head and retched out the lunch and breakfast and everything else his body rejected. He felt like he was going to pass out, and he did, on the cold bathroom floor.

When he came to, he dragged himself back to the couch. He had emptied himself and slipped back into his stupor. He woke up suddenly, sweat pouring out of him, shaking, and terrified. He had been walking through the park in the early morning hours, just minding his own business, coming back from Haley's apartment. The path was well lit, and he could hear the fountains that were not far away. Without warning, something slammed into his back, throwing him to the ground. He felt himself being dragged by his feet, his face scraping the sidewalk onto the grass, his hands groping for something to stop the backward thrust. He felt another jolt, this time landing into his side, that caused him to double up.

He caught a glimpse of his attackers. He thought there were three of them, though he couldn't be sure. It was dark, so he couldn't see anything other than shadows and flailing feet and arms. They were spewing obscenities at him, sounding like he had done something to them. Each kick seemed to lessen the pain until he no longer felt anything. Then everything stopped and went black. He was left for dead.

Nate had a hard time pulling out of the nightmare. In some sense, he did feel as though he had been beaten up, but not by punks in the park. Trying hard to orient himself, he turned on the light. He rocked himself on the edge of the couch. He lit a cigarette to ground himself. "Holy shit," he said. "Where did that come from?" Nate never had nightmares. In fact, he never remembered any of his dreams, if he had any at all. It left him trembling more than his hangover did, which he knew he deserved. He saw the time. 3 a.m. *3 a.m.?* He thought, *Jesus, I'm in deep shit!* He got up, started pacing around, rubbing his hands into his face to erase the pain in his head and the anxiety wracking his nerves. He had told his grandfather that he would be back before noontime yesterday. "Now what the fuck am I going to do?" he said out loud to no one.

He went into the bathroom, looked at himself in the mirror, and didn't like what he saw. Splashing cold water on his face, Nate took the towel and just held it there. He felt miserable and was listening to the same old accusatory voice in his mind that he had been listening to for months. *You're such a piece of shit. You're useless. You're a burden to all who know you. You've let everyone down, the spirit of your father, Jack, Haley, and now your grandfather. I don't want to live like this. I can't do it. Maybe I'm just not meant to be here. No one would miss me anyway, or if they did, they'd get over it. They'd understand.* Talking to himself in the mirror, he angrily said out loud, "I don't want to do this anymore. I don't know how to do this anymore. I'm tired." He started to cry into the towel. "I'm so tired of it! I don't have anything left."

He thought of his plan. The one he had and fought and had and fought, trying to grasp onto something that would give him a desire to keep going. His self-talk was eliminating his options. There was only one choice, one decision. And it was gaining on him. In the past, he would just put it off. One day at a time, he would allow himself to live, perhaps a flicker of hope that he didn't have the will to kindle or blow out. He didn't know if he had the courage to end it, but he was caught in the minefield of ambivalence. He couldn't live and he couldn't die.

He went back to the couch and lay down. He pulled the afghan that his mother had made long ago over himself. His tears grew. His agony grew. His grief erupted from the depths of his slain spirit, from his gut. He wrenched, clutching himself, as if he would split apart. He sounded like a mother mourning her child. He could not stop it. In his primitive state, in his fragile mortality, in his darkest hour, he pleaded for mercy. "Oh God, I don't want to die ... I don't want to die ... I don't want to die." Yet he felt as if he were dying. After a while, his pain subsided into sobs, like a child, trying to catch his breath. As his breath returned to a more normal but shallow rhythm, he fell back to sleep, exhausted from the fight.

When he woke up, he couldn't think and didn't want to. He didn't move. He didn't want to move. He didn't want to think. He didn't want to feel. It was as if he were waiting to be taken. He wanted to just stay there in his lifeless, fetal position. But the urgency to urinate grew. He felt intruded upon. His body was prodding him to move, and he didn't want to. He knew if he didn't move soon, he would wet himself. He wished he didn't care, and part of him didn't, but his anger forced him to yank off the cover and sit up. It took an enormous effort to get up and go to the bathroom, but his anger motivated him to respond to this need.

Back to the living room, he looked at the clock. It was just after nine. He felt empty, but he wasn't hungry. He was awake, but not aware. He was disoriented, but he knew where he was. He wandered around the house with his hands in his pockets, not looking for anything, not noticing anything. He sat back down on the couch. The din of the TV, which had been on since he had gotten home, was there like white noise. He didn't really hear it, nor did he even look at it. He was mesmerized and paralyzed. The room, generally darkened, was brighter than usual. He hadn't drawn the drapes the night before. He had passed out before he knew it was dark.

Staring at the carpet, he saw a patch of light and traced it back to its source. A ray of sun was poking through the shades. He watched the dust floating in the light and stared as it shifted closer to the window, and as the sun rose further into the sky, it disappeared, the room returning to the shadow. He lit a cigarette and noticed he only had two left in the pack. He knew he couldn't get through the day, let alone the hour, with just two cigarettes.

Once again, he felt the frustration and resentment at having to respond to his body and his addiction. If he had to be awake, he would have to smoke, which meant he would have to go to the store. The store nearest to him didn't sell liquor, so he decided to take the truck and drive to the strip mall down the road. He knew that he would need to get gas. It was now a matter of survival, and he was pushed into action, hoping he could manage to do these things quickly because he didn't want to see anyone or talk to anyone. He just wanted to get it over with. So, wearing the same clothes, looking unkempt, he angrily put his jacket on, grabbed his keys, and went out the door.

There was a liquor store and laundromat in the plaza. He could handle one stop, that's it. The store he had in mind was about a mile away. Pulling into the gas station, he saw that two cars were ahead of him at the gas pump. He sat there, punching his fingers on the steering wheel. He had shut the radio off when he got in the truck, another intrusion. Pulling up to the pump, he got out and opened the cover to the tank, twisted off the lid, and jammed the nozzle into the inlet.

Nothing happened. He squeezed the trigger again. Still nothing. He waited for the idiots inside to clear the pump. Squeezing the trigger over and over again resulted in nothing. Then he looked at the pump and realized that he hadn't selected the 'pay inside' option as directed. He did so, squeezed the trigger, and the gas started flowing into his tank. He stood there holding it until it jarred off. When he went into the store, he looked around and thought he should pick up some food. Even though he wasn't hungry now, he might be later. He grabbed a basket and filled it with groceries. He went back to the cooler and got four cases of Bud Light and bought four cartons of Marlboro Lights. He asked the cashier to add in a cup of coffee and paid for it all. He didn't plan on going out again for a few days.

Loading it all into the truck, Nate glared at the person who blew the horn. Then he got into the driver's seat, and sped away to park in front of the liquor store. He decided to treat himself and bought four large bottles of Johnny Walker. In a hurry to get home, he floored it, doing sixty-five in a forty-five. He didn't care if he got stopped. He pulled in front of the house and jammed on the brakes, made two trips into the house, and slammed the door.

He unloaded the bags, leaving the stuff that didn't need refrigeration on the counter. He opened one of the cartons and grabbed a pack of cigarettes, grabbed his coffee, and went into the living room. Sitting on the couch, he turned up the TV that he never shut off, lit a cigarette, and drank the coffee. He surfed the channels, giving each one five seconds to capture him, and finally settled on the weather channel. It was something that he could watch with some degree of interest. He didn't want to be outside and didn't want to go anywhere in the country, but he still wanted to know what nature's plan was. Meanwhile he went back and forth to the kitchen, snagging one beer after the other. His routine was reestablished, and he found comfort in his solitude.

Chapter 18

For two weeks he lay there. He drank and passed out. Drank and passed out. He paid no attention to the time, gauging it by the rising and the setting of the sun. He slept for the most part, and when he awoke, he drank himself back asleep. He was passed out when he felt something shaking him. Then he heard a voice. The voice of his grandfather. He didn't want to turn and face him. So, he didn't. How did he get in? He couldn't remember whether he had locked the door or not. Why was he even here? His grandfather had never come to visit him since the funeral. Now he felt his unwelcome presence over him.

"Nate, get up," his grandfather said, gently but firmly. Nate did not respond. His grandfather gave him another shove. "Nate, get up, now!"

Nate turned onto his back and stared at the ceiling, not daring to look at his grandfather. His grandfather persisted.

"Nate get up and get your things. You are coming with me."

Nate resisted the commands and did not move or speak. His grandfather left his side and went into Nate's room. He saw the duffle bag packed with clothes. He picked it up and dropped it by the back door before going into the kitchen. Nate heard him rummaging around. It sounded like he was filling bags. He then shut off the TV and came back over to Nate. He picked up one of Nate's cigarettes, lit it, and handed it to him. He then popped open a beer and handed it to Nate.

Nate sat up, still not looking at his grandfather, and gulped it down. He put out the cigarette that he had smoked down to the filter. His grandfather handed him the bottle, from which Nate took a swig, opened another beer, gave it to him, lit another cigarette, and did the same. Nate didn't understand why his grandfather would do this since he never drank. And while he did smoke a pipe, it was more ceremonial than anything.

Meanwhile, his grandfather grabbed his bills off the kitchen table and loaded them, the beer, and the liquor into the truck while Nate guzzled down the second beer and put the can on the floor with the others that he had lined up for days. His grandfather handed him another without saying a word. When Nate had downed the fourth one, he gathered enough courage to speak.

In his hungover state, he tried to clear the hoarseness in his voice and asked, "What are you doing here, Grandfather? Why'd you come? I blew you off."

His grandfather repeated the same directive. "Nate, get up."

Nate got up. His grandfather put his hand on his back, moving Nate toward the back door. He set the lock on the knob and closed the door behind them, prodding Nate to the passenger side of his beat-up truck. He opened the door and ordered Nate, "Get in."

Nate got in, and without a word his grandfather got behind the wheel and drove away from the house. In silence they rode. Nate recognized the route. They were headed to his grandfather's house. He didn't have the strength to dissent. He just sat there staring ahead at the road while his grandfather drove in silence. In time, they came to the dirt road that headed back into the woods. Going over the ruts made him want to puke.

In the same fashion as when they left Nate's house, his grandfather went around to Nate's side, opened the door, and gestured for him to get out. He did and followed his grandfather into the cabin. With groceries in hand, his grandfather led him into the kitchen. Motioning for Nate to sit down at the table, he fished through the bags, took out another beer, opened it, and put it in front of Nate with an ashtray and the Marlboro Lights. Nate lifted the beer to his mouth, took a drink, lit a cigarette, and stared at the table while his grandfather put the rest of the beer, the two whiskey bottles, and the groceries away.

Nate sat there, now drinking with less intent, listening to his grandfather's movements. He could hear him filling the coffee pot then mixing something, and the frying pan responding to the fire under it. He could smell something cooking, something sweet. He didn't look up, not curious enough to do so.

His grandfather did not speak. He filled the two plates with the French toast and came over to the table, setting one down in front of Nate. He put the utensils, orange juice, and coffee in front of Nate. He poured the syrup over Nate's food and then his own. He sat down across from Nate and began to eat. Nate picked up the coffee and took a sip, having emptied the beer. He then took a drink of the juice. He picked up his fork, pushing around the toast and then cut into a corner. He took a bite, then another, still looking down at his plate. He had not looked at his grandfather's eyes since he woke him earlier in the day. He could not. In silence they ate.

His grandfather got up and poured more coffee into Nate's mug. He had finished the food on his plate and lit up another cigarette. His grandfather cleaned up the kitchen while Nate sat and smoked and drank his coffee. After he finished washing the dishes, his grandfather came over to Nate and put his hand on his shoulder. Once again, he said, "Get up." Nate got up, head down, while his grandfather escorted him into the extra bedroom where Nate had slept a couple of weeks ago.

He pulled down the covers, told Nate to take off his shoes and lie down, then pulled the covers over him and left the bedside. Nate heard him close the door quietly behind him. He turned to face the wall, looking at the grains in the wood. He listened to the sound of the axe splitting the dried-out firewood, connecting with a rhythm that allowed him to close his eyes. Feeling held by the sounds of nature around him, he drifted off to sleep.

He opened his eyes, seeing the same wood grain that he had before he went to sleep, hearing the same sounds of the axe, the breeze, and the melodic sounds of birds and insects outside the window. He didn't have to think long to figure out where he was and felt better after having had a good nap on a full stomach. He wanted to just lie there, taking it all in. He had no questions or thoughts. He wanted to just close his eyes again and recapture the elusive comfort.

The mattress was supportive of his weariness. He wanted to stay there, but as usual he had to use the bathroom. When leaving, he again caught himself in the mirror. He couldn't figure out why he had to stop and look. It wasn't vanity---but more a way of measuring himself. He didn't like what he saw and decided to move on. He smelled the coffee and another unfamiliar but not unpleasant scent. He passed through the living room, not looking for the source of this aroma, but headed directly for the coffee that beckoned him.

Nate noticed the clock. It was after one o'clock. He had slept for at least three hours since breakfast. Pouring the coffee, he summoned up the will to go outside. He stood on the porch. It was a beautiful and rather warm day. Indian summer. He heard his grandfather's labor behind the house. Despite his shame, he couldn't just stand there. He went around the back to where his grandfather was hard at work.

"Well," his grandfather said, seeing him appear in the clearing, "I was wondering if you were ever going to get up. I've been at this since eight this morning. I think it is time for me to stop and get some lunch."

Nate was totally confused. He knew he hadn't gotten here much before nine. Then they ate breakfast, and now he had just woken up from a nap. His grandfather couldn't have started much before ten or eleven, yet he said he had been working since eight. What day was this? Then it dawned on him—he had been asleep since yesterday. Feeling shame, thinking that his grandfather looked down upon him, he started to walk away.

"What do you want for lunch?" asked his grandfather. "I have some bologna and cheese, thanks to you, as well as some chips. How about we go in and get a sandwich."

"That sounds OK to me," and he followed his grandfather inside.

He sat at the table and lit up a cigarette while he sipped the now lukewarm coffee. His grandfather opened the refrigerator, pulled out another beer, poured some whiskey in a glass, then gave them to Nate. Nate hesitated, but since his grandfather had given it to him, it must be OK. Besides, he was feeling shaky and his hands were trembling. He knew that the alcohol would calm his nerves. He downed it quickly, along with the sandwiches and chips. His grandfather handed Nate another beer. Nate gratefully accepted both the food and the drink, thanking him. Those were the only words spoken during the meal.

Opening the refrigerator, his grandfather pulled out another beer, aware that withdrawal from alcohol is to be done gradually. He handed it to Nate and said, "Let us get back outside. There is still a ton of wood I need to deal with."

Reaching the clearing behind the house, his grandfather picked up the axe and put the log on the block. While doing so, he said to Nate, "You just have a seat over there on that big rock," pointing to one that was in the sun.

"But I thought you needed help."

His grandfather responded, "You need the rest. Just go over there and sit down."

Nate did as he was told, sat on the rock, and opened the beer. He could feel his hands steadying, his body reaching for balance. He watched his grandfather work. He felt guilty, but also knew that he was too weak to do much of anything. He had buried himself over the past few weeks and months. He knew that he could barely push himself out from under it. So, he just sat there.

He felt the warmth of the rock beneath him and the sun above. He was being taken in by it, and it soothed him. He could hear leaves falling through the trees, the gentle breeze urging them to give it up for now. He looked up and watched one. It floated in the air, the breeze holding it, directing it tenderly to the ground below. It joined the others, mixing in with the mosaic of color. He watched another, and another, mesmerized by the repetition. He felt the coolness of the air on his face, superseded by the warmth from above and below. He noticed a dragonfly hovering about the bushes and then another meeting it and then parting, the blueness of their transparent wings distinguishing them from the green around them.

Looking up through the clearing, the sky was perfectly blue and brighter than he had seen in a long while. He hadn't been out much. He watched in fascination as two hawks glided in a circular pattern, perhaps looking for a prey, perhaps just enjoying the freedom. At home he rarely saw a hawk, making this moment one of the special ones he remembered as a child. Each time he saw one he marveled because they were only seen by accident, appearing just for moments and, unlike crows, were never a nuisance to humans. It was almost as if God placed them in the sky to remind us of what it means to have a free spirit. Nate longed for that.

His grandfather just kept chopping, not in a pressured manner, but methodically and purposefully. He'd occasionally stop and rest on the handle of the axe, go over to the hose and drink some water, and go back to it again. Nate wondered how a man of his age had the stamina to do this for hours on end, somehow wishing he could do the same at his present age, let alone as an old man. The afternoon was waning as the sun began to set earlier each day now. The air was getting colder. Nate, feeling the chill, went over to where his grandfather was working and started to pick up the short stack that had already been cut, piling them on top of the growing heap. He did this until his grandfather stopped. It was around five.

They went inside. Without asking, Nate grabbed a beer and a bottle, then sat down at the table. He smoked and watched his grandfather prepare dinner. Nate noticed that they were going to have a kind of fish with rice and a mixture of zucchini, summer squash, and onion. Despite his lack of activity, he was starving. His grandfather just let him sit there with his drink and cigarettes. Nate felt his shame gradually diminishing, allowing his grandfather to take care of him. He didn't have his truck with him, so he was stuck here. If he got to the point where he wanted to leave, like the last time, he would have to ask his grandfather to take him home. He would never steal his grandfather's truck. What's more, he didn't want to leave.

Grandfather had not realized just how much Nate had been drinking. After a few days, he knew that it would take some time to get it out of his system. He began to ration the amount of alcohol he gave him over the course of a couple of weeks, a little at a time, detoxing him from the poison in his system. Nate did not object. Frankly, he didn't know where his grandfather was storing the liquor and didn't dare ask. The food and fresh air seemed to be helping. Nate was sleeping better, and though still irritable much of the time, his grandfather attributed most of it to his withdrawal from the liquor and diminished cigarette smoking. In time, the alcohol was gone and there was to be no more of it in the house. His grandfather was adamant. No more drinking. Nate didn't argue. He was able to admit to himself that he was starting to feel a little better, at least in his body.

He put the suicide stuff on the back burner, always knowing that it would still be an option if things didn't get better in his life. His grandfather was not pushing him, and he pretty much did what he wanted. He'd help a little here and there, which his grandfather appreciated, but Nate didn't feel like doing much of anything, especially since he wasn't expected to. Encouraged to be outside as much as possible, he would take long walks in the woods, kicking up the leaves in the brisk fall air. His grandfather was relentless in getting the wood cut and some of the chores done outside.

Nate instinctively made his way down to the creek. Sitting down, he found himself wandering back in time to the better moments of his relationship with Haley. They were so good together, both having a quick wit and a keen sense of humor. They kept things fun, laughing at the stupidest things. One day in the car, for some reason they were focusing on the different road signs they passed. One sign read, 'rough road ahead.' They had driven by this sign and over all the bumps and ruts many times before. On this day, though, they were laughing because nothing had been done in so long, yet the sign remained. They both decided it was a lot cheaper for the state to put up signs rather than fix roads.

Then his mind shifted to the love and passion they shared. Whenever he would be able to get free from work, they would often just plan to have dinner at Haley's apartment. She would cook. He would set up the atmosphere. They both enjoyed listening to light jazz and classical music while they ate and talked. That, the candlelight, and the wine always set them up for a night of romance and lovemaking.

Looking around the water soothed him, the sun warmed him, and the breeze consoled him. He noticed the rocks in and around the creek bed, seemingly lifeless, yet leading the water around them to guide its path. He noticed the trees and wondered how they could stand against the seasons and all the changes they brought. He heard the leaves rustle, the breeze getting under them just enough to lift them gently from one resting place to another. He was in tune with them, feeling calmness come over him. The smell of the wood burning in the stove brought him back. He didn't know how long he had been sitting there.

Turning back, he climbed the slope to the clearing behind his grandfather's house. His grandfather was sitting on one of the rocks in the sun, motionless, with his eyes closed and his hands palms-up on his knees. Nate thought for a moment that maybe he was sleeping, but then it occurred to him that he might be praying. That would be like Grandfather, to sit alone in silence. Nate thought that he must have just gotten used to it. Nate doubted he ever could. As Nate walked into the clearing, his grandfather opened his eyes and looked over at him.

Nate asked what time it was. His grandfather looked up into the sky and ventured, "It is probably around two."

Nate, surprised as he always was when it came to measuring time without a clock, said, "Geez, I didn't know I was gone for that long."

"Well, I am glad you're back. I need you to help me get those shingles replaced on the roof up there."

Nate looked up and saw what he meant. Some of the shakes were quite warped, and a couple of them were missing. But inside he could feel the challenge. *OK*, he thought, *here it comes again, payback time*. He could feel the peace that had accompanied him back from the creek slipping away. He knew this 'vacation' wouldn't last forever and that his grandfather would be putting on the pressure again. Without showing his sense of resignation, he said to his grandfather, "Where's the ladder?" His grandfather pointed and told him that it was on the other side of the cabin. Nate crossed over into the shade to get it. It was an old, heavy, wooden one that had seen its day. He picked it up and lugged it to the back of the cabin.

His grandfather suggested, "How about you set it up over there," indicating the roofline near where the work was to be done. Nate did so, but not without a struggle. He couldn't believe that something once so easy to him was now causing him strain. His grandfather got up, strode over to where the new shakes lay, brought them over to Nate, and said, "I will hold the ladder. Let me get the crowbar, hammer, and nails first."

Nate thought he was kidding. He had never fixed a roof before. He had done many things because he was generally handy but getting up on ladders was something he tried to avoid. He hated heights. His grandfather returned with the tools, and Nate, having to make two trips up and down the ladder, felt increasingly anxious. When he was finally up there, he gingerly made his way to the spot where the shakes were missing, sure that he was going to slip and meet his end. He didn't. He followed the explicit instructions his grandfather was shouting up to him. When he didn't do it perfectly, he could hear his grandfather's agitation, which wasn't typical for him, but his grandfather would be damned if he were going to get up there when he had someone much younger to do it.

When the job was finished, Nate climbed down, meeting his grandfather at the bottom of the ladder. "Well, that is one way to get past your fear. Let us get the ladder back and get inside, my hands are getting cold."

As his grandfather went around the front, Nate took the ladder around and slammed it against the house. He knew what was pissing him off was not the cold and sore hands but his grandfather's words. 'Fear.' *I didn't tell him that I was afraid. It's as though he was reading my mind. 'Getting over my fear.' Give me a break, this was nothing compared to the fear I've been dealing with since my father died. Damn it,* he thought, *he really knows how to get to me, and I'll be damned if I'll let him know it.* With that, Nate took his time going back.

Stepping inside, Nate smelled chicken roasting in the oven. His anger at his grandfather quickly subsided. He loved roast chicken. His grandfather was peeling potatoes over the sink, basically ignoring him. Nate thought that he probably heard him slam the ladder against the house.

"Sorry about the ladder, Grandfather," Nate said as contritely as he could. "It slipped out of my hands," he lied.

Without turning around, his grandfather said, "Apologies are meaningless without the truth. Just set the table."

Nate went to the bathroom to wash his hands. In going through the living room, he smelled that same aroma he noticed when he had first come here. It had a pleasant enough scent, but it was not familiar to him. Maybe he would ask his grandfather about it, hoping the interest might ease the tension. When he got back to the kitchen, he started to set the table.

Nonchalantly he asked, "Grandfather, what do I smell?"

His grandfather said, "It is chicken."

Feeling ridiculous, Nate said, "I know that. I'm not talking about the chicken, what's that smell in the living room? I smelled it last time I was here. I'm just wondering what it is."

He put the peeled potatoes in the pan of water, turned on the stove, and said, "It is sage."

Nate said, "I thought sage was for cooking. What else would you use it for?"

"I use it to neutralize negativity," he said as he turned around to get something out of the refrigerator.

"What negativity?" Nate asked without thinking about it.

"Yours," replied his grandfather, looking directly at Nate.

"What are you talking about? Up until the ladder incident I was doing fine. I thought my attitude has been good. Why do you think I'm so negative?"

"I suppose that is a question you should answer for yourself."

Grandfather would never give him a straight answer. Nate asked a simple question, and his grandfather put it right back to him. It made him not want to ask anything. Why would he ask a question if he already knew the answer? In school, if he had a question, he would just raise his hand and the teacher would answer it. Then he would learn. His grandfather was a lousy teacher.

Nate allowed his agitation to seep out with his question, "Why is it that when I ask a question you play mind games with me?"

His grandfather retorted, "I did answer your question. I told you why I use sage."

Frustrated, Nate said, "You know damn well I'm not talking about that. I heard what you said. Then I asked why you think I'm so negative, and you tell me to answer the question!"

His grandfather replied, "It is like this. There are some things I know, and some things I do not. I feel your negativity when I am around you. I use sage to keep me centered. You are angry and resentful, even over little things. You are afraid and doubtful. You do not trust me, nor do you like to be told what to do. You get into your negativity. You let it run around you and inside of you, and it leaks out. Now I get to ask the questions. Why are you so negative? You tell me."

Nate was angry now, so much so that he pounded his fist on the table and yelled, "I don't know the answer to that! All I know is that you piss me off and I don't want to be around you!" Nate stomped out of the room, went to his bedroom, and slammed the door. His grandfather just continued to prepare dinner.

Nate flopped down on the bed, not bothering to take off his boots. He lay on top of the covers, his jaw clenched, his arms folded tightly over his chest, his mind racing, and his heart pounding hard. He couldn't believe that three hours ago he was sitting peacefully by the creek, and now he was ready to explode. How was he going to deal with this? He didn't have his truck. There wasn't any beer to calm him down. He could try that 'breathing thing' but was too angry to get into it. Besides, his grandfather taught him that, and for that reason alone he didn't want to do it.

As he let himself stew, he could feel his stomach growling. He was hungry. If he stayed in here for too long, he would miss dinner, one of his favorites. While he could resist his grandfather's suggestions, it was another thing entirely to resist his cooking. Nate started to slow down his breath. He kept doing it until he felt more composed, not to please his grandfather, but to get to a place where he could at least be a decent human being and once again apologize for his behavior. He hated that.

Nate hated to admit that he was wrong. He hated owing anything to anyone, let alone an apology. He remembered what his grandfather had said. There is no apology without the truth. Nate thought about this as he continued to calm himself. In time, he swung his feet over to the floor and sat on the bed, trying to get himself ready to go out to the living room, where he knew Grandfather would be sitting while the potatoes were cooking. He got up and opened the door. With his head down and hands in his pockets, he sat down across from where his grandfather was sitting, lit a cigarette, and let out a long sigh.

His grandfather said, "Better?"

"Yes. Thank you, Grandfather. Listen, I'm sorry I blew up at you like that. You don't deserve that. You've been treating me well."

His grandfather said, "You sure it's not because you are hungry that you came out here?"

Nate felt the ping and pushed it down. "You're right. I am hungry, and it is one reason I came out here. But it's not the whole reason. I've been acting like a spoiled brat. You've asked little of me, and I'm grateful for that. It's just that I get so upset when you challenge me. I don't understand you. I don't understand a lot of things around here. I don't understand why I smell whatever it is all the time." He watched the smoke wisps from the bowl. "I don't understand your silence. I don't understand your humming."

Nate felt anger stirring up in his gut but went on anyway, his curiosity overruling his emotions. Looking straight at his grandfather, he said, "I don't understand how you can almost read my mind, or, as you say, feel my negativity, even when I'm not angry. I don't understand how you think I know the answers about myself, or what's inside of me. I just don't get all of this, and it does piss me off. I don't like not knowing. I haven't liked not knowing, especially when I once did, or thought I did."

His grandfather asked, "And do you want to know the answers to all those questions, Nate?"

"I'm not so sure. Maybe I'm afraid of what I'll find."

"You will be."

"So, then," asked Nate, sincerely this time, "What do you think I should do?"

114

His grandfather said, "We have many things to talk about and many things to do to help you get better. All you need to do is cooperate and try to trust me. But right now, I need to mash some potatoes and make some gravy. We can talk about this more after dinner."

Nate, getting up when his grandfather did, said, "OK, then we'll talk. I'll mash the potatoes. I'm good at that."

"That would be a big help," said his grandfather. They both went into the kitchen to finish making and eating their dinner.

Chapter 19

Nate cleaned up the kitchen willingly while his grandfather went out to the living room. He put another couple of logs into the stove, which by now had embers that were keeping the cabin comfortably warm. When he was finished, he went out to sit with his grandfather. He lit a cigarette. He enjoyed smoking after a meal. Nate had noticed that his smoking habit had decreased in a relatively short time. He had to admit that the lack of alcohol and fewer cigarettes were making him feel stronger, at least in his body. His mind was still in turmoil.

As his grandfather smoked his pipe, they sat in silence. Nate was getting more used to the silence. What could he do, after all? He would read now and then, but his grandfather's books did not appeal to him. He enjoyed novels of high suspense. He also enjoyed historical epics like *Pillars of the Earth* by Ken Follett. Set in Medieval times, it was a story about a stonecutter who wanted to build a cathedral. Nate could identify with this book on many levels. What books his grandfather had around were not fiction. They were books about spirituality, a subject that Nate was not much into. Eventually, his grandfather spoke.

"So, Nate, before dinner you had many questions. Why did I know this, or do that, or say that? What specifically would you like to talk about?"

Nate thought for a moment. Many things swirled around in his head. He was trying to prioritize them, for some things were more important than others. "Grandfather, I think what I'd like to know most about is why you say that you can feel my negativity. What do you mean?"

His grandfather pondered and carefully chose his words. "Nate, you must understand that all things have energy. All things and all people. In its essence, energy is positive. Negativity or darkness exists when that energy is blocked. When you consider your recent past, what is it that keeps you so pessimistic and angry?"

Nate had to think about this, because certainly many positive things had happened in his life. On the other hand, particularly over the past year, a lot of negative things had occurred, starting with the death of his father. Once that happened, life had become a battle. But who was he battling? He wondered. No one had done anything to harm him. Sure, he had experienced some major losses, and there was the accident when he was eight. But otherwise, he had always considered himself to be lucky compared to many people. He always had food and shelter. He always had family and friends. He always had the things he needed and many things that he just simply wanted. So why was he now facing turmoil and despair? Why was his life force leaking out of him?

So, he answered. "I think at this time in my life it's my negativity that has consumed me. It has pushed away all the people that gave me a positive outlook on things. Now I see the glass half empty; before, it was just full."

"You are right. So, there is part of the answer. Negativity has taken you over, and it has an impact on others around you. That is why your friends disappeared. That is why Haley left you. That is why you have not been able to get back to work. That is why you feel angry, fearful, and empty inside."

Nate then asked, "So, how is it that you know so much about this so-called energy? Everything you have created here is beautiful, peaceful, and simple. You seem so much at peace, even though you're alone all the time. I don't see you as having anything negative about you, other than your lack of conversation. You don't have a great sense of humor, but I think you find me amusing. We come from the same roots, yet you are so different from me, even from my father and mother. What makes you so different?"

"Well, there are many reasons, I suppose. In a big sense, I have been where you are. You know the story. When we left Belize, your father was young and lost until he met your mother some years later. I cannot say that he welcomed his new life in the States."

"But he had you, Grandfather. He had you to lean on."

"And now, so do you. But you are different from him. And you are different from me." Nate listened intently as his grandfather spoke.

"When I left Belize, I was lost. I had lost everything that meant anything to me, except for your father. My wife, my relatives, my job, my home, and all my possessions were gone. Like you, I did not have a clue as to what I was going to do. The only thing I knew at the time was that I had to leave. My grief was unbearable, and everything that was left in Belize haunted me. But there was one thing I had, though, that you do not."

"And what's that?" asked Nate.

"I had my history. I knew my ancestry. I knew where I came from and what I had to do to heal from all the pain that filled me. I had to unblock my pain. I had to become open to the energy that could help me."

Nate asked, "Well, what do you mean by that? I mean, OK, so you lost a lot, more than I have, for sure. What did you have to do to make peace with it? How did you manage to go on, start a successful business, and help my father too? How did you pull it together?"

118

"That is a good question, but with a complicated answer. I went inside myself. I talked to my father, and my grandfather, and truthfully, others before them. I listened to what they had to teach or to reinforce what I already knew about myself. Do you think I managed to get to this point without help?"

Nate stated, "But you didn't have help. You were all alone. Your parents and relatives were all dead. What friends you had, you left behind in Belize. What do you mean?"

"As you know, we have a great heritage behind us."

"Well," said Nate, "I know, and I don't know."

"What you know is that your parents were good people with many gifts and talents, which they passed on to you, even though you haven't been using them. What you should also know is that your father, and my father, and my father's father are of Mayan descent. This is and has always been important to me. The Mayan culture was highly advanced. It embraced all of life and allowed them to learn. Why is it you think we can build with stone the way we do? It is more inherited than taught, and sometimes it's hard even for me to understand."

His grandfather continued. "Some Mayans were so open to the spiritual world that they were gifted with special powers. They were seemingly chosen to be the spiritual leaders, teachers, and healers of the communities. Through their connection to the spiritual world, they discovered their power and used it to help others and the environment. They were shamans. They had many ways to draw negative influences out of people. Much like the Chinese, and truly, many other spiritual groups, they were able to communicate with the Great Spirit. They were willing to and they listened. This is what I did. I listened."

"Is that why you are so quiet most of the time?" asked Nate.

"You might say that. Part of it is quiet, part of it is discipline, and part of it is keeping yourself open to the positive energy that surrounds you by not allowing the negative to defeat you, much less kill you. Believe me when I say this, and do not question it. The answer lies within you, and you must be willing to cooperate with it and listen to it. That will help you find yourself and get you back on your feet."

"Grandfather, I don't mean to be disrespectful, but this doesn't sound like the life for me," said Nate with a little laugh.

His grandfather laughed at this and then grew quiet. Then he said, "Well, it is up to you. There are many paths, many ways to go, but you will not be happy until you find your own."

Nate lit a cigarette, feeling a little uncomfortable, because he knew that he was unhappy and didn't know which way to go. He sat there and thought about things. He knew this was the end of tonight's conversation. His grandfather had grown silent.

"Well, I guess I have a lot to think about."

"Yes, you do," replied his grandfather. "And while you do that, I am going to bed. This is late for me."

He got up from his chair and went to his room. Nate sat there, not knowing exactly what to do. His mind was tired, and he couldn't think about much more. He too decided to go to bed.

Nate woke up in a cold sweat. He had a nightmare, the same one he had not long ago at his house when he had been drinking heavily. Now, the same thing, and he couldn't attribute it to anything. He knew that he fell right to sleep when his head hit the pillow, so how could such a disturbing dream shake him loose again? He had trouble pulling out of it, it was so vivid. He was in the park, at night, alone, three attackers, a brutal beating, dying. 'Shit,' he said to himself. 'What the hell is going on?' His clothes were soaked with sweat and he was shivering. He got up, pulled on his jeans, and went out to the living room.

Sitting in the dark he lit a cigarette, trying to still himself. It all seemed so real. He could feel the fear and helplessness.

He could feel the assault and almost the pain and his powerlessness over what was happening to him. He could feel their rage and struggled to figure out why they chose him to kill. He could touch death and his fear of it. He knew he would not be going back to bed. He went into the kitchen and put on a pot of coffee. It was only four thirty.

Passing by his grandfather's room, he stopped and listened. *There he goes again*, thought Nate. He was hearing his grandfather's humming and the faint scent of sage seeping through the door. Now he was wondering if his grandfather did this every morning or if it was just because Nate was here with all of his bad energy. He vowed he wouldn't be afraid to ask when his grandfather came out.

Nate sat thinking about the previous night's conversation with his grandfather. He was right about his anger, his fear, and his emptiness, though Nate couldn't figure out how his grandfather knew these things. As before, Nate felt that his grandfather could read his mind, though he didn't influence it. He had always thought there was something different about his grandfather. Nate had never met anyone like this before. He remembered his parents being spiritual in many ways, but nothing like this. Nate wanted to learn more, just out of curiosity.

His grandfather came into the kitchen around six. Seeing Nate sitting there, he said, "Well, it looks like you have been up for a while. There are quite a few butts in that ashtray."

Nate said, "Yeah, I've pretty much been up as long as you have."

His grandfather, pouring himself what was left of the first pot of coffee, just looked over at Nate and smiled a bit.

"So, you have noticed."

"Yeah, it's that humming you do that gave it away," said Nate. "Is that something you do every morning, or just when I'm here?"

His grandfather laughed. "No, it is not because you are here. If that were the case, I would be up at three." He paused, waiting for a reaction, smiling. Nate smiled back. "No, it is something I do every morning about the same time."

"But why at four thirty? You're here by yourself most of the time. Why not one or two in the afternoon?"

"It is my discipline. It is also a time of day when there are few distractions."

"So, what's the point of it?"

His grandfather thought and responded. "Remember last night when I was telling you about our heritage?" Nate nodded. "The basic beliefs of our ancestors are that we are all given gifts and that we are only a small molecule in the big picture of things."

Nate said, "I know that part of it. Life here is only temporary. Then we die and go to heaven or something like that."

"Or something like that," his grandfather replied, "but at the same time, it is more than that."

"How so?" asked Nate.

"Our souls can have many lives, each evolving to a higher level. There are ways we can know where we come from and where we are going. There are ways that we can communicate with God, or the Great Spirit, if you will, and others who have gone before us. They are all our teachers. Everything in life has something to teach us. I meditate in the mornings so that I can learn and stay in tune with the greater truth."

"Grandfather," asked Nate, "are you saying that you can communicate with the dead?"

"They are not dead, Nate. They are here with us, much like the angels you learned about when you were young. If you are in the right frame of mind and are willing to listen, they will teach you."

"Hmmm," Nate thought some more. "So, when you meditate and hum and stuff like that, what's that do for you?"

"It does many things for me, Nate. It quiets my mind and my body. It lifts me out of this world, in a way. I feel peaceful, and full, and grateful."

"You're full of it, all right," Nate laughed. He then asked, "So is this why you can feel my negativity, and when I'm lying, and when I'm afraid?"

"In a manner of speaking, yes. When I feel a harmful presence around me, I know where it is coming from. It's not always a person, but usually. Sometimes it comes from the sky, sometimes the earth. There is the story of a town that was experiencing a drought. They asked a shaman to come and help them. He did. By gathering all the people together to pray to the Sky Spirit, all that positive energy put together for one purpose resulted in rain. That is why it is so important to recognize it. You cannot recognize the negative if you do not fill yourself with the positive. I have learned and practiced staying in touch with positive energy."

"Well, there's something else," said Nate.

"Yes?" said his grandfather.

"I feel like you can read my mind."

"In some ways, I can," said his grandfather. "I knew when you were coming to see me that first time. Then I knew that you were not going to come back unless I dragged you here. I knew you were going to lie to me before you even came in the door after fixing the roof yesterday. I knew that you were going to ask me all these questions this morning."

"How do you do this?" asked Nate.

"You are probably not going to believe it, but it is one of my gifts."

"Like the shamans?" Nate said in disbelief. "I thought that was just an alien thing. You can do that?"

Hesitating, and feeling Nate's skepticism, his grandfather said, "Yes, I can. It is one of my gifts. If we can get outside of ourselves, we can use our gifts. But you have to go inside before you can go outside." His grandfather got up to make a pot of coffee.

"I'm not so sure I could ever do that," said Nate. "I can't sit still that long. I wouldn't even know where to start."

"You already have," said his grandfather.

Nate didn't get this at all but didn't take time to think about it. "I do have some other questions for you."

His grandfather simply said, "That is enough for now, Nate. Go wash up. We will eat breakfast and get to work."

"And just what is it that we're doing today?" Nate asked with a little edge in his voice.

He just wanted to talk. The questions were coming fast and furious, but the answers weren't sinking in. He was struggling to understand. Some of it he did, like the discipline piece and praying. His parents taught him that. But this other stuff sounded like a lot of hocus-pocus to him.

"Today," his grandfather said, interrupting Nate's thoughts, "we are going to split more wood. We are about two thirds of the way there, most of which I have done myself, I might add."

Nate shrugged his shoulders and left the room. It was late September. He knew that it was going to be a long winter.

Chapter 20

For the next couple of weeks, Nate did exactly as he was told, believing that his grandfather might know how to help him. His grandfather began to knock on his bedroom door at six every morning and would say to him, "Nate, it is time." He wouldn't say, "It's time to get up," or, "It's time for breakfast," or, "It's time to get working." He would just say, "It is time." The rest of the day would follow.

There were many chores to do outside before the first freeze and first snow. They caulked all the windows, cut, stacked, and covered all the wood, replaced some of the floorboards on the front porch, cleaned out the stove chimney, preparing for the coming winter. All the work made for a long day.

It wasn't like Nate didn't have any time to himself though. He would still take walks in the woods, still be able to sit and have a cigarette, and still go down to the creek bed just to sit and think of Haley or his father. Most often he would feel his sadness. Most often he would think about his work and the business. He struggled to deal with the anxiety and uncertainty that followed his thoughts.

One day as he was sitting there listening to everything around him, he heard a shrieking sound from the sky. Looking up he saw a hawk circling above. He was hoping it wasn't looking to pounce on him. An old Hitchcock movie came to his mind. He kept his eye on the hawk, still in awe of its ability to soar without much effort.

It was becoming kind of a ritual to sit and talk after dinner. Much time was spent on figuring out what Nate had to do to get the business up and going again. He would ask his grandfather lots of questions. His grandfather would give many answers to each question, letting Nate decide for himself what would work for him. Most of the time, though, they would just talk about their day.

When Nate saw the hawk, he told his grandfather about it and how it reminded him of some scary movie. They had a good laugh, but then his grandfather had some questions for Nate.

"So, Nate, when you see a hawk, what do you see?"

Nate said, "Well, I see a magnificent bird of prey that knows how to take care of itself."

"And?" his grandfather would follow.

"And I see freedom."

"And?"

"And I see keenness. They have sharp eyes, you know. They always seem to know what's going on around them."

"True, very true," his grandfather remarked. "The hawk is trying to tell you something."

"Like what?" Nate asked.

"Think about it, that is all."

So, Nate would think about it, and that would be the end of the conversation. His grandfather, without saying it, was telling him to pay more attention. Nate began to pay more attention to things he saw and what they might mean to him.

On a day in early October, his grandfather made a trip into town to get more groceries. Alone in the house, Nate became bored. He had cleaned the bathroom and even his bedroom. Everything else was in good order. He didn't feel like reading. There were times when he was interested in the books his grandfather had around, but they were a dry read. Nate couldn't concentrate well enough to get through them. Sometimes he would end up reading the same paragraph over and over again, still getting nothing out of it. He would either give up or go to sleep.

This day he just gave up and wandered around the house instead of his head. There wasn't much wandering to do though, back and forth from the living room into the kitchen, where he would sometimes pour himself a drink of something, mostly coffee, and back again. Sometimes he would detour into his bedroom and sit on the edge of the bed for a while.

He never went into his grandfather's room. The door was always closed. In turn, his grandfather never came into his bedroom. But today Nate's curiosity got the best of him. Knowing his grandfather wouldn't be back for at least another hour, he decided he would go in for just a couple of minutes, just for a change of scenery. At first, he just peeked in, but his eyes caught something that pulled him into the room.

Nate was surprised by what he saw and smelled. The aroma of sage filled the room. He noticed that there were other herbs and some oils. There were all kinds of books, even a Bible on a shelf built into the wall. On the floor was a piece of woven material with rocks and crystals lying on it.

A wall hanging with a Southwest kind of pattern and bright colors was embroidered with animals—a bear in the middle, a hawk overhead, wild horses, wolves, and hummingbirds. It was beautiful. He saw a small fountain on top of a block of marble in the middle of the room. It was surrounded by a miniature stone wall with a tree formed from copper in its center, allowing water to flow over the wall and around the tree.

There were candles, incense burners, and statues. Of the many statues, the one that caught his attention was one of an Angel. It was made of marble, a highly polished, quite detailed work of art, most likely sculpted by his grandfather. He meant to be in there for only a couple of minutes, but he was captivated by a world that was unfamiliar to him. He couldn't decide if his grandfather was more than weird, was crazy, or if all these objects had a deep meaning. He felt as though he had intruded upon some sacred space. Indeed, he had.

His attention focused intently on the nightstand next to the bed. On it lay crystals of many shapes, and colors. Some were rather small, uncut and unpolished. Others looked like diamonds. These were clear quartz crystals, precisely cut and polished, with all kinds of different facets, sizes, and shapes. They fascinated him more than the other things he saw. He wondered why his grandfather had such a collection. Maybe they were worth something. When he became aware of how long he had been in there, he left, leaving it undisturbed. He decided to go outside for a walk. He was counting on the cold air to clear his head.

It was cold outside. Nate guessed that the temperature was in the mid-thirties, which was unusual for October. Fortunately, the air was still. The ground underneath his feet was hardening as he walked into the woods. His boots crunched the fallen leaves into crumbs. The trees were bare except for the pines that seemed to reach their glory in the winter. They stood majestically over the others, as if they were protecting them from the wrath of the winter soon to come.

The sun didn't lend itself to warm the atmosphere at this time of the year. The first snow had not yet fallen. Nate moved through the forest with ease. Going ever deeper into its shadow. Then he heard his grandfather's truck coming up the road. He decided to turn back. He knew his grandfather would need some help with the bags of groceries. Two weeks of food filled them.

Nate was able to keep busy the rest of the day. He was responsible for dinner that evening, so he decided to make some chili. It was one of his favorites, especially in the colder months. Normally he would have some beers with it and eat in front of the TV watching football. He didn't have a favorite team per se because he never had the time to follow one. But when he did have a chance, he normally would stand behind the underdog. He got great satisfaction in watching these teams overcome the odds, even though he would never bet on it. He didn't need another vice.

His grandfather puttered around that afternoon too. He spent a long time in his room, which Nate could now picture, and wondered what he was up to. Neither of them was much for naps, especially since they went to bed relatively early, so he was certain that his grandfather was doing something else. Nate was dying to ask about all the things he discovered in his grandfather's room but didn't dare. He knew he had invaded that sacred space and felt a little guilty about it. Little did he know that his grandfather was spending so much time in there these days so he could help Nate grow into himself.

Chapter 21

It was getting closer to November. Over the past week there had been some snow that lightly dusted the ground. It sparkled on the days that the sun decided to show itself, but didn't stay there for long. The foundation had not yet been established. Usually, the bigger storms didn't hit until December, and even then, there was no guarantee of a white Christmas. Last year's winter had been mild, the snowfall well below average. As much as Nate liked to look at the snow, he didn't care for dealing with it. Since his grandfather still insisted on doing the errands into town, maybe he wouldn't have to deal with it at all. He thought it might be a hard winter this year. The region was overdue for one.

The evenings were still spent in relative silence. He discovered a beautiful chess set in a box in the closet of his room, all hand carved. Half the pieces made of white opal, the other half made of black obsidian. He and his father had enjoyed playing chess, especially during the winter months. He had gotten better at it and every now and then would win a game over his father.

He pulled out the pieces and set them up on an old coffee table in his room. After a couple of days playing against himself, he asked his grandfather if he could bring it out into the living room, where it was somewhat warmer and more comfortable to sit and ponder his next move. He played both sides of the board, which made it more challenging. One evening his grandfather pulled up a chair on the opposite side of the table where Nate sat staring at the board. Nate looked up at his grandfather, who smiled at him. Nate smiled back, knowing that he had a real-life competitor. He cleared and reset the pieces and held black in one fist and white in the other. His grandfather, pretending to not know which hand had which color, chose the right hand. It was white. Smoke before fire. His grandfather made the first move. Nate countered with the next, which took him ten minutes to think about. The game was over in fifteen minutes. His grandfather had defeated him in only four moves. Nate was astounded. He had never been beaten that badly.

He looked at his grandfather in disbelief, saying, "How'd you do that?"

His grandfather, with a slight bit of conceit, said, "And who do you think taught your father?"

Nate should have known better. Many skills and talents had been passed down through the generations, each one teaching the next. Nate had learned a lot from his father, but not enough about chess. It seemed the more he learned, the less he knew. He now realized he didn't know much about chess at all.

He flopped back onto the couch. His grandfather rose and took his usual and more comfortable chair across the room. Nate crossed his arms over his chest, almost as if he were pouting. Again, he thought about how his grandfather had a knack for mind reading. Maybe that's how he was able to win so handily. They sat in silence, his grandfather allowing Nate to process all of this. Nate hated losing. He was not accustomed to being the underdog. One negative thought fed another, and Nate could feel himself sinking.

The thoughts pushed down into his gut where he could feel unwanted emotions being stirred up. He crossed his arms over his stomach, holding them in. His grandfather sat, waiting, and watching the anger tighten its grip on Nate. He gently prodded Nate to focus on his breath. Nate resented this but tried to cooperate. The more he did it, the more he could feel the familiar angst surging in his gut.

His resentment was evolving into anger, then rage. His breathing became even more labored and shallow. He was beginning to panic. His stomach started cramping, and his arms moved down to the center of his pain. It was not the kind of pain caused by eating bad food; it was much, much deeper than that. It was ripping him apart. He clenched himself tighter and tighter, his entire body tensed as if it were ready to explode. It did.

The tears that followed were bitter ones. He doubled over, losing himself in the depths of his darkness. He cried out in his defeat, dropping to his knees, rocking himself, trying to hang on. He was begging for mercy, begging for his life. "Oh God," he wept, "I can't go on like this. I don't know what to do. It hurts so much. I don't know what to do. I don't know what to do ..." Over, and over again, spilling out his guts, unaware of where he was. Unaware of his grandfather approaching him and getting down on his knees, giving him consolation, and then instructions.

His grandfather told him to lie on his back. Nate tried to uncrumple his body, but he struggled in his agony. His grandfather took Nate's hand, still clenching his belly, and in it he placed a stone. He then instructed him to close his eyes and to start breathing the way he had been taught. With great effort, Nate forced himself to do this. His grandfather then positioned himself behind Nate's head, still encouraging him to breathe deeply. Putting both hands at the nape of his neck, he started blowing out air over Nate's body. Nate then heard the clacking of what sounded like small stones hitting against one another. With one hand under his head, his grandfather passed his breath and the stones over Nate's body. Nate was aware, but not aware of what was happening. As his grandfather did this, Nate could feel the tension leave his body, his sobs diminishing into stillness.

After what seemed like a long time, he lay there on the floor, as if in a trance. Maybe Grandfather had hypnotized him. Nate didn't know. But he was content just to lie there, and his grandfather let him. He then smelled the odor of the burning sage around him. Nate probably could have stayed that way for a long time, but his grandfather said, "Nate, it is time to come back. When you are ready, open your eyes."

Nate wanted to stay put and had trouble complying with this instruction. But his grandfather gently repeated it until Nate opened his eyes. He stared at the ceiling and struggled to reorient himself. Shortly thereafter, he got up and sat back on the couch. He didn't feel humiliated, which was something that he expected while being in this condition with his grandfather, but he did feel humbled, which was hard for him to figure out— the difference between humiliation and humility. All he knew was that one felt better than the other. He sat in silence and was not afraid of it. He knew in his heart that his grandfather understood without having said a word. He understood Nate's pain as if he were experiencing it himself. Maybe he had. Nate was sure he had.

Sitting there for a while in the quiet after the storm, Nate had to ask. He wanted to know what his grandfather had done to him. He wanted to know what the blowing and rocks were all about. Then he realized that he was holding a stone in his hand. He opened his hand to look at it. It was not a big stone, but was rounded and smoothed, the kind that he saw settled at the bottom of the creek bed. It was reddish, maybe sandstone. Examining it, he turned it over, and on it ink defined the shape of a bear. He looked up at his grandfather, who simply said, "Nate,

133

now is not the time to ask questions. This is not something you can figure out, at least not yet. You need to get out of your head. Take the stone with you and go to bed. Hold the stone over your stomach and go to sleep."

Nate did as he was told. Pulling the covers over him with the stone in his hand and the smell of sage permeating the room, Nate allowed peace to envelop him.

Chapter 22

The next morning Nate awoke to gentle tapping on the door. It must be six, he thought. He was lying there, not wanting to get up at all. He had slept so deeply, unlike most nights. He desperately wanted just to turn over and go back to sleep but knew his grandfather would not allow it, and as much as Nate disliked it, there was something about routine that made him feel more grounded in life. He then recalled the events of the previous evening.

Lying in bed, staring at the ceiling, he tried to figure out what happened to him. He hadn't remembered ever crying so hard, as if he had saved it up for years. It was as though a river had broken through the cracks in a dam, bursting through with a thundering rush. His body ached, he was emotionally drained, and his mind too foggy to be of any help. He got up and rubbed the sleep out of his eyes. It was still dark outside. The clocks had been set back a couple of weeks ago. He still wasn't used to it. He hated getting up in the dark. Reluctantly, he got up and got dressed.

He passed through the living room where he smelled a faint scent of sage that was overruled by the smell of coffee coming from the kitchen. He was looking forward to that first cup and the first cigarette. He hadn't yet given up this habit, but justified it because of his grandfather's occasional pipe smoking. Nate thought, *if he smokes inside of his house, so can I.* He entered the kitchen and poured himself a cup of coffee. He swung his legs over the bench, sat down and lit up. Grandfather had started to cook some bacon, filling the room with a smell that Nate could never resist. While watching the bacon cook, his grandfather turned his head around toward where Nate was sitting. Nate peered over his mug, locking eyes with his grandfather.

"How are you feeling this morning, Nate?"

Meekly, Nate replied, "I'm OK. To tell you the truth, I had the best night's sleep I've had in a long time."

"That is good to hear," said his grandfather. "I was frankly a little worried that too much had happened last night. I was not sure how you would handle it."

"I don't know what you did, and I don't understand it, but I do feel better than I have. You know, well, of course you know that I have a lot of shit to deal with. In some sense I feel that last night was only the tip of the iceberg."

"Then you do understand. You have begun the work. As painful as it was, it was honest, and I honor that," said his grandfather.

Feeling somewhat validated, Nate replied, "Last night I learned something important. I learned that I could trust you, and that you do care about me and what happens to me."

"I do," said his grandfather with all sincerity. "I have always cared about you. I have been worried about you, but at the same time, knew I could not force you to trust me. I had to earn it."

"I guess I can be pretty stubborn at times. I don't mean to be, but I'm not used to showing you my feelings. I find it difficult unless I am totally desperate. I guess I was feeling pretty desperate last night."

His grandfather put the bacon on a paper towel to soak up the grease. "Yes, you were desperate and have been for a long time. It is amazing to me that you have been able to live with it, and I am not necessarily talking about this past year. You have had some difficult things in your life to deal with. Your father's death just seemed to reinforce this in a big way."

Looking out the window, Nate noticed that it was beginning to snow. He pointed this out to his grandfather, wanting to change the subject. It was coming down quite heavily.

"Yes," said his grandfather. "Maybe you could go out and bring in some more wood. It feels like this storm could last for a while. Afterward, breakfast will be ready."

With that, Nate got up and grabbed his coat, which he now had the habit of hanging by the front door near the log carrier. Going outside, Nate saw the ground was getting covered. It was coming down hard. There was an inch of snow on the ground already and it had only begun a short time ago. It was hard to look up because the snow was melting on his face, so he kept his head down, pulling up his collar. He piled wood onto the canvas, bringing in several logs at a time.

He made three trips. Satisfied that they were good for the next twenty-four hours, Nate took his now wet coat off and hung it up. He sat down where his grandfather had just laid down the plate of food for him. He poured the orange juice and refilled Nate's mug with hot coffee. They both ate and talked about the weather. His grandfather predicted a foot of snow. Nate took a bet that it would be more than that. His grandfather said, "In any case, we are going to have to plow our way out of this one."

Nate was wondering if his grandfather would ask him to do this. He was kind of hoping so. He had not driven his truck or even his grandfather's truck since he was dragged back here two months ago. He felt that now he could be trusted not to take off again. Besides, he was curious to know what else was up his grandfather's sleeve. Nate felt that he had a plan for him.

Nate cleaned up the breakfast dishes, wrapped the extra bacon up and put it in the refrigerator. He knew he would be having bacon again this week. The stove in the corner was fired up with some of the fresh wood, making the kitchen warm and pushing the heat out into the rest of the cabin. Nate had left his bedroom door open for some of the heat to fill his room. His grandfather's door remained closed. With the snow falling and the comfort of the air inside, he felt quite comfortable, which made him want to fall asleep again.

Sitting down in his usual spot, he lit up a cigarette, joining his grandfather in a leisurely smoke. His grandfather had a book in front of him and a slight smile on his face. Nate knew he was up to something but didn't ask. He went to place his mug on the coffee table in front of him and saw what his grandfather was smiling about. He had moved the knight on his side of the chessboard. Nate looked up and smiled. His grandfather looked up over his book and smiled back. "It is your move," he said.

Nate didn't move any piece for quite some time. He studied the board intently, weighing all his options, trying to figure out what his grandfather would do next. As time passed, his grandfather kept on reading. Nate still had not made a move.

His grandfather said, "Are you afraid of losing again?"

Nate admitted that he was. His grandfather put his book down and started up a conversation. "So, Nate, what do you think last night was all about?"

Nate replied, "I'm not so sure. I think it must have had something to do with my past."

"You are right, and there is more in there. That was only one layer. There are many, much like an onion." Nate understood the concept but wasn't quite sure how it applied to him. His grandfather continued.

"If you can trust me, I would like to do more work with you so we can get to the bottom of all of this."

"All of what?" Nate asked, feeling curious.

"We need to get to the root of your pain. Let us talk about it."

Nate's mind knew exactly where to go, but it made him feel small. He knew that he had felt enormous grief when his mother died. She had been sick, but it didn't seem as if she had been sick all that long. He just figured she would get better, just like he had after the accident. He had never known anyone to die and didn't know anything about it. Kids don't spend time thinking about death. Kids have a way about them that makes them feel immortal.

When she died, he just couldn't fathom that he would never see his mother again, angry that she had been taken away from him. He grew envious of the other kids who had mothers. Yet, he felt he had to be a man about it. Other than crying for that first week, he went on with his life with his father, not talking about it, and living his life as if it had always been that way. He still felt the grief about his father's death, though later in life, just piled on top of what was already there. He felt it would just always be this way. Nate started talking. His grandfather would nod and through his silence encouraged Nate to go on. Filling with sadness, Nate started to get angry.

"Why are you asking me to talk about this? You're just making me feel worse! I was feeling fine this morning until you started all of this! What the hell are you trying to do with me? Are you trying to ruin my day?"

His grandfather got up and went to his bedroom. He came right back out and told Nate to lie down on the floor as he had the night before. Nate resisted at first, but he did trust his grandfather. So warily and with a deep sigh, he got off the couch and lay on the floor. His grandfather placed a stone in Nate's hand and told him to breathe into it three times. He then placed Nate's hands on his stomach, still holding the stone. Getting behind him, as he had done the night before, he told Nate to close his eyes and start focusing on his breath.

As Nate did this, his stomach tightened up and his entire body became tense. Before long, everything he felt was like the night before and the agony that accompanied it. Feeling as though he would split apart, his grief pushed through. He cried the tears of a little boy who had just lost his mother. He heard his grandfather blowing his breath over him again, and the sound of the rocks hitting together. His grandfather repeated the motion, starting at the top of Nate's head, then moving down to his feet. In time, Nate's tears subsided, and he felt calmness coming over him. His body slowly relaxed. Like the night before, he lay there for some time, as if basking in the sun. Like the night before, his grandfather let him stay that way. He eventually called him back into the room.

Coming alert, Nate realized that he had been in a different place, a place of peace and comfort. It was almost as if he had recaptured the time of his mother's death, but this time allowing himself to pour out his heart that was so badly broken. Getting up and back onto the couch, he fell asleep. He dreamed about his mother and met her in his dream. He talked with her and told her how much he missed her. She held him in her arms, telling him how much she loved him and that she would always be with him.

Chapter 23

After Nate woke up from his unplanned nap, he and his grandfather continued their game of chess. This one lasted much longer than the first, mostly because Nate was taking longer for each move. He studied his grandfather's decisions carefully and was learning through his own mistakes. After dinner, he spent more time at the board while his grandfather read. He got up occasionally to stretch and get something to drink. He would sit back down, light a cigarette, and stare at the board. The evening was fading. He still hadn't made a move.

Finally, as it was getting toward bedtime, his grandfather said to him, "You know, Nate, if you let your fear of losing get in the way, you will never move. What are you waiting for?"

With that, Nate moved the piece he had been focused on for the past hour, looking at it from every angle he could. "There," he said, "I think I've got you."

His grandfather got up from his chair, looked at the board, reached down, moved his bishop, and said, "Checkmate."

Nate was dumbfounded. But he could also see where he went wrong. He graciously shook his grandfather's hand and said, "Congratulations, old man." They both laughed and soon went off to bed.

Nate had another good night's sleep. The snow had stopped, and, as his grandfather predicted, there was about a foot of snow on the ground. Nate was glad he hadn't put money on the bet.

After bringing in more wood, they ate a breakfast of bacon and pancakes and then sat for a bit drinking their coffee. Getting up, his grandfather went to his coat pocket, reached in, turned, and tossed Nate the keys to his truck.

"I'll clean up the kitchen. I need you to go out and clear off the truck and plow the road."

Nate couldn't believe it. It had been a couple of weeks since they had attached the plow to the truck. Now, to his surprise, his grandfather was letting him drive it. Keys in hand, he jokingly said to himself, *Man, I could plow my way right out of here.* He had no intention of doing so but was glad for the opportunity to get outside and behind a wheel.

Before getting out the door, his grandfather cautioned him.

"Be careful plowing. The road is full of ruts and potholes, as you know. Do not go too fast or you will smack your head on the steering wheel."

Nate returned, "OK. Thanks for the warning."

Stepping out, he kicked through the snow down to the truck. The snow was deep but not too heavy. It was cold outside, and the air was still. He looked around at the forest and took it in. The pine trees were clothed with a frozen shroud. Other trees had white markings, creating a scene that only the best artists could duplicate. The sky was mostly bright blue with wisps of white clouds floating. Flying below them was the hawk.

Nate brushed the snow off the driver's side door with his gloved hands and got in to start it. He put on the heat and defroster and then got out to clean off the rest of the truck. Done with this, he got back in. He started in the area in front of the cabin. Pulling up, he dropped the plow, scraping the snow away from the house, moving forward and backing up again until the area was cleared. Then he slowly proceeded down the road. Mindful of what his grandfather had said, it took a while. He went over it a couple of times to widen it enough to leave a little room to spare on each side of the vehicle in case they would need to pull over and let another car get by. He knew that this was highly unlikely to happen, but he cleared it anyway.

Stepping into the kitchen, he appreciated the stove's generosity. The coffee pot sitting on top of it invited him to stay a while. Hanging up his coat, he went over and filled his mug, the steam filling his nostrils and the mug warming his hands. His grandfather understood how simplicity was a gift. Nate was grateful that it had been given to him.

He walked into the living room where his grandfather sat reading, puffing on his pipe. Nate loved the smell of his grandfather's pipe much more than the smell of his own cigarettes, but not as much of the smell of the sage he had grown attached to. When he would eventually return to his house, he would be sure to have it.

He sat down across from his grandfather, this time ignoring the chessboard in front of him. His grandfather hadn't started a new game. Nate didn't feel like it anyway.

"Grandfather?" His grandfather looked up and put his book down. "I have something I'd like to ask you."

"Go ahead. I may not have the answer, but I will give it a shot."

"I'd like to know about the stone. You know, the one you always give to me before you do your thing."

"My thing, huh?"

"Well," said Nate, "I don't know what else to call it."

"No matter," said his grandfather. "You want to know about the stone. What would you like to know in particular?"

"I want to know why the shape of a bear is imprinted on it. Does that have some special meaning? Does the stone have any special meaning? I'm curious. You know me."

"Yes, Nate, I do know you. I've known you since you were a baby. Your curiosity got you into a heap of trouble sometimes."

"Then I shouldn't ask?" Nate inquired.

"No, it is fine. I will tell you." And so, he began to explain with his questions. "Nate, when you think about a bear, what comes to mind?"

Nate thought for a moment. "Well, when I think about a bear, I think of strength and power. I wouldn't want to be in the woods alone with one."

His grandfather smiled. "And what else do you know about bears?"

"They forage for food and are not too picky about it. They'll eat berries, fish, and garbage."

His grandfather smiled again, trying not to laugh. "And what else?"

"They hibernate."

"Why do you think they do that?"

"I don't really know," Nate remarked. "I guess they don't like the winter either."

Now his grandfather was laughing. When he grew quiet again, he asked another question. "Now, I want you to think about this one in relation to the bear. What have you been doing over these past couple of months?"

Nate was beginning to get it. "Well," half laughing, "I guess I've been hibernating."

"OK, and in your hibernating what have you been doing?"

"I've been doing a lot of thinking." He thought some more. "I've been seeking a lot of answers."

"About what?" asked his grandfather.

"About me," Nate replied. "I'm trying to find myself, in a way. And you've been helping me to do that. There have been many things that I've been hiding from myself, things I haven't faced about myself. I've never taken the time to look inside long enough to do this. Until recently, I never even took the time to sit still and pray, or meditate, or whatever you call it. I was always too busy and look where it got me. I suppose if I had taken the time to deal with me, I wouldn't have needed to hit the wall."

"And so it is with the bear," said his grandfather. "The bear hibernates in the winter to gather its strength. It goes into a cave and stays there until spring comes. Then it knows what to do. The stone I give you is the power of the bear. It helps you to go inside yourself to find your strength and purpose."

"So, the stone is helping me to do this, to find the part of me that has been hiding behind my emotional wreckage."

"Exactly. And do you find that it is helping?"

"Yes," said Nate, without further comment. After a few minutes, as if the conversation never stopped, Nate said, "And the blowing, and the stone clacking. What's that about? Oh, and the sage too. Why do you use it after we go through all of that?"

"They are to help unblock whatever it is that keeps you from receiving positive energy. I also use a pendulum that you never see."

Nate blushed because he knew that his grandfather had a pendulum next to the crystals he saw, having gone into his room that one time. So, he decided to confess.

"Grandfather, I never told you this, but, uh, one day when you were out doing your errands, I went into your room and saw all of those things." Nate looked up, expecting a reaction from his grandfather. "I'm sorry. I know I shouldn't have done that, but I did see the pendulum and many crystals. I just don't know why you have them."

His grandfather spoke. "You are right. You should not have gone into my room. Not because of what is in there, but more because it is my private space. I would have hoped you would respect that."

"I do, and I'm sorry. I won't do it again."

"Good. Now, since your curiosity did not get you in a heap of trouble this time, I will tell you why I use the crystals. I mostly have clear quartz. You probably noticed that." Nate nodded sheepishly. "The theories about clear quartz have been in existence for centuries and are still used today. Look at a watch, for instance. Inside is a crystal that keeps it going. Crystals have energy and can also create magnetic fields. They can be used in modern technology for many things, but that's not why I use them. Crystal energy can be powerful."

Nate listened intently.

"There was a guy by the name of Marcel Vogel who discovered this years ago when he worked for a technology company. As part of his work, he found that by pointing quartz crystals at another person their thoughts and emotions were amplified. After leaving the company, he continued his research on the healing energy of crystals by creating different shapes and sizes. The number of facets determines the charge capacity. I could go on and on about this, but just know that Vogel knew what he was doing. The most powerful of his crystals is one with twenty-one facets. It can help heal individuals as well as social groups. Even the environment."

His grandfather stopped to see if Nate was listening. Satisfied that he was, he continued.

"The pendulum that I suspend over you helps me to find where you are blocked in your body, sort of like dowsing for water. It helps me to know where healing needs to happen. Your body is made of energy. When energy is blocked it causes illness, like your depression. I believe that clear quartz crystals help absorb that blockage and infuse positive energy in its place. It emits powerful energy, and needs to be treated with utmost respect and care. Knowing what it can do is a gift not to be abused. It is a sacred gift and only meant to be used for good purposes."

Nate was amazed. Not just about the crystals, but about his grandfather's ability to use them.

"Oh, and by the way," interrupting Nate's thoughts, "I use them on myself too."

Chapter 24

Nate thought about the conversation with his grandfather, mystified by what he was learning. He wondered how his grandfather had acquired this knowledge. Not just about stones and crystals, but about life in general. Nate secretly wished he had his grandfather's wisdom. But he also knew that his grandfather had acquired it, and so he imagined that he could too. After dinner, they talked about getting the business up and going again. Nate didn't know if he could or would be able to do it. As the conversation petered out, they eventually called it a night.

Nate's head was spinning again. He was trying to find answers. Trying to figure out how he would keep it together once he left his grandfather's house. He knew he would eventually have to leave, and he was already anticipating it, even though neither of them had spoken about it. The more he thought, the more anxious he became. He knew that if he didn't slow down his mind, he would never get to sleep. He made a conscious decision to focus on his breathing, and every time his mind went off, he would make himself get back to listening to his breath. After a few repetitions he finally fell asleep.

Not even two hours later he sat straight upright, sweat pouring off him, cruelly jarred awake by the same vicious attack. Angrily he threw off the covers and got up. He was shaking and shivering, pacing around in the small room. *What the fuck?* he thought. He held his hands on his head, rubbing them on his face, feeling the tension in his gut. He wanted to hit something. He wanted to scream, *leave me the fuck alone!* But there was no one to scream at. They weren't there, only in the nightmare. He couldn't fight them off, and they continually beat him to death.

"Damn it," he said out loud, "another night's sleep gone to shit." He went out into the living room and tried to figure out where all this was coming from. He hadn't been drinking. That ended a while ago. He wasn't angry with anyone that he knew of. He didn't know anyone who wanted to kill him. He just couldn't get his mind around this. Why the same nightmare, over and over again? He couldn't figure it out.

It was just before two a.m. He didn't want to start with the coffee yet. He sat in the living room and lit a cigarette, a habit that was slowly diminishing. He decided he would just try to calm down enough and go back to bed. He initiated the breathing, hoping that it would work for him again. It did, and he fell asleep, waking only to the gentle tapping of his grandfather's knuckles on the door. "It is time," he heard him say.

When Nate finally came out, the smell of coffee mixed with the familiar scent of sage permeated the cabin. His grandfather was banging around some pans in the kitchen getting prepared to make breakfast. Nate had grown to love breakfast. Now it had become his favorite meal. He walked into the kitchen seeing his grandfather grinding up some leftover corned beef. He had already diced some potatoes and onion.

"Ahh," said Nate to his grandfather, "looks like corned beef hash today."

"Yes," said his grandfather, "with eggs over easy."

"God, that sounds great, especially after the night I had."

His grandfather turned away from the counter toward the stove where Nate was pouring out the coffee for them. Curious, he asked, "You did not sleep well?"

"No," said Nate, "not that great."

"Are you sick?"

"No," said Nate, hesitating. "I keep having this same dream, over and over again. Well, I shouldn't even call it a dream. It's a goddamn nightmare."

Nate usually didn't swear in front of his grandfather, but he didn't know how else to get across how bad it was. His grandfather, looking concerned, said, "So, do you want to tell me about it?"

"Yeah, I do. Maybe you can help me figure it out."

Nate related the nightmare. Every detail. Every punch. Every emotion. He ended the story by saying, "And every time I have the nightmare, I die. Every single time."

His grandfather was filling the plates. Coming over to the table, he set the plates down and swung his legs over the bench. He could see the anxiety in his grandson's face. Nate was eating, but finding it harder to swallow the food. He was so tense, and in between bites, his jaw would clench as if getting ready for a fight. His grandfather could feel what Nate was feeling. It was uncomfortable for him too. Nate was indeed fighting something, and he wasn't winning the battle. Nate shoved the food down his throat, not tasting it, and was angry because he couldn't enjoy it. His grandfather wanted to tell him to slow down and chew, but he knew how Nate would react to it at this moment.

"Looks like this has got the best of you." Nate nodded, clearly not wanting to talk about it anymore. His grandfather then said, "Nate, do you want to do something about it? Or do you just want to leave it alone?"

Nate was sipping his coffee, the muscles still tight in his face. With resignation he said to his grandfather, "I don't have a choice, do I? I can't stand it! If you can make it stop, then I am willing to. I want it to stop!"

150

His grandfather cleared the table. Nate got up to help. He threw another couple of logs into the woodstove and took his coffee into the living room. His grandfather followed and took his chair. Nate sat, looking around the room as if he would find something. He didn't know what he was looking for. He had trouble focusing. He was tapping his fingers on his leg, then clenching his fist, tapping, clenching, tapping, clenching. His grandfather watched and felt it. He knew a battle was about to ensue. He asked, "Are you willing to cooperate?"

"Yes, Grandfather. I want you to help me get rid of this."

"OK," said his grandfather, "finish up your coffee and lie down on the floor like I taught you. I will be right back."

Nate did as he was told. He didn't know how to fight off an enemy he couldn't see. He lay there as his legs shifted restlessly on the floor. His grandfather came back and brought the pendulum and a large quartz crystal with many facets cut into it. It was about an inch in diameter and came to a point at the end of its six-inch length. He also had the stone that had become Nate's and a rattle. He lit the end of a cone of tightly wrapped sage. Nate knew he usually did this after the work.

Today though, his grandfather circled him three times with the smoke and then circled himself with it too. After this ritual, as Nate anxiously watched, his grandfather knelt beside him and started moving the pendulum slowly above Nate's groin. He didn't go any further.

The pendulum started circling over Nate's pelvic area. He laid the pendulum down on the floor and put a stone in Nate's hand. He instructed Nate to blow into it three times, then placed Nate's hands just below his abdomen. He told Nate to start focusing on his breathing. Nate complied. His grandfather got behind his head as he had before and let his breathing fall into the rhythm of Nate's. Nate quieted into a hypnotic state.

His grandfather then picked up the crystal, and with the pointed end, pushed down into Nate's belly, holding it firmly there. Nate felt as though something was squeezing him, and he could feel his lower torso trying to push it off. His grandfather kept it there for a few moments, then put the crystal down and moved back behind Nate's head, placing his hands underneath. He could see Nate's eyes rapidly moving under his eyelids, as though he were watching something happen.

Then Nate started to struggle. He could feel enormous cramping in his lower abdomen. It was painful. He wanted to get up and run for his life. It felt like panic. His grandfather spoke out loud, asking the Great Spirit, the guardian spirits, the earth spirits, and the animal spirits to come and intercede, especially the bear. He asked for their protection and for them to help him and Nate. He joined his spirit with theirs and Nate's.

He then asked, "Nate, what do you see?"

Nate was trying to hang on to himself, massively confused, not able to answer. His grandfather asked again, "Nate, what do you see?"

He strained to answer; he could barely get the words out. "I don't know. I don't know." He was panicked, whimpering, trying to focus, and struggling to keep his body on the floor.

Again, his grandfather asked, more emphatically, "What do you see?"

Nate blurted out, "I see a car," sounding more frightened.

"What is it doing?"

"I don't know ... I ... I think it's coming at me!"

Nate was truly terror-stricken. He clenched his gut, writhing in agony. "Oh, God ... oh, God ... it's coming right at me!"

"How old are you?"

"Argh!" He could barely speak as he doubled up on the floor, crying out, "I'm little! I'm just a kid!"

"What are you doing?" his grandfather pushed on.

"I'm just riding my bike! Oh God, argh … argh … I'm going to die! I don't want to die!" Sobbing in agony, "I don't want to die! I don't want to die! I don't want to die!"

Now on his knees, his head burrowing into the floor, his emotional guts spilled out. His grandfather loudly asked, "Nate! What are you feeling? Tell me!"

Nate, barely able to speak, trying to breathe, trying to move, screamed out, "I don't know! I feel like I'm dying!"

"Name it!" his grandfather commanded.

"I can't! I don't know what it is."

"Nate, it doesn't belong in you! Name it! What is it?" Nate was struggling to breathe.

"Name it!"

Nate let out a loud cry from the depths of his gut, from the depths of his soul, "It's fear … it's terror … it's death!"

He wept in anguish as his grandfather blew out air above his body. He shook the rattle over him from his head to his feet. He blew and shook, as if blowing it out of Nate's body, giving energy to Nate's body to push it out.

"Tell it to leave you, Nate! It doesn't belong in you! Tell it to leave!"

Nate, still grinding into the floor, spilled out the words, "I don't want to die! Leave me alone! I don't want to die!"

"Tell it to leave!" his grandfather shouted.

Nate, as if taking in his last breath, screamed, "Leave me! You don't belong in me! You're killing me! I don't want to die! Leave!"

His grandfather shouted as he shook the rattle over Nate, "You have no home here! You have no power here! Leave him now!"

He then asked the Great Spirit and all the others to return that part of Nate's soul that was lost at the time of the accident. He blew it into Nate while Nate sobbed inconsolably the tears of the world. His grandfather turned him over to his side and then his back. Nate felt water spraying over him. He felt his grandfather's hand anointing him with oil from his forehead down to his feet. Nate's tears began to subside as his grandfather placed his hands under Nate's back. Then, reaching for Nate's hands, which still held the stone, placed them over Nate's heart as he cried the cries of a little boy.

His grandfather started to hum a sound of comfort. Nate tried to catch his breath between sobs, tried to listen. His grandfather continued to hum as Nate's breathing slowed into a tranquil place. Getting up, his grandfather, still humming, circled Nate with the burning sage three times and then himself. He placed the burnt sage down and went to sit in his chair. Still humming, he let Nate lie there for a long while.

Chapter 25

The rest of the day was spent in quiet solitude. Nate's grandfather spoke little as he allowed Nate time to rest. His grandfather was weary too. So, while Nate rested on the couch, dozing on and off, his grandfather did the same in his chair. They stayed that way for most of the afternoon. The morning had been exhausting, more so than splitting a cord of wood. Splitting a gut is much harder work for a man than heaving an axe.

As dinnertime approached, Nate's grandfather went into the kitchen to begin cooking. He wanted to keep it simple this evening, for there were more important things to do. He took a couple of burgers out of the freezer and put them in the pan on the burner over low heat to thaw. He had no rolls but did have some unsliced whole grain bread. He sliced off four thick slabs. While the burgers were frying, he took out some leftover home fries and heated them up. Nate, smelling the food, came into the kitchen and quietly sat down.

He felt emptied out. He was more in a daze than anything, but still present. He had no thoughts, yet felt calm, almost peaceful. He didn't try to figure out what had happened to him, nor did he even ask questions. He just knew that something had left him, and he felt better than he had in a long time. The gnawing anxiety that he usually felt was no longer there. He didn't feel a need to talk or do anything for that matter. He knew this was a gift, to be able to spend time with his grandfather, dealing with himself and not having the pressure of needing to make money or raise a family. He was genuinely grateful.

During dinner, his grandfather talked to him about gratitude and how important this was, especially considering what happened earlier in the day. His grandfather said that they would need to symbolically give thanks to God, the Great Spirit, and to all the elements that lead toward that Spirit, including the spirits of the animals and the natural world. After dinner, he led Nate outside to the back of the cabin in the clearing. There, Nate saw that his grandfather had shoveled the snow away from the fire pit that they occasionally used during the summer evenings.

The circumference of the pit was laid out with many rocks. The pit itself was about three feet wide. In the pit Nate saw that his grandfather had placed some logs in the form of a square. There were spaces in between them that would catch the air and sustain the fire. It was cold out but without wind. The night was crystal clear with the full moon rising in the horizon through the trees. His grandfather lit the kindling, which soon ignited the logs.

As the fire grew, his grandfather instructed him to follow in his steps. Folding his hands, his grandfather circled the fire three times, stopped, and bowed to the rising moon in the east, thanking the Great Spirit for the strength and clarity given to them. Circling the fire again, his grandfather, now facing the south, bowed and asked that things from the past be taken and healed. Nate caught on and spoke for himself. They then circled the fire again three times, bowing as before, this time to the west, accepting the gifts that they were being given to find the answers within. Nate followed his grandfather once more, this time stopping and bowing to the north, thanking the Great Spirit and all the other spirits for all he had been given so that he would grow into his higher self. Finally, they stopped to face the rising moon in the east, bowing, standing in silence, and honoring that which transcends the earth.

They stood in silence as the fire warmed their bodies. Tears flowed from Nate's eyes, knowing that something special had happened to him today, but he still felt sadness within. He was thinking about his father, and Haley, still feeling like a part of him was lost in their leaving him. He let the sadness fill him. After the fire had died down, his grandfather extinguished it with the snow around them. They went inside and silently parted ways, each going to his room for the night.

Waking in the morning, Nate was aware that he had slept well, yet he still felt depressed and tired. He awoke just before his grandfather arrived at his door. Sitting up, he put his feet on the floor and sat for a few minutes listening to his breath, allowing himself to listen, and to thank God for helping him. Tears welled up and sadness overtook him. He shook it off as best he could and went out to the kitchen to greet his grandfather.

"Good morning, Grandfather."

"Well," his grandfather said, smiling, "and how did you sleep last night?"

"I slept well, certainly better than the night before. No nightmares. I think I probably got a solid eight in."

"Good for you," his grandfather responded.

Nate tried to put on a good front. He felt too vulnerable. He tried to keep the conversation filled with small talk. He noted to his grandfather that it was snowing again, but only lightly. After clearing the table, Nate told his grandfather that he was going for a walk. His grandfather simply said, "Have a good one."

Nate went outside and made his way through the snow down to the creek. He sat listening to the creek, it was still running despite the snow. He thought about how badly he missed his father. He thought about how much he was missing Haley. Tears started to well up and flowed down his face. He managed to shake it off and go back to the cabin.

Sitting down, Nate thanked his grandfather for the coffee and told him that the snow had melted into the water down at the creek. His grandfather said that in the early winter the creek always won. Later in the winter, the ice had a way of slowing down the flow, but underneath it could still be heard. The depth of the water and the life within it never stopped.

His grandfather looked at Nate, waiting for his eyes. When they met, he said gently, "You still miss your father, yes?"

Nate should have known he could not hide from his grandfather, and said, "Yes, I do."

"And Haley too."

"Yes," admitted Nate. "I feel like a part of me died with them." He sat there, head down, trying to not give in to it, but needing to say more. "I can't get over it. It still feels like it all happened yesterday. It feels even worse now. I feel like all the work we have been doing is not helping. I feel OK for a while, and then it's as if nothing has changed. I can't hang onto it."

"That is because there are other layers to peel away," said his grandfather. "Are you willing to cooperate?"

Nate knew full well what this meant, and said, "Yes, I am."

They both got up and went into the living room. Nate did not have to be told to lie down. His grandfather repeated the steps he had taken yesterday. This time, though, placing the stone in Nate's hands, he took them and laid them over his heart, which his grandfather knew was blocked in its brokenness. His grandfather invoked the Great Spirit to assist Nate in finally freeing the intense grief he had been holding onto. When all had subsided, Nate visited a place of light and peace that filled him and held him. He lay there for a long while.

His grandfather went about his business. He brought some wood in, swept up the kitchen, and started putting together the makings for chicken soup. Soon the cabin filled with the smell of simmering broth. Sitting back down in his chair, he saw that Nate had not moved. Feeling that it had been long enough, his grandfather prodded Nate back. It took a few minutes, which was OK, for his grandfather wanted to be as gentle as possible.

Finally, Nate opened his eyes, lying still, staring at the ceiling. He wanted so much to stay where he was and where he had been. He opened his eyes and knew where he was. He looked over at his grandfather and smiled. His grandfather smiled back. They both knew of this place now, and Nate finally realized what he had been missing. He felt as though he had been made free.

His grandfather was sitting in his chair reading the Bible, which in some ways surprised Nate, but on the other hand he knew that it too had been a part of their heritage. His parents read the Bible, his mother more than his father. There was no contradiction as far as Nate was concerned. God had many ways to teach us.

Sitting down on the couch, Nate's eyes roamed the room and settled on the coffee table in front of him. He laughed and looked up at his grandfather. He had made the first move. As Nate studied the board, he and his grandfather talked. Nate talked about how different he felt since coming here a little over two months ago. He couldn't believe that he had been so close to the brink, and now he saw the brink from far away.

They continued their discussions about the business, the house, and the work that would need to be done to reclaim the losses. As they discussed these things, Nate could feel his confidence grow. He dared to think that maybe he could make it happen. Eventually he would.

Both then got up and went outside. They spent most of the day cutting some more wood. The stack had been diminishing since the weather continued to be below freezing. After a couple of hours his grandfather went back inside while Nate continued chopping. Nate's stamina was now well beyond his grandfather's, so he remained outside until the pile had been fully restocked. The sun was beginning to set, and he was losing light. He had to quit. He went into the cabin that was filled with the aroma of a dinner about to come.

Chapter 26

After dinner, Nate and his grandfather started up another game of chess. His grandfather had won the last one, as usual, but in doing so he was teaching how he did it. Nate was learning how to make the right moves with the right pieces at the right time. He learned that he didn't have to capture so many of his grandfather's men to win. His grandfather never needed to capture any. Nate was getting better at it. He was getting better at a lot of things. Soon after the game, his grandfather went to bed. Nate started to doze off and decided to go to bed.

He was hoping for a dreamless sleep. He would be happy with no visions and no nightmares. It was too late. He was on the ground. He didn't hear them sneak up on him. He felt the blow on his back and his head slamming on the ground. He felt the skin being torn from his face as the cement scraped it away. He tasted dirt in his mouth and closed his eyes to protect them. He felt the boot, and another, pounding into his ribs. He heard them and their rage spewing out at him. The beating continued until he could barely breathe. He couldn't respond. They began to leave him in darkness and death. But somehow, he came to.

He could see them walking away. He struggled to his feet, trying hard not to let them see him. Straightening himself out, he brushed off his clothes and then stepped out into the lighted path. He was bruised but not broken. He found new strength in his weakness. He called them out, each of them. They turned around as if to come at him again. But they didn't dare and backed away slowly until it was safe enough to run. And they ran. They ran as fast as they could.

Nate woke up, startled. He was shaking but not afraid. He couldn't believe it. He said out loud, "Holy shit! Holy shit! I didn't die! I didn't die this time! Oh my God! They ran away! They actually ran away!" His grandfather woke up, his sleep disturbed by the commotion coming from Nate's room. Something was wrong, he thought, and bolted out of his room over to Nate's. He opened the door to see Nate sitting on the edge of his bed talking loudly. He was wide-awake.

"Grandfather, you won't believe what just happened. I can't believe it myself." His grandfather sat down on the other end of the bed, intently listening, and monitoring Nate's behavior. Nate went on.

"You remember the nightmare I told you about, the one with the three guys beating me to death? The one I've been having over and over again?" His grandfather nodded.

"I had it again. I just had it. It woke me up. But it was different this time. I didn't die! Do you believe that? Grandfather, I didn't die this time! I was able to get up somehow. They saw me. They thought that they had killed me! They almost did, but they didn't! They ran away from me. Damn, they ran for their lives! What do you think of that one, huh? Is that unbelievable, or what?"

His grandfather knew that this was the beginning of a new chapter in Nate's life. The rest of the night was short for both of them, but the sleep was deep and satisfying.

The following morning his grandfather walked into the kitchen.

"I'm making breakfast today," Nate announced.

"I guess you slept, despite it all."

"I did. In fact, I slept great! And I have you to thank for it."

"Do not thank me," said Grandfather. "Thank the Great Mystery above."

After they ate his grandfather reached into his pocket and gave Nate a stone. Holding the stone in his hand, he turned it around, looking at it, thinking, and staring at it. He then held it out and said to his grandfather, "It's a turtle."

His grandfather smiled, "Yes, it is a turtle."

"And so," said Nate. "Don't ask me. I'll tell you."

"OK," his grandfather said, urging him on.

"The turtle is about as close to the ground as you can get, other than the snake. A turtle has a hard shell, not because it is a hard creature, but in order to protect itself. It is purposeful and steady—the old hare and turtle story. It's about staying grounded on the earth and not rushing into things."

His grandfather sat back. "You are getting wiser in your old age, Nate."

His grandfather sat in silence, thinking about what Nate had just told him. Nate was frustrated by that. He said to his grandfather, "Please talk to me, Grandfather. Tell me what you're thinking. I want to know. I need to know what you think about all of this. Tell me what you know. Please."

After a few minutes, his grandfather said, "Nate, one of the reasons you came here was to find yourself." He stopped. Nate did not interrupt. His grandfather squared himself and looked directly into Nate's eyes and said, "You just did."

Nate smiled. Now he understood. His grandfather spoke no more. He got up, and left the room. He left Nate alone, where he needed to be.

PART III

GRANITE

Chapter 27

Nate returned to his house early in January and was appalled at what he saw. He was met with the thick odor of stale tobacco. The place smelled like a sleazy bar and looked like one too. He wasted no time, determined to bring the house back to life. Remembering how disgusted Haley had been with the bathroom, he decided to start there and attack it head-on.

It took him close to a month to clean and paint each of the rooms. The hardest room to paint was his parents.' After his father died, he had just closed the door. He couldn't go in there. Now he felt ready to deal with it.

Nate wondered how his father managed to sleep in the same bed after his mother died. He imagined that his father's emptiness had been much like his own. His father handled the death of his wife courageously, and probably left his grief in that one single room. Nate's respect for his father deepened as he realized how difficult it must have been for him to keep Nate's life as normal as he could. His father was a hero, and by living with his grandfather over the past three months he grew to know what that really meant.

His parents' room felt like sacred space, much like his grandfather's room at the cabin. He felt that he was somehow intruding. There were two sculptures on the dresser that Nate's father had made. One piece was a pair of wings delicately carved in white marble, polished to such a gleam that light was drawn to it. The other was a vase carved out of limestone. Its slender base rose out of its square footing with graceful lines carved with detailed vines, leaves, and blossoms. It was a gift to his wife on their fifteenth anniversary. There were fresh flowers in it at all times until his mother's death; the vase had grown lifeless without her.

On the wall was a crucifix. On the dresser, a silver tray full of various stones and natural crystals. Nate had never seen either of his parents use them despite their inclination toward spiritual expression. He found this particularly true in their connection with the earth—his father with his stonework, his mother with her gardening.

He looked in the closet. In it hung his father's clothes. Toward the far side Nate was surprised to find some dresses of his mother's. His father couldn't give them away, so they were left in the shadow in the corner. Nate didn't know if he could give the clothes away either. He would wait on this one. There were enough other things to do now.

Working on the house was cathartic Everything was painted, washed, and steam cleaned. He bought new furniture for the living room. By the time he was finished, some two weeks later, he opened the windows for some fresh air. The traffic didn't bother him anymore.

He also cleaned up the studio addition and the storefront. He even bought some new, more comfortable furniture to replace the old, beaten-up vinyl chairs. The place was sprucing up nicely. He wasn't quite ready to go back to the shop where his father had died. That would come in time.

His grandfather came regularly into town to help Nate get things set up again. He organized the paperwork for Nate and showed him where all the important files were. He suggested that Nate find someone to help him with the business. Nate knew of only one person whom he might be able to ask, even though they hadn't spoken in months— his best friend, Jack O'Leary. Nate would need to call him.

He sat at the kitchen table with the phone in his hand, drumming his fingers, trying to decide how he would start the conversation. It had been so long since he had seen Jack. He didn't know where to begin and was trying to think of an opening line that would break the ice. It felt like a cold call. Maybe Jack wouldn't want anything to do with him. He had tried so hard to pull Nate out of his slump and Nate wouldn't even laugh at his jokes. Jack didn't understand depression. He felt that if he could just get Nate off the couch and out the door, he would be fine. Nate couldn't get off the couch.

In school Nate and Jack were in a couple of classes together. After a while Nate learned not to sit next to Jack because he couldn't stop laughing and would find himself getting into trouble too. In their senior year, Jack won the class award for the best sense of humor. Nate won the award for most likely to succeed. Jack had a great time with that one. He would say that his award was a fact. Nate's was only speculation.

Sitting at the kitchen table, Nate smiled to himself as he thought about his friend. Jack was probably the best mason he knew. He worked hard and played hard. Jack had learned his trade from his father too, but they didn't have their own business. They contracted for work through the union. There was always plenty of work, but Jack often complained of how boring bricklaying had become. He knew he had to make a living, though, and made sure he had a life beyond it.

Nate felt sorry for having pushed Jack away and hoped he wouldn't now regret it. But in sitting there thinking about their friendship, he somehow came to feel that Jack would forgive him. He longed for the old times he had with his buddy. Finally, he dialed.

"You haven't reached Jack, and won't if you're trying to sell me something," the answering machine said. "For the rest of you, leave a message and I'll get back to you in the order your call was received."

Nate started laughing as he left his message. "Uh, Jack, you're still an ass, and I'm off mine. Call me back. You've got my number."

Nate hung up and had just gotten up when the phone rang. He turned back and picked it up. "This is Nate," he announced.

"Excuse me," said the guy at the other end, "is this a dead man talking?"

"Talking and walking the other way," Nate laughed. "How are ya' Jack?"

"How am I? You son of a bitch! Where the hell have you been? I tried to get a hold of you around Christmas time, mostly out of guilt, but then I thought you had died! Jesus, man! I mean, what the hell? What was I supposed to think?"

"Yeah, I know," said Nate, feeling guilty. "I should have called you, but I think my pride got in the way. The last time I saw you, I couldn't have cared less."

"Yeah," retorted Jack, "I got that feeling, all right. I just decided I'd better leave you alone to deal with your shit. You weren't much fun to be around."

Nate said, "Yeah, I know," feeling contrite. "It wasn't much fun to be around myself, but hey, here I am, and I'm ready to get back into it. I'll tell you the sad story sometime."

"Nate give me a break. I know the sad story already and don't want to hear it again. You sound better. That's all I care about."

"When am I going to see you? I can't do anything tonight, got a hot chick on the line, you know?"

"That's OK. Do I know her?"

"Don't think so, maybe never will. Who knows? How 'bout tomorrow night?"

"That would be great. I can't wait to see your ugly face."

Nate laughed and said, "Eight at the pub?"

"I'll be there."

Nate felt wonderful. Jack was back in his life. He wondered what it would be like to see him again.

Chapter 28

The following day Nate put in a full day's work before going out. He was tired, having spent most of the day in the shop, moving stones and slabs around with the forklift, and organizing the tools and cleaning them.

Nate worked on half of the shop. He wasn't ready to deal with the other half yet. The slab that killed his father still sat in the broken sling and was partially propped up with blocks on the side where his father's body was pulled out. He knew he would need help.

Nate should have known when he walked into the pub that evening that Jack would already be there. As soon as he entered, he got a fist in the shoulder and a bear hug that lifted him off the floor. "Nate Bearing! You son of a bitch! Get in here, you bastard!"

Putting Nate down, he said, "Man, it is so good to see you. I missed you. I was getting bored without you around. What'll you have?" he asked.

Nate had thought about this moment for a long while that afternoon. He had essentially stopped drinking, and even though he was in a much better place emotionally, he didn't want to risk it. He had taken to heart everything his grandfather had taught him. He even carried over the morning ritual of starting his day with focused breathing and meditation, finding peace that would carry him through the day. The aroma of sage he burned as part of his ritual lingered in the house.

Nate frequently found himself reflecting on his grandfather's words. "Nate, you have been given special gifts." He still wondered about this. The only thing he ever got from his silent listening was that he would know it when it was time. He learned to be content with that. Now, here he was with Jack at their favorite haunt, and he knew how he would handle it.

Matching Jacks' boisterous voice, he said, "Get me a Buckler."

"A what?" asked Jack.

"A Buckler, I said, me lad," faking an Irish brogue. "And if they don't have that, make it an O'Doul's."

"Shit, OK, OK, I'll get you your goddamn fake beer. So, you gave up the real deal? This I gotta' hear about. I'll be right back."

Nate scooped up a basket of peanuts and claimed a booth by the door. It was a great place and being here made him feel part of society again.

Jack came back to the booth with drinks in hand.

"Here you go. Now tell me what's gotten into you. How long have you been on the wagon, and why?"

Nate related as much of the story of the past few months that he dared to share. He mostly focused on his need to get physically and mentally back in shape and get his life together. This Jack could understand. He talked some about his grandfather's propensity toward spiritual things and how some of it rubbed off on him. Jack could relate to it in some ways. He would occasionally go to church, and he did pray every now and then. But Nate knew that Jack would never buy into what he had learned about himself, and about his relationship with the world around him, so he spared him the details.

Jack too had the opportunity to talk about what he had been up to over the past few months, mostly about dating. He wasn't quite sure what he was looking for in a woman. He could never figure out what they wanted from him. He had a hard time identifying with their need to talk about their feelings and relationships. He was more interested in how well they cooked. It seemed that in many ways he was looking for someone to take care of him. That wasn't going to happen, Jack decided, not with the women he had met so far. He guessed he'd be waiting a long time for the right one to come along. Nate got brave, and in a nonchalant way asked Jack if he had seen Haley at all.

"Just once, right before Christmas. She was shopping at the mall with some guy. Big dude. Looked kind of creepy to me." He paused. "Too bad you guys broke up. I thought you were good together."

Nate commented, "Yeah, I thought so too. But like you, she got kind of sick of me. I can't blame her." After a pause, Nate broached the subject of work. "I've been thinking about getting the business up and going again."

"That's a good idea you lazy shit," Jack said.

Nate pressed on. "I've been cleaning up the place and getting things organized. I haven't officially opened the business, but I'm hoping to do that in March sometime. I still have a lot of inventory, all paid for. I've ordered updated catalogs for people to browse through. I think that people will still remember the company's reputation. I figure it will take about two months of hard work to make it a viable business again."

Jack was listening without interrupting. "I was wondering if you would ever get back into it. When I last saw you, it didn't seem to matter to you. I tried to kick your ass. It's good that you're going to give it a shot again. You're one of the best, Nate."

"Thanks, Jack," replied Nate. "But I've got to ask you something, and I don't need an answer right away. I just want you to think about it, that's all."

"Think about what?"

"Well," said Nate, hesitating, trying to figure out how to put it. "Well, uh … I was wondering if you would be willing to come and work with me."

Jack was silent, which wasn't always a good thing. Nate was feeling like he was in for a letdown. After a few awkward moments, Jack said, "Geez, man, I didn't see that coming. I don't know what to tell you."

More silence while Nate waited in his anxiety. Jack then said, "You know, Nate, I've been a mason for quite a while now, and I have a certain amount of job security through the union, not to mention the benefits. Tell me exactly what you have in mind."

Nate, feeling more hopeful, then replied, "Well, you know, you think I'm one of the best. And I, well … I think you're one of the best. I mean, I think you and I together could make things happen."

"Go on," said Jack, still listening.

"What I was thinking is that maybe you could start doing something part-time with me, just so we could test it out. It's not like I would expect you to drop everything. As you said, there is a lot of security in what you're doing now. I can only hope that I can generate enough work to make it feasible for you. We can always work out the benefits. My father and I did. Whenever we wanted to take some time off, we would just close the business for a couple of weeks. You can do that sort of thing if you own your own company."

"But what about salary?" Jack finally interrupted. "I'm making fairly good money now. What would that look like?"

Nate nodded and replied, "This is what I can tell you. My father and I were doing well. We always had projects going. We didn't work by the hour but rather by the job itself. Most often we would get half of the cost right up-front. We could engrave five or six monuments a day, depending on how complicated the design was. We had such a good reputation that most funeral homes in the area referred customers to us. I'd say we were clearing at least fifteen thousand dollars a month. Maybe you and I wouldn't make that much right away, but I still have a lot of connections."

Jack mulled this all over and got up to get another beer. He turned to Nate. "Do you want another drink of that shit?" he asked.

Nate looked down at his bottle. It was still about a third full. "No, I'm good," he said.

It took Jack a while to get back. "Well, Nate, I don't know what to tell you. I've got to think about this for a few days. I mean, you know I'll help you out any way I can, but if I were to do this, it would be a big risk for me."

"I know. Take your time. I've still got nearly a month's worth of cleaning up to do. My grandfather has been a big help, whenever he wants to leave his life of solitude. He doesn't even mind staying with me for a couple of days at a time. He's glad to see I'm back to my old self, or, as he would put it, into my new self. I can't tell you how lucky I am to have him." They talked late into the evening, being joined every so often by old friends who were glad to see Nate again. As he was saying goodbye to everyone, Jack saw him to the door.

When there, Jack said to him, "Nate, I'm glad to see you again, no kidding. And I want to tell you something else."

"What's that?"

"If I do decide to do this thing, I want you to know that I will work *with* you, but not *for* you."

"Good enough for me."

Chapter 29

It was early February and Nate was making good headway in preparing the property for a new start. He even had new gravel spread out in the parking lot. He planned on paving it when the weather was warmer. He had made a sign that sealed his fate. With a deep breath, he put it in the window of the storefront: REOPENING FOR BUSINESS, MARCH 15.

"Well, that's it," he said out loud to himself. He walked back into the studio. He sat on his stool in the middle of the room. He looked around, satisfied with the cleanup job he had done. He fixed his eyes on the far-left corner of the room. There on the shelf was the piece he had been working on before his father died. It wasn't for anyone, but he always spent his spare time carving away for his own need to create. He never sold any of his pieces. Sometimes he might give one away as a wedding gift, but most just sat on the shelves. He often thought that he might have a showing of his work someday, but he never took the time to do anything about it. It was enough for him to sculpt for himself.

Nate had a knack and a passion for creating intricate pieces by hand, even though smaller power tools made the work go faster. By using small rasps and rifflers he was able to carve even the smallest detail. It took a great deal of patience and focus, but it was the detail that brought his work to life.

Just about a year ago he had been chipping away at a statue in that corner. He had chosen black marble, a block left over from one of their bigger jobs. He had chiseled away angles of the block to size and started to rough out the form of a man sitting with his head down. That's as far as he had gotten. He planned on finishing it, a figure of a boxer who had just lost a fight. At the time that's how he felt inside. But as he thought some more, he decided to make another sculpture beside it—a boxer in his glory. Now that would be a finished piece.

Nate stood up and stretched. As he walked across the lot, an old familiar Chevy pickup pulled in. His grandfather got out and made his way over to his grandson, whom he hadn't seen in a couple of weeks.

"Well, how are things going, Nate?" he asked, perusing the area around the yard. "I saw the sign in the window. Looks like you're just about ready."

Nate felt encouraged by his grandfather's confidence in him. His grandfather by now knew him better than anyone ever had, and maybe ever would. They had a connection with each other that few people could ever hope for, the depth of which few could understand.

They both walked into the shop, and Nate showed him what he'd accomplished over the past couple of weeks. Everything had been done except for moving the slab out from under the hoist. The straps had not yet been replaced. Bill was coming to connect new straps next week Nate told his grandfather. Meanwhile, he would just let the slab stay there until it could be pulled up and away. His grandfather nodded. He understood.

They talked about the long winter together and how the snowmelt was filling the creek. Nate told him that he would be out there in a couple of days for a visit. He wanted to see the creek rushing into spring. As they were talking, they heard someone calling.

"Nate! Are you here? Where the hell are you? I don't have a lot of time, so get your ass out here, you bastard!"

Jack was making his way through the lot, he looked up to see Nate and his grandfather. He stopped in his tracks.

"Oh, Mr. Bearing, uh, I didn't know you were here. Is that your truck out there? God, I haven't seen you in ages." He went up to shake his hand. "How are you, sir? And hey, sorry about my mouth, but ..."

By now Nate was laughing. His grandfather played stoic just to egg Jack on. When he broke out with a smile, Jack started laughing too. "God, I'm such an ass," he said, "I mean, jerk." He raised his hands helplessly, shaking his head. With the three of them laughing, Nate invited them into the house for some coffee.

After a few minutes of banter, Nate poured the coffee and sat down. Looking at Jack, he asked, "So, what brings you by today?"

Nate knew all along why Jack was there. In fact, he knew that he would show up today. Nate seemed to have developed his grandfather's intuition. He could feel what another was feeling. He also had a good idea of what someone else was thinking. Nate realized that this was a gift that was growing inside of him. He waited for Jack's response.

"Well, you remember what we were talking about that night? I've been thinking about it. How's this for an idea? I'm about to finish up a big job. We just got done repairing the stonework for the cathedral downtown. Frankly, I need a break. I told my contractor I may want to take some time off for some personal business. He also knows that I haven't taken any time off in a long time."

"So, I've been thinking. What if I was to, say, take six weeks off and give it a shot. You know, to work *with* you, not *for* you, but *with* you."

Nate knew what he was going to say next, so he offered it up. "I'd cover your expenses at least." His grandfather nodded in approval.

Jack said, "Geez, I didn't even get a chance to ask. Well, yeah. That would be what I would need to pull this off. If you can do that, well then, I guess it's a done deal. I'll come in, and we'll see how it goes."

Nate was thrilled, and relieved. "Jack, look, I know we can make this work."

His grandfather simply said, "I know it will work. The two of you are meant to do this." Nate looked over at his grandfather and simply smiled.

Jack added, "Well, we're going to be finished up in a few days. And, hey, I saw the sign you put out in front there. Boy, do you have faith or what? What were you going to do if I said I couldn't?"

Nate shrugged it off. "I don't know. I would have figured something out."

"Yeah, you probably would have, knowing you. Not to mention this old guy sitting next to me, with all due respect, sir."

They all laughed at that and knew they had formed a bond. Jack was going to become part of the Bearing tradition. Both Nate and his grandfather were proud to have him and told him so. Understanding that a final decision had not been made, they let Jack know that there was no one else they would rather have.

Over the next couple of weeks, Nate spent most of his time ordering headstones to add to the inventory. When Jack showed up, he was surprised to see how much Nate had accomplished.

"Man," said Jack. "You expect me to work that hard?"

"Somehow I think you'll keep up. You're no slouch."

"Yeah, you're right. I wouldn't ever want you to get one up on me. Where do you want me to start?"

"How about giving me a hand getting that slab over there out of the way?" Nate said pointing over to the hoist.

"Sure," Jack replied. "This has got to be pretty tough for you."

"Well, it is, but it's got to be done, and I couldn't do it by myself."

They went over to the place where his father died and just stood there. Looking at it, both felt a need to remember the tragic event, the place where his father's soul was freed. Eventually Jack asked, "Now, where do you want this to go?"

"I think we should put it back outside with the other stones."

Back inside the shop, they went over to the empty space where the stone had sat for months. They had to leave the hoist and pulley where they were and wait for the repairs to be done.

After showing Jack around, Nate invited him back over to the house for some coffee and to talk about getting ready for opening day. The two of them talked all afternoon, planning and brainstorming. Jack wondered what Nate would have done if he hadn't agreed to come in for a few weeks. He was equally impressed by the condition of the house, especially knowing how it looked the last time. The old couch was gone and replaced. Nate had even hung new curtains and got the stains out of the carpet. *Now, that took some doing,* Jack thought.

Chapter 30

Opening day came. Calls came in immediately. There was no one in the office, as Nate learned quickly. He put his cell phone number on the voice mail message so that people could call him if there was no answer at the desk. He also installed a buzzer at the customer service desk that would automatically sound off in the shop. One way or the other, the customer would be attended to. So far, so good, but he knew it wouldn't be long before he would need to get more help.

The constant interruptions were starting to get to him. But at the same time, Nate knew what his customers were going through. He held even greater empathy for these people since the death of his own father. He was able to help them choose the stone, but also took time to listen to the stories they told about their loved ones. If he didn't have a monument that met their wishes, he would guide them through the catalogs until they saw what they had in mind. Sometimes, though, they wouldn't find what they were looking for, so he would sketch out their thoughts on paper and make the stone to order. Even though it took longer, it was important to Nate to give them what they wanted instead of opting for an easier way out.

Nate had always been a kind man, and a compassionate one. But now as he met people, one by one, he could often feel their sadness as if it were his own. It was clear that it wasn't his, but that it was somehow his responsibility to lessen the pain for them by joining in it and giving them comfort in a way he hadn't before. They knew he was genuine. Nate would take the pain away from them if he could. He often found that this giving of himself, so to speak, was more exhausting than the physical labor of his work. All he knew was that when people left the store, they felt better, even if only a little bit.

Many times, after a customer had chosen a monument, Nate found himself thinking about the headstone his father had made to place on his mother's grave. It was unique. He had chosen a white marble block that had blue veins throughout. Nate remembered that the rounded stone, lying flat on the cutting block, looked much like a wedding cake.

It took his father months to cut, grind, hone, and polish the stone. It was flawless and elegant. Stacked in tiers, in the center of the smallest stone on the top layer he carved a hummingbird. On the middle stone, around the circumference, he had engraved the dates of her birth and death. He surrounded the dates with a delicately carved vine of roses. On the circumference of the last and largest tier, he carved her name, 'Augustina Marie Bearing. A free spirit.

When he set the monument at the cemetery, he planted a garden of lamb's ears and miniature red rose bushes in front of it. It was his father's last sculpture.

After his father's death, Nate could only manage to set a marker at his father's head. Although he often thought about a monument, he still couldn't formulate a vision. Until he could, he would not begin.

Into the third week of opening the business, it was clear to Jack that this arrangement with Nate just might work out. Nate made sure that Jack always had money up-front each week, and the business was already growing. He was seriously considering joining Nate instead of going back to his regular job with his contractor. He would decide soon.

Nate and Jack were putting in long days. A couple of times Jack stayed over at the house rather than bothering to go home. Jack reserved Friday and Saturday nights for himself to keep up with his dates. But on the nights that nothing was happening he got Nate to stop what he was doing and dragged him out to the pub. Though Nate wasn't drinking, he made up for it with wings and pizza. Jack continued to entertain him and anyone else who would listen.

There were times when young women would flirt with Nate. While he was polite and interested, he wasn't ready to date anyone. His heart still ached for Haley. He hoped that once he could prove he was stable and moving forward, he would have the courage to give her a call.

There had been a lot of rain in this early spring. The dead could now be buried in the thawed earth. Nate and Jack could barely keep up with the orders. Funerals seemed more ominous, dark clouds descending over the already dark days. The soaking rain melded with the tears, dropping grief into the graves. It seemed as if nature was rubbing it in. Spring was supposed to be a time of new life. The irony made death more pronounced.

The weather, as usual, shifted for a few days. Mud started to dry. The April sun was lending its warmth to the air, and some of the crocuses were peeking up from the dead weeds in the garden. When he had a little downtime, Nate took advantage of it weeding, trying to fulfill the promise he had made to himself to care for the gardens as his mother had.

One morning, when Jack was into his fifth week of working with Nate, he showed up for duty with a big grin on his face. Nate knew something was up. Even though Jack was generally full of energy, it usually took a second cup of coffee to jump-start him. This morning it seemed that he'd already drank a pot.

When Nate saw the look on his face, he couldn't help but ask, "What's up, Man, did you finally meet someone who could stand you?"

Jack was still having a lot of single date experiences, and usually couldn't get a second one. It had much to do with his old-fashioned approach to male-female relationships. Women saw right through him, though he didn't know how. It was usually when hen he started joking around about their cooking skills and how he always loved coming home from school to find milk and cookies.

Jack, in response to Nate's question, said, "No, although when that happens, you'll be the first to know. No, it's better than that. At least I think so. OK. So yesterday I told my contractor that I wouldn't be coming back. I told him I had an opportunity that I couldn't refuse. I tried to let him down easy, but he was bummed. It's your lucky day, man, 'cause I'm coming to work with you, the venerable Nate Bearing."

Nate pumped his fist and said, "Yessss, this is awesome! You and me—the best in the business—working together!" He jabbed Jack in the shoulder. Jack jabbed him back.

They worked particularly hard that day, driven by their comradery. Nate was so relieved and had a feeling that somehow his father had a hand in this. He secretly thanked him, God, and all of God's spirits for giving him the gift of Jack and hope for a new and prosperous future. Nate was deeply aware that he had been given another chance at life.

Chapter 31

Nate went out to his grandfather's place regularly now. He would be sure to help him with any work that needed to be done on the property. After the long winter, many things needed attention. The wind, always more adamant at the higher elevations, had ripped off a few more shakes from the roof. Nate replaced them even before his grandfather asked.

The winter had also haphazardly trimmed the trees around the house. Many branches had barely missed the cabin. Nate used the chainsaw to cut through the thicker limbs. He had decided that for some things power tools made more sense, just as they did for cutting through stone. His grandfather would acquiesce, even though he hated the noise. In this regard, he gave Nate the liberty, admitting that as man's mind evolves, so do his tools.

Nate had been looking forward to today's visit. After dinner, he went to go outside to walk around. It was such a far cry from his life at work. The need to keep track of time, people, and money was wearing on him. Being at his grandfather's, even if for only a few hours, allowed him to be more aware of his surroundings. Most of the time he was able to find balance through his daily meditation, but here in the woods he didn't have to seek it. He decided to stay the night.

The next morning, after one of their he-man breakfasts, Nate went outside to the clearing behind the cabin. He looked around to see what else needed to be dealt with to finish the winter cleanup. He had only to split the logs that were remnants from the fallen trees. He decided there would be plenty of time for that. He then walked over to the fire pit. He could tell that there had been a fire in it recently. He surmised that his grandfather had used it for a ceremony. Nate had not done anything like that since his return home, but now he was reminded of how important it was. The fire ritual was one of gratitude. He had a lot to be thankful for. He decided that he would need to make time for it.

"Well," Nate began, "things are looking good out there. There're still a lot of tree branches to cut up, but I left it for you."

"You are ever so thoughtful, Nate," his grandfather smiled.

"You're welcome" said Nate with a laugh. "I still have some time before I need to get back to town."

"So," his grandfather asked, "what do you want to talk about?"

"You know, I don't have a lot of time on my hands for the most part, but when I start thinking about things, I still look back at this past winter with you." He paused. Looking down at the floor, he tried to collect his thoughts. "I'm still trying to sort it all out. I still have a lot of questions about what you did and how you did it."

"OK," said his grandfather. "So, you still need to have answers. What do you want to know?"

"Yeah, well, you had said that you use the pendulum on yourself. I wonder if that would help me. I mean, I know you used it on me, but why do you use it on yourself?"

"It is like this. I used it on you to find out where your energy was blocked in your body. Very often the body tells us more than the mind. Different parts of the body tell us different things."

"Like what?" Nate asked.

"When your father died, it affected us both. I too wanted to retreat from the world. I found myself immobilized. I was not eating well. I had no desire to pray. I could not sleep. I found myself stuck in the past, all the memories, all the regrets. And yes, I do have regrets. I will not get into that now."

Nate was riveted. He didn't believe that his grandfather went through the same kind of torment that he had. "Now, Nate, you should know that most of this is normal. We are only human. Our hearts break. Death is a part of life. Most of our grief is focused on the loss. But sometimes it brings us face-to-face with our fear, our fear of death, our own death. Losing your father was as devastating to me as it was for you. But it was taking too long for me to get back. I could not let go of it."

"So, what did you do? I couldn't seem to do anything about it."

His grandfather replied. "That is where the pendulum came in. As I had done many times before, I lay down and passed the pendulum over my body. It started moving right where I started, over my groin. It is the area of survival in the body. It was my own fear of death that was keeping me from moving. Yes, my heart was broken, but it was my fear that took over."

Nate had to interrupt. "You mean that you're afraid of dying? I find that hard to believe."

"I am not afraid now. I was able to unblock myself. Once I knew where the energy was stuck, I asked for God's help to move it out. Your father's death brought me back to Belize and the hurricane, a time when I was terrified of life. I continue to need healing from that catastrophic time. So, I released it. Let go of it, so to speak. I let go of your father. I let go of my fear. I allowed the Great Spirit to move through me. I reconnected."

"But I thought that you were always connected."

"We can only try. Sometimes life throws us off."

Nate could understand this, especially the part about being thrown off balance. He knew that even after a morning of good intentions, it didn't take a whole lot to disturb his sense of peace. Nate yearned to stay with his grandfather longer. He still had many questions. He wanted to know what he was supposed to do to receive his gifts. He wanted to have some certainty about his future. But he had to go, and he knew it wasn't all that simple. Or maybe it was. He didn't know. He just knew it was time for him to get back home. There was a lot of work to do. In leaving, he promised his grandfather that he would be back the following week.

Jack and Nate had plenty of work to do to keep them busy. One by one a customer would come to silently browse the various headstones in the yard. Nate would just stand off to the side and wait. Selling headstones was not like selling cars, and Nate's respect for their privacy overruled his sense of urgency to get back to work on something else. Jack too understood this and never questioned why it took so long for Nate to get back to the shop. Working with people was like working with stone— neither should be rushed.

Nate was keeping up with the paperwork and finances, most often reconciling accounts and paying bills after hours. He would make regular trips to the bank, mostly on Saturday mornings, putting money into various business and personal accounts. It was early May, and spring was coming into its own. He was at the bank for his usual Saturday transactions, patiently standing in line, when out of the corner of his eye he caught a glimpse of something that made his heart jump. Adrenalin rushed through his body. He pretended not to notice and hoped that she wouldn't notice either. But there, two lines down from him, was Haley, looking more beautiful than he remembered, even in her Saturday sweats.

Nate felt paralyzed and nervous. His mind was racing, trying to decide if he should say something to her or just let her go.

He stepped forward as the line moved, trying to concentrate on why he was there to begin with. He took an occasional peek as she kept her head forward, waiting for the teller as she too moved up in the line. She was one person ahead of him, so he knew she would get her business done first. He was also acutely aware that his banking transactions always took more time than most. This was not the branch that Haley generally used. She usually walked to the one that was a couple of blocks from her apartment. She probably just stopped in to cash a check on her way to a store. Nate felt a sense of panic. *What am I going to do?* he asked himself. He didn't want to let her go again and watched as she stepped up to the teller.

Haley had caught sight of Nate too. She too was hoping he wouldn't see her and kept her gaze straight ahead. She too didn't know what she wanted but felt that she needed to decide quickly. Either she would bolt out of there or stall. She wasn't sure what she would say. She was embarrassed and intensely self-conscious. She knew she didn't look that great. She never fussed on Saturdays. She took the day off from her daily ritual of makeup and picking out the right clothes for work.

He looked great, she thought. Not that he was all dressed up. She couldn't believe the difference in the way he looked now compared to when she left him last September. She stepped up to the teller to cash her paycheck. After putting the cash in her bag, she walked out the door, and walked slower and slower and slower, hoping with all her heart that he saw her.

Nate saw her leave. He was next in line. The bank wasn't going to be open much longer. If he didn't take care of this stuff today, he would have to take time on Monday morning to do it, which wouldn't make Jack happy. But she was leaving. He would need to make a spit-second decision. Without thinking further, he turned to the person behind him and said, "You go ahead,

I've got to catch someone." The person behind him was surprised and expressed his thanks. "No problem," said Nate. He wanted to run, but instead walked quickly and with purpose out the door with his papers in hand. He looked to the right and then the left. She was nearly at the corner. He broke into a run. "Haley! Wait up!" She stopped and turned and stood there, watching the man she loved rush toward her.

She stood there, saying to herself, *Cool, calm, and collected. Cool, calm, and collected,* over and over again. Nate slowed to a trot. It was a long block in more ways than one. He was trying to catch his breath as he pulled up about ten feet in front of her and started to walk toward her. He felt god awkward. She felt god awkward. Nate broke the ice because he didn't know what else to do. He wanted to just grab and hold her. She wanted to just grab and hold him. Then he said, as calmly as he could, "I thought I saw you at the bank. But … I wanted to be sure. And here you are."

"Here we are," she said.

Nate, trying to hide his exhilaration, said, "So, how are you? Long time, no see."

Haley, as calmly as she could, said, "I've been good, Nate. How are you?"

"Good, really good. It seems like ages since I last saw you. What have you been up to?"

"Oh," faking indifference, "you know, same old, same old. Get up, go to work, come home, go to bed, pretty much the same. How about you? You certainly look different from the last time I saw you."

"Yeah," said Nate, now feeling a little shame. "I've come a long way since then."

"So, I see," she said. "You look great. You really do."

"And so do you," Nate said. He felt himself blushing.

"Who are you kidding? I look like shit today. It's Saturday. I wasn't even planning on going out, but my cousin called and wanted me to come over. She's having some trouble these days, so I couldn't say no. So here I am, in my Saturday uniform."

"You still look wonderful. Beautiful. I'm so glad I caught you. I just wanted to say hi. So, hi."

"Hi Nate." And then she smiled. Nate smiled back. He couldn't help himself and then, like a bashful schoolboy, asked her, "So, have you been seeing anyone?"

"Well, yes." His heart started to sink. "But only a couple of guys. It was pretty short-lived with both. I don't know. I think I like my alone time. I get tired of running around, especially after the days I put in at work. It's not any better than before. If anything, it's probably worse."

Haley worked as an administrative assistant in one of the largest planning and development corporations in the region. She had always had trouble with her boss, the CEO. She never trusted him, and he acted like he never trusted her. It was a strained relationship. But he knew how valuable she was to him. Haley was excellent at her job, and he knew it. Even though she didn't like him much, he paid her well for her position. She put up with a lot and used to talk to Nate about what a jerk her boss was. But the money and benefits outweighed her desire to go somewhere else. Golden handcuffs. She did what she had to do.

"I'm sorry to hear that," said Nate, pausing. "Well, maybe one of these days something better will come along."

"Maybe," she said, looking at her watch.

"Well, maybe I should let you get going."

"Yeah, I told my cousin I'd be there by noon, and it's almost that. A little behind schedule, as usual," she said.

"OK," said Nate, hesitating, challenging his fear of being rejected. "Uh, listen, would it be OK if I called you?"

"Yes," said Haley, hesitating herself, "I'd like that."

"OK then. I'll call. I hope things work out for your cousin."

"Thanks, Nate. I hope so too."

Haley turned and crossed the street to her car. Nate waved as she pulled away. She waved back. Both felt that this was not just a coincidence. Nate walked away. The bank was closed, but he didn't care. Something much more important had occurred, and he would not take it, or her, for granted. When he arrived home, he spent his time in quiet, reflecting on the events of the day and thanking God for giving him yet another chance. He would go out to his grandfather's as he did on most Saturdays. He debated with himself if he should talk about it with him, or anyone else for that matter. It's not that he didn't trust his grandfather. He just didn't want to get his hopes up that Haley would come back to him. He would keep it to himself for now and let it stay quietly inside of him, in his own sacred space.

Chapter 32

Weeks passed since their chance meeting at the bank. Nate and Haley were getting reacquainted with one another. Nate told Haley all about his recovery and the time spent with his grandfather over the winter. With her, unlike with Jack, he could talk about the spiritual healing and the unleashing of emotions that had kept him locked up inside. She admired his courage, saying that most men would never allow themselves to be so vulnerable. She had always thought of Nate as being a man of compassion and sensitivity, especially toward her and others. She had never imagined that he didn't have the same consideration for himself.

Their conversations became deeper and more meaningful, both openly sharing their thoughts and feelings about their lives and each other. Haley had always had a connection with her spirituality. She had gotten that from her mother, who gave freely of herself to others. Haley knew that her mother's faith was powerful, and learned to live in that faith herself. Now, in her conversations with Nate, she knew that she could not only talk about it, but that he understood her and how important a role it played in her life.

They were dating regularly now, though both restraining their physical desire for one another. They would hold hands, caress each other, and share an occasional kiss, but nothing further. Their passion for one another was deepening at another level. They could almost feel their bodies reacting and joining together without even touching. They were becoming soul mates in the true sense of the word. Both knew that they were meant to be together and allowed the other to grow in love.

Nate and Jack were doing so well together that Nate was considering asking Jack to be a partner in the business. He struggled with the idea, having some difficulty adding O'Leary to the Bearing nameplate that had embossed the family business for generations. He spoke with his grandfather about it on several occasions, but his grandfather always deferred to Nate's instincts, having grown to trust him in all matters and intentions. Nate knew that he didn't need his grandfather's permission, but he did need his blessing. When the time was right, he would know it, and if it were meant to be, it would happen. Sooner or later Nate knew that it would, and so did his grandfather, without needing to say it.

Nate and Haley didn't see each other every day. She needed her sleep and alone time. Even though Nate did too, he never wanted to admit it. They talked to each other every morning and evening though, catching up on the activities of their days on the phone. Haley always had a lot to talk about. She was always under a lot of pressure at work. It was a fast-paced environment with people coming in and out of the office all day long, interrupting the flow of her work. She would often talk about the 'suits' that came in, apparently for important planning and strategy meetings. Most times she was asked to take the minutes for these meetings. That was part of her job.

Haley grew to understand a great deal about commercial real estate, acquisitions, mergers, and zoning regulations. She sometimes felt smarter than some of the people who came into the office and that she should be the one in the power chair. But Haley was too honest a person to do that kind of wheeling and dealing and knew it would compromise her integrity. There were many times when she was not invited into these meetings. On the one hand, the exclusion gave her more time to get her work done, but on the other, it made her more suspicious about what was going on. She was mostly content with the 'don't ask, don't tell' position she was in.

After their evening phone conversations and after his paperwork, Nate often went into the studio to work on his carvings. He would spend time working on a sculpture or sit and stare at a block of stone he had chosen, waiting to discover it. He had been working consistently on the boxer, which was still in its rough-cut form. He continued to grind it down into a more definable shape, using the flat-edged chisel to round out some of the corners. It would go a lot faster if he were using the power tools, but Nate preferred the sound of the ping on the stone rather than the magnified sound of a dentist's drill. Especially since he was around the noise made by the sandblaster all day long. Whenever feasible, he did his work with hand tools.

At the same time, he was also working on another piece, his father's headstone. He had chosen a block of marble, much like what his father had chosen for his mother. He had decided that he would create the same form, uniting them in death as they had been in life. He studied the stone for hours, looking at the grains, looking for cracks as he began to cut away at it. It was remarkably like his mother's stone, the blue grains deepening in color as he cut deeper into it. There was no deadline for this piece or any of his other works, unlike in the business, which is why the time he spent in the studio by himself was so special.

Nate and Jack were keeping up with each other, and not just with the work. At every opportunity Jack would ask Nate how things were going with Haley. Jack had no problem talking about his social life, still perplexed on why he couldn't find someone like Haley. Nate came into the shop and looked at Jack as he handed him a cup of coffee. Jack was covered in powder from sandblasting. His face was flushed and dripping with sweat from the respirator helmet. It was heavy as hell and made him look like a spaceman, but it protected his lungs and face from the flying dust. Nate had yet to get into the building, having met with one of their customers first thing in the day.

"Man, you're a sight for sore eyes," said Nate.

"You aren't kiddin'," said Jack. "My eyes *are* sore. For one thing, I stayed up too late last night. This girl was as cute as hell, and man, was she built. She was all Irish too, something that she had in her favor for sure. But like an idiot, this morning I forgot to put my goggles on when I started polishing the back of one of the monuments, stupid ass that I am. I think some of the dust got in my eyes. So yeah, my eyes are sore, and yours are looking at them."

Nate commented, "Well, mine really weren't sore until I saw you. Now they're killing me."

"Ha, ha, ha," said Jack, looking offended. Changing the subject, he asked, "What's up with the new customer?"

"Ah," said Nate, "it was so sad. God, I nearly cried myself, right in front of them. It was a couple of middle-aged parents. They were just broken. Their son was in an accident while he was away at school. He was in a car with his buddies. It was so stupid. The kid who was driving was drunk, their son's best friend. They were probably both drunk, though the parents didn't say so. Their son died when the car slammed into the rail. He got thrown out of his seat down the embankment. No seat belt. He died on the spot. His friend broke his back ... doesn't look like he'll walk again. The parents, especially the mother, could barely speak. It was a hard one, man. They're all hard, but when it's your kid, it's the hardest. I can't even imagine it."

"Know what you mean. When I was a kid, there was a little girl across the street from me who was about the same age as me. She had some type of brain tumor. I guess there was nothing that could be done for her. My parents were close friends to her parents. The day she died I remember how sad my parents were. They both cried, even my father. I figured it had to be bad. Then I cried too. I'll never forget it."

Nate said, "Yeah, I don't know why these things happen to people. Some people just get more than their share of suffering, you know. I don't know. I guess I'm amazed at their ability to go on."

"You should know. I mean, I've never had anyone close to me die. I might have wished it, but you know, I just haven't experienced it myself. You have, so you know what you're talking about. I guess I'd rather deal with the stone. You're better with people."

"Maybe so ... so, who's the girl?" Nate asked, his turn to change the subject.

"Well," said Jack, hesitating, "you know her."

"I do? So, who is she? Where do I know her from?"

Jack said, hesitating again, "From the pub. She works at the pub."

"Not Katie! You went out with Katie O'Brian? You're kidding. She went out with you?"

Jack said, incredulously, "Yeah, she went out with me! Why not?"

"Because ... well ... I don't know. I guess I can't see it. She doesn't take shit from anyone. And everyone loves her because of that. She deals with all the drunks, no offense, and she has no bones about cutting people off. She's great lookin', no doubt about it, but ... she went out with *you*? I don't believe it!"

"Well, believe it. And we had a great time. I wasn't wasted, so I asked if she'd go out with me."

"Where'd you go?"

"We went over to this café, the small place over near the movie theater. There was some folk singer there that she knew and wanted to see. So, that's where we went."

"But they don't serve alcohol there, do they?"

"No, they don't," said Jack. "What do you think? You think I can't have fun without it?"

"Seeing is believing," Nate responded.

"Well, believe it. We had coffee, and some vegetarian burger. It was OK, but what was better is that she really wanted to talk to me. I mean, she wanted to hear the singer, but during the breaks, she wanted to know all about my work, and asked me all kinds of questions about how I do what I do, and, well, she knows you. And I guess she figures that if I work with you, I must have something going for me, which I do, as you know."

"You do, and not because of me."

"So," Jack continued, "she was really into me. And, well, I've always liked her. I just never thought she would go out with me, so I never asked. I gotta' tell you. I'm not going to blow this one. Maybe you can give me some good advice, you know? I mean, you seem to know what women like."

"I *seem* to know, but what man really does? They're all different. I guess that's the first thing to know. Take your time to get to know her, you know? Don't do your usual hit-and-run act, that is, if you want it to work out. You've gotta' go slow, man. You know?"

Jack pondered, and said, "Yeah, I'll challenge myself. I think she's worth the effort. So, how's Haley?" he added getting the heat off himself.

"She's great. It's going great. I'm lucky to have her back."

"That's for sure, and lucky to have me back too, might I add."

"So much for humility. Let's get back to it, huh? And put your goddamn goggles on this time."

"Yes, boss, sure thing."

Nate and Jack went back to work, both stopping every now and then, thinking about the women in their lives and how much of a difference they made.

Chapter 33

It was mid-June. The days were getting warmer and longer. Nate loved this time of the year. It was a motivating force to get done with work sooner so he could take advantage of the sun. Last year he passed it by. One of the things that he enjoyed most was going to the semi-pro baseball games. The stadium was on the other side of town. He'd pick Haley up on the way. She too enjoyed the crowd and the distraction from her work. They were like kids, yelling and jumping out of their seats when the home team scored, especially if they came from behind. Afterward, they would excitedly talk about the plays, making the success of the team their own.

In the nicer weather, Nate and Haley also loved to go horseback riding. Neither of them had grown up around horses or even knew much about them. They just happened upon it on one of their excursions to the country. They dared each other to try it. They did, and ever since would go a couple of times a month when the weather was decent. Nate had grown more interested in horses. Like the horse, he often found himself helping others carry their burdens when they came to him in their grief. It was a personal thing that he never talked about, even to Haley. There was no room for pride in his spiritual life.

One Saturday, after Nate returned from his grandfather's, and after Haley had run her errands, the two of them decided to go out to dinner. They chose a restaurant they could walk to, near the park, one where they didn't have to overdress to be acceptable. It was an Italian place known mostly for its excellent bread and homemade pasta, somewhere that they had been many times before. It was good food by Nate's standards, though no Italian restaurant could match his mother's cooking. Maybe it was nostalgia more than the truth, but it was how he remembered it.

They ordered a bottle of Chianti. There were certain social occasions when Nate would allow himself to drink, ever cognizant that too much of a good thing could end up badly. Nate proposed the toast.

"To life and love," Nate said, lifting his glass to kiss Haley's.

"To love and life," she returned, taking their first sips in unison.

"What do you feel like eating?" Nate asked.

"I don't know," replied Haley, "but I don't want anything too heavy. You know, summer's here, and my clothes can't hide me."

"What's to hide? You're beautiful just the way you are, always have been. I'd say, eat what you want. Dieting is for weekdays."

"Yeah, right," said Haley. "You don't have to worry about it. You move around all day long. I essentially sit on my butt all day. Everything I eat sinks to my bottom."

"And a cute bottom it is," said Nate, with a provocative little smile

"So, what's it going to be? Salad or pasta?"

Guiltily, Haley said, "Well, I shouldn't, but I would rather have pasta. After all, as you said, it is the weekend."

"Now you're sounding more rational." He poured a little more wine in their glasses. The waiter came over and Nate looked to Haley and said, "Order up, sweet cheeks."

Haley laughed, and said, "And that's exactly where it's going to land."

The waiter smiled, knowing what she meant, and said to her, "Don't worry about it, honey. Most people who come here come to eat."

"Then I guess I'm going to eat," she said and ordered the lasagna.

Nate said, "And I'll have the same, and antipasto for two with anchovies on the side." Haley loved them. Nate couldn't even stand looking at them, often saying they reminded him of worms.

"So be it," said the waiter as he turned away from the table.

"Thanks," they replied in unison.

They lingered over dinner, which was particularly difficult for Nate. He was starving and just wanted to wolf it down. But Haley was such a slow eater that he forced himself to pace it, delaying gratification, much like their love life. Maybe tonight, he thought.

Nate didn't order dessert. Surprisingly, neither did Haley. They ended the dinner with decaf. Both were feeling mellow and didn't want the caffeine to counteract the wine. They left the restaurant and walked to the park for a stroll through the gardens and fountains. It had been dark for a couple of hours, but the air was still warm. It was a clear night, and the moon was rising from behind the trees, a perfect night for romance if ever there was one. But Nate didn't want to push it now. They had only been dating again for a few weeks, testing one another, and waiting to return to a time when both were sure of their future together. After a while, he walked Haley back to her apartment. He gave her a kiss and then let go, wondering if Haley would invite him in. She didn't, and he was OK with that. Saying goodnight, he walked back through the park, headed toward his jeep.

Reaching the fountains, Nate paused and decided to sit for a while. He never lost his love for the sound of water. He sat there listening to the water fall on itself. The solitude though was short-lived. Something disturbed his peace, shattering the quiet of the night. He heard a commotion not far from where he sat. It sounded like a fight, a bad one. Some loud male voices were heard throwing obscenities and anger toward someone.

Nate couldn't help himself. He had to move. He had to see what was going on. The voices continued spewing out vulgarities. He moved ever closer to the path where the sound was coming from. Then he stopped. Déjà vu. Suddenly everything became surreal. He had been here before, and he saw what was happening. It was his nightmare, so vivid, as if he were in it. He saw three young men, no faces, but they were all dressed much the same. Maybe they were in a gang. They were the ones who were yelling. There was someone on the ground, moaning, begging them not to hurt him anymore. They were kicking the shit out of him. It was too much for Nate to bear, and despite his fear he started toward them. They were too intent on what they were doing to notice him coming.

Nate felt the boots against his ribs. His fingernails were broken, a couple of them ripped out of their beds. His face was torn, skin hanging, bleeding raw. He felt himself losing his grip on life. He was in pain, especially when he tried to breathe. His ribs were broken. He tried to get up, but they kicked even harder. He could still hear them.

"Man, I didn't think mugging could be this much fun! Son of a bitch, you fucking scumbag," one voice said as he slammed his foot into Nate's side.

"He's a goddamn asshole, walking through here at night. He gets what he deserves for being so fucking stupid!" another said.

"I think this prick has learned his lesson. Grab his wallet, and let's get the fuck out of here," said the third.

They left, leaving him for dead. Walking away, they reveled in their victory. One of them flipped open the wallet. "Holy shit!" he said. "There must be three hundred bucks in here!" He started doling it out. "One for you, one for me …"

Howling with laughter, punching, and slapping each other on the back, they suddenly stopped dead in their tracks. Someone was yelling something from behind them. They turned around and saw someone emerging from the bushes. It was their victim. "Hey! You bottom feeders! Want to try that again?" said the voice while spitting out blood.

It was Nate's voice, and he was stunned. The gang turned silent. They were stunned too. This wasn't the guy that they left lying there, though it was hard to tell. He was a bloody mess. They stared, not believing what they were seeing. They cautiously started to walk back toward him to get a closer look. They were confused as hell. They looked at each other saying things like, "Holy shit! Who is this guy? What the fuck? I thought we nailed him! What's happening here? Do you see what I see? Shit, man!"

They stared at him. He stared at them. And in their disbelief, they saw the truth. This was no ordinary guy. Then they felt fear and started running, dropping the cash on the ground. Nate stood there and watched them run. He knew they would never do this again.

Nate brushed himself off. He was in a state of shock. He was confused. He hurt all over. He couldn't figure out if this were real or if he had fallen asleep into his nightmare. He felt a little blood from one of the scratches on his arms. He felt a bump on his forehead. He heard the fountains in the background and smelled the scent of roses that were blooming all over the park. This was no nightmare, he thought, baffled. This was real.

As he turned around to walk back toward his jeep, a man was standing in the walkway in front of him. He was in his early twenties, maybe a college kid. He just stood and stared at Nate, then asked, "Are you OK?"

The young man reached out to shake Nate's hand, looking massively confused. Nate said, "So how are you feeling?" The young man was shaking apart. "I'm Tony. I, uh … you won't believe it, but I think I was the guy they tackled down. I mean, it *was* me, but then, well, and then it looks like it was you. They were kicking me hard. Shit. I'm sorry, man. It should've been me. It *was* me! But look, I mean, there isn't a scratch on me, and look at you …"

"Yeah, look at me. Do I have a black eye?"

"A shiner all right … your face is a mess," said Tony. "Here," he reached in his pocket. "Here's a clean handkerchief."

"Thanks, Tony," said Nate as he dabbed the blood from his face.

"I feel like I'm tripping, man," said Tony, rubbing his forehead.

"Yeah, it doesn't seem real to me either," said Nate. "I don't know how to explain it."

"I don't know who you are, and I don't understand what you did. I'm so fucking confused. Maybe this was some kind of a miracle! My mother believes in shit like that. But she'd never believe this one, even if I told her. But that isn't gonna' happen. I've got to think about this. I've been drinking and drugging pretty heavy. Maybe it's getting to my brain. I've been hopping into one bed after another … not a nice guy. Maybe this is a wake-up call."

Then it hit Nate. Tony *had* been given another chance. He would turn his life around, but he couldn't even think about it now. He was overwhelmed, and he couldn't imagine how overwhelmed Tony must be.

"Listen, man, I should thank you. You saved my life, for what it's worth."

"It's OK," Nate replied. "At least I think it is."

They shook hands, and as Tony began to leave, he turned back and said to Nate, "Man, I don't know. It's almost like, well, like you took the hit for me. I don't know why, or how, but you did, and I can only thank you, really, for saving my life. I'm sorry that you got hurt, but amazed that you aren't dead. I thought that they were going to fucking kill me … I don't know. But thanks, whoever you are. You're some kind of guy, or something. I gotta' go. I don't know where. But I gotta' go. Thanks again. I don't even know how to pay you for this."

"Even if I could figure that out, I wouldn't let you. I don't think this was about me anyway."

"Maybe, maybe not, but thanks anyway. Geez," said Tony, bewildered, shaking his head. Then it occurred to him. He asked Nate, "Hey, what's your name anyway?"

"What's it matter?" said Nate. "We'll probably never see each other again anyway."

"Probably not, but I'll never forget this for sure." Tony turned to leave.

"Neither will I," said Nate. "And hey, watch your back."

"Damn straight I will!" said Tony as he shuffled off. "Thanks again."

"Welcome," said Nate for lack of anything better to say.

Chapter 34

It was around one thirty in the morning when Nate got home. He was exhausted. It had been a long day to begin with, and the event in the park left him wasted. He was still confused and feeling pretty beat-up. He went into the bathroom to clean himself. He looked in the mirror, shocked at what he saw. There wasn't a scratch on his face. There was some slight bruising around his right eye, and his sides hurt where he had absorbed most of the assault on his body, but otherwise, nothing. He looked at his hands. His nails were perfectly manicured, just as they were when he left the house much earlier. He was even more surprised that he wasn't angry with the guys who pummeled him. He felt grateful that he and Tony had gotten out alive. Trembling inside, he made his way to his bedroom, but he didn't go to bed.

Much like his grandfather and his father, Nate had created a sacred space for himself in his room. His bed was in the middle of one wall, the door to the left, and windows to the right. In the far-left corner stood his 'altar of peace,' upon which were crystals, stones, a cross, ointments, candles, and a bowl for his bundled sage. He lit the sage, and the aroma filled the room. He then sat cross-legged on the floor and started to breathe deeply and slowly as he had been doing every morning, slowly calming himself down. In his trance state, Nate sat quietly, thanking the Great Spirit for protection and for his ability to help Tony. He cleared his mind, and then just waited.

What he saw amazed him. Michael the Archangel appeared. Then an old, bearded man appeared, and then an older woman. Nate recognized them. He waited, watched, and listened. He saw a vision unfolding before him. It was the same vision that he saw at his grandfather's the previous winter. Nate was in awe. As in the vision, the angel, the man, and the woman stepped forward and presented Nate with a crystal. Nate knew about this crystal and its amazing powers. It had the ability to detect blocked energy and clear it, thus allowing light from the higher realm to enter. The three handed the crystal to him, and he heard them say, "Nate, this is your gift. Always remember where it came from, and never take it for granted."

Then they left. Nate stayed in the quiet for long afterward, allowing himself to be filled and transformed in the experience. It was just before four when he brought himself back, all senses awakened. Opening his eyes, he smelled the sage, listened to the intermittent traffic outside, and felt his body returning to the present. He went to bed, relaxed enough to drop off immediately.

Nate slept until seven thirty, feeling well-rested despite the short sleep. He decided he would see his grandfather later that day. He knew it was early, but he showered, dressed, and went over to Haley's. She liked surprises, especially from him. It was a beautiful morning, not too hot, not too humid. He rang the bell when he arrived. No answer. He figured that she was still sleeping. Feeling a little sorry about this, he rang the bell a second time anyway. Haley showed up at the door. She had just woken up but was happy to see him. They held each other for a minute or so, until she decided she needed coffee more than a hug.

Then she noticed his eye. "How'd that happen?" she asked as she gently touched the bruise.

He was caught off guard. He had forgotten about that. Flustered, but not showing it, he said, "Oh, I'm just an idiot. I was half asleep last night when I was getting a glass out of the cupboard to get some water. I forgot that I left the cupboard open all the way. When I lifted my head, *smack!* Just a klutz," he said as he lifted his hands as if to say, what the hell.

"Poor baby," Haley said with sympathy. "You're tired. Go sit down in the living room. I'll make you some breakfast."

Haley went into the kitchen. Nate did as he was told and sat down on the couch in the living room. It must have been fifteen minutes later when he came to, hearing the clatter of pans in the kitchen. The aroma of bacon urged him to get up. Besides that, he had to go to the bathroom. He had already had a couple of cups of coffee at his house.

Washing his hands, he looked at himself in the mirror. Other than the bruise, he looked good. He was clean-shaven and tanned from the summer sun. He had come so far from the desolation of last summer. He liked the person he was looking at. He didn't dawdle, though. Haley and breakfast awaited.

Haley was over the stove, wearing one of Nate's denim shirts that he had left there some time ago. Nate smiled as he came into the kitchen. She looked so sexy in his shirt. Her long, beautifully toned and proportioned legs were arousing him. She turned and smiled at him as he came up behind her to hug and hold her. They gently rocked together until the bacon was done. Setting the last piece on the paper towel, she said, "Now there's a beautiful thing," and gestured toward the perfectly straight strips aligned on the towel.

Nate then turned her around. Looking in her eyes, he said, "Now here's a beautiful thing." Then he kissed her. She kissed him back, both feeling a sense of urgency and passion. She caressed his back, ever so gently, and then reaching her hand under his tee shirt, felt the warmth and strength of his body. He did the same, slipping his hand under the denim, feeling

210

his rough hands against the softness of her skin. As their kisses deepened further, so did the desire they had for one another.

Nate stopped, and quietly and breathlessly asked, "Do you want to do this?"

Haley said, breathless as well, "Yes, Nate, I do. I've wanted to for a long time."

She turned off the stove and he led her into her bedroom. It was late morning before they decided to get up.

Haley was first in the shower. After she dressed, she went into the kitchen to make the coffee when Nate appeared at the door. She asked, "So how do you like your eggs?"

Nate smiled, and said, "Over easy, please."

"You've got it, and I'll have the same." Shortly after, Haley brought the plates to the table and sat down.

"Here you go, honey."

"Thanks, sweetheart."

They started to eat. Haley stopped and looked at Nate, her beautiful dark eyes meeting his. "You know," she said, "I think I'm falling back in love with you."

Nate replied, "I was so hoping that you would. I've never stopped loving you."

"I know that. I could feel it since we got back together. But I, well, to be truthful, I was afraid. I wanted to wait until I knew that you had decided to live and take care of yourself. And you have."

"I knew that I had to prove myself," said Nate. "I didn't want to blow it this time, and well, I didn't want to lose you again. I guess you'd say that in some sense I was testing myself too. I've changed a lot in the past year, and I think for the better."

"No question about that," said Haley, broadly smiling at him. "I'm so proud of you."

"You can't know how much that means to me, Haley."

They ate their breakfast in peace and in quiet, not needing to fill the space with anything but their presence to one another.

Finishing up, Haley said, "You know, I need to get moving. My family is expecting me for our weekly reunion. You're welcome to join me if you'd like. You know they all love you."

"No thanks," replied Nate. "I love being around your family too, but I do need to catch up on my paperwork. Most of the time I love running my own business, but as you know, it can be overwhelming at times. Later I'm going to go see my grandfather."

"No problem," said Haley. "I could probably sit here all day just talking to you, but then I would feel guilty for disappointing them."

Nate then said, "I'll clean up. You just get yourself together. By the time I'm done here, maybe you will be too," he laughed.

"Very funny. Don't worry. I'll be done sooner than you think. I don't need to get made up so much to impress my family. They're not in the corporate world."

"Race you," said Nate. "On your mark, get set ..."

Haley was out of the room before he could say "go!"

When they were ready and left the house, they kissed good-bye, and went their separate ways.

Despite the need for him to get down to business, Nate had an overwhelming urge to go see his grandfather first to tell him about last night. But he had just seen him yesterday, and Nate decided that he needed more time to digest the experience. Even if he were to ask his grandfather what he thought about it all, he would most likely just say, 'The answer to that lies inside of you. It is up to you to find it.' That's the kind of response that always frustrated him. So instead of going to his grandfathers', he drove home, not knowing what he would do there, but decided he would do whatever was in front of him, and there were lots of things in front of him. He kicked himself for not stopping to pick up some groceries, but knew he could make do until tomorrow. Maybe there would be a lull in the work activity. If not, he would do it after work.

Nate was thinking about giving Jack a call, maybe to get together that evening. So instead, he decided he wanted to be alone, so he didn't. He also knew that Jack spent a good deal of time with his brothers and his current girlfriend on the weekends. That space allowed them both to work well with one another during the week. Every now and then they had to come in on Saturdays to catch up with the orders, but overall, they worked so efficiently that this was an exception. "Work hard, play hard," was Jack's motto. It was rubbing off on Nate too, giving him more balance in his life, helping him to not take himself so seriously.

Nate had trouble concentrating as he tried to pay the bills and reconcile the budget. He didn't get far, so he decided to go to the studio. He felt inspired to work on his sculptures, but wasn't quite sure where it would lead him. He sat on a stool in the middle of the room, turning every now and then to a different form or rough stone block. Then he set his eyes on the boxer. Still rough-cut, there were many intricate details to finish. But the more he stared at it, the more he decided that other than polishing, the piece was finished. Instinctively, he knew that the stone had spoken. No need for detail in the downfall of a man. The form took on the defeat of the spirit that was now a part of Nate's past. He then went about polishing the squared-off edges. After several hours, the work was completed. Satisfied, Nate was moved to go outside to the back of the house.

It was getting darker. Not long after the sun had set, the full moon rose from the horizon. Behind the house, Nate had built a fire pit, much like his grandfather's, though somewhat smaller.

Nate felt called to perform a fire ceremony. It took him a while. The wood was still damp from a thunderstorm a couple of days ago. Soon the fire grew. Nate bowed to the moon, thanking the God of the Sky, and the spirits of south, west, north, and east.

He circled the fire three times, expressing words of gratitude. He also thanked the spirits of the bear, hawk, turtle, hummingbird, horse, and eagle, all of which significantly appeared to him over the past year, reminding him of his heritage. He then sat on a boulder that he had moved near the pit, silently watching the embers extinguish themselves. He spent time meditating on the events of the night before and the vision. He still wondered what it all meant and what was to be expected of him. As he had learned, though, he would need to be patient and let it unfold. When it was revealed to him, he would know.

Chapter 35

On Monday morning, Jack was already in the yard when Nate came out of the house. It was around eight. The store didn't open until nine. Nate took inventory, looking at his orders. Some of the monuments that people wanted were in stock. He noted that he should order more of the more popular shapes and colors soon, especially those that were polished. Polished stone was always more expensive. It was becoming more of a standard.

Most people were satisfied with having just the front and back of the stone polished, leaving the sides in their roughed-out form. Having the sides polished as well was even more expensive. People bought what they could afford. The size, shape, type of stone, and polish, as well as the complexity of the engraving influenced cost. Nate treated every customer with dignity and respect, no matter what they could or could not afford. The reason they came to him was always the same. Grief was grief, and it did not make exceptions.

Nate was still outside looking things over when he heard the diamond blade saw stop. Shortly, Jack emerged, standing at the opening of the shop when he spotted Nate. "Hey, you lazy shit, when are you coming into work?"

"I am working, buddy. Just checking out how much stone we'll need to order."

"I'd say a lot, especially the red granite. It doesn't take a rocket scientist to figure that out." Coming over toward Nate, Jack asked, "So, how was your weekend?"

Nate filtered his reply. "Good, really good. I saw my grandfather on Saturday, and then that evening Haley and I went out to dinner, he lied. It's a great Italian place, plenty of food for a reasonable price. Luigi's, ever hear of it? You should go there sometime with Kate."

"I may take your advice on that. The problem is that she works Friday and Saturday nights. It sucks. When I want to play, she's working, and when she wants to play, I'm working. I don't know how people do it when they work different shifts. It must be hard to have a life. On the other hand, when we do get together it can be pretty hot. We have time to miss each other. Distance makes the heart grow fonder. My mother used to always say that. Not about my father, no way, but more about her family and friends who lived farther away."

Jack had been dating Katie for over a month now. Given his history, it was so out of character for him. Yet he seemed happy and content. He also had lost that hungover look that was his usual morning face. He was starting to look healthier. It was amazing to Nate to see how much influence women had over men. They slowed men down, not particularly wanting their boyfriends getting plowed every night. They had a way of grinding away the rough edges. Most men, Nate decided, needed a woman in their lives. It humanized them.

Later that morning, Nate had to meet with customers. Some were old, some new, all looking for the right headstone to honor their deceased loved ones. This was the hardest part of the job for Nate. He hated to see people suffer. It touched him deeply. He most often wished he could just take it away from them. Even though he knew that suffering was a part

216

of life, he still didn't understand why it had to be this way. Maybe, he thought, people had to suffer in order to bring out the good in others. That was the only thing that made any sense to him at all.

Coming back to the yard, Jack saw Nate coming inside and stopped the overhead rail that was hoisting another stone to the rubber stencil area. "So, what's up?"

"The usual. One woman just lost her husband to cancer. He was only forty-four. Another guy came in with a couple. His fiancée was killed two nights ago in a horrible accident. They say the guy who hit her was drunk. They could barely hold back the tears. The wedding was going to be in three weeks. I don't know. I can't imagine losing Haley like that. I needed to spend some extra time with them."

After a respectful pause, Jack asked, "You know, we're getting busier here all the time. Have you thought of getting more help?"

"As a matter of fact, I was just thinking about it this morning. You and I are swamped, and I'm finding it harder and harder to be in two places at once. Why, do you have anyone in mind?"

"Not really. But if you're serious, I can start asking around. There aren't a lot of stonecutters out there to begin with. And those that are good generally have their own businesses. You know that. But let me start snooping around. I've got a lot of friends out there who know a lot of people. That is one benefit of hanging out with the guys. We help each other out."

Nate paused to think about all of this. He was particular about who he would work with. It was easy to come up with Jack. And Jack did know a few good men. So, he gave Jack the go-ahead to look for someone else for the business.

Then Jack said, "Have you also thought about getting some office help, even part-time?"

"Well," Nate hesitated. "I know we're making a good profit right now. I just get worried about too many expenses. You know, the more we spend, the less we have. I want to come out in the black this year, especially after the miserable way I left things last year."

"I understand, man. But think of it like this. The more people we hire, the more work we can do. Then the business grows. I see it as a win-win."

"You're probably right, Jack. Let me think about that one." Then, suspiciously, he asked, "I don't suppose you have someone in mind for this job?"

"Me? Nah," he said with a little mischief in his voice. "But if you decide you want someone, I'll put the feelers out, and we'll have someone ready to go. Just let me know."

"OK. I'll let you know. In the meantime, I've got to run into town to get some stuff into the mail. I shouldn't be too long. I'll flip the sign in the storefront and say I'll be back around one o'clock."

"Later," said Jack.

"Later," Nate said as he turned out into the yard.

Nate had to park a couple of blocks from the post office. He should have known not to come there at lunchtime. Too many people trying to fit it in during their lunch break from work. The lines were always longer. Invariably, there was always someone sending packages. They always took longer, sort of like being in a convenience store line waiting for someone to redeem their handful of winning lottery tickets. Nate hated standing in lines and was angry with himself for not planning better.

He walked down the sidewalk to the post office. He ended up tripping over a rise in the concrete. The sidewalks were old, with crumbling, cracked cement giving into the elements. The winter was never kind to the roads or sidewalks. The trees were also doing their damage as their old roots ran out of room under them, heaving the vulnerable concrete enough to make people watch where they were going in a serious way. Nate was angrier at tripping than at the condition of the walk. He was embarrassed and hoped no one saw him. No one likes to be seen falling. He kept on going, now more wary of where he planted his feet, and slowing down enough to notice things. This 'trip' was just going to take longer than he had planned.

He passed people along the way, all also in a big hurry. Some looked up, and if Nate caught their eyes, he would always nod as if to say "Hi, how are you?" Most didn't make eye contact, though, probably concentrating on their feet too. In the din of the constant traffic, people were yelling to each other, horns honked every so often, the street very much alive. As he was approaching the next block, he heard someone yelling loudly. It was a man, and a woman was yelling back at him. Nate heard them, as others did, but continued to finish his business.

At the post office he got lucky. There were only four people in front of him, and all were holding envelopes and not big packages. Like himself, they probably only needed to get stamps. He guessed right and was at the teller in less than two minutes. He bought his stamps, peeled, and stuck them on the envelopes, and flipped the envelopes into the box. Going back to his car, he took his time because now he had some to spare. But in his leisure, as he was coming to the corner, he again heard a lot of yelling. He couldn't make out what was being said.

Out of curiosity he turned down the side street to see what was going on. There were people around, but no one seemed to notice or care. As he was getting closer, it was clear to him that something terrible was happening. He heard the woman screaming for help, sounding desperate. "Stop it! You're hurting him! Oh, God, please stop!" She was crying loudly.

Then he heard a smaller voice begging for mercy. "Daddy, stop it! I'm sorry. I'm so sorry. I'll never do it again, I promise!"

The father screamed back at him, "You bet your ass you'll never do it again. Keep crying, and I'll give you more to cry about!"

Nate saw where it was coming from. It was a brick apartment building, surrounded by weeds, and people sitting on their stoops ignoring it all. This sort of thing happened every day in this neighborhood. He saw that a second-floor window was open. The closer he got, the worse it sounded. He couldn't help himself. He ran up the steps into the building and bolted up to the second floor.

The man inside was furious. "You little son of a bitch! I told you not to throw things in the house! How many times? Over and over and over again!" Outside the door, Nate heard what sounded like a whip, landing apparently on the boy, who cried louder and louder each time it cracked.

"Harry, stop it, or I'll call the police!"

"Get out of the way, you bitch!" Nate heard a thud, and the man continued ranting at the boy. "I'll tell you this, you will *never* break another goddamn window in this house!"

Nate heard the crack again. He was at the door, daring to try the knob. It wasn't locked. He hesitated, a voice in his head telling him over and over again to mind his own business, but he knew he had to do something. He threw the door open. They were all in the kitchen. He could see the woman on the floor, crying, clearly in pain. The boy was screaming. Nate got to the kitchen door.

He could feel the sting of the strap as it ripped into him. He was crouched on the floor, against the wall, curled up as much as he could to protect himself. The man was relentless, furiously attacking. "Do you think you'll remember this time, you little worthless bastard?" He cracked the belt again, digging in deeper with every blow. Then he stopped. No one was crying. He looked at his wife, who sat on the floor, clutching the boy to her, rocking him, soothing him. Then he looked down where his son had been cowering beneath him.

Massive confusion overtook him. He backed off, the belt dangling by his side as he watched this man rise from the floor onto his feet. He was bleeding through his shirt and in obvious pain. Nate turned to the woman and her son. He looked to be around six years old. He asked if they were all right. They nodded rapidly, fearful of what they had seen and in awe of this man who seemed to appear out of nowhere. The father backed up against the wall, dumbfounded. Then Nate looked at the man, and said, "You know, maybe this is how your old man treated you. I feel bad about that. Let me say though, don't ever do this again." Nate knew he never would.

Then he quickly left the apartment, walking briskly back in the direction of his truck. Behind him he could hear sirens approaching. He glanced over his shoulder and saw that they were pulling up to the apartment. Someone must have called 911. He turned and walked faster, knowing he had blood on his shirt. The walkway was fairly cleared out, so no one noticed him as he got into the truck. It was one fifteen. He was late, and Jack was probably pissed, especially if he had to wait on customers. Nate hadn't planned any of this. It just happened. It was so freaky, so much like the other night. He was shaking as he drove, trying to get his head around it, trying to focus on his driving, trying to focus on anything other than what just happened. He had to come up with something plausible to tell Jack. He spent the rest of the ride thinking about it.

Chapter 36

Nate pulled the truck up onto the gravel lot just as Jack was walking out of the store. He looked irritated as he came over to Nate, who was swinging his feet onto the ground.

"Where the hell have you been? For god's sake, you said you'd be back by one. Two customers came in during the last forty-five minutes! You know how I hate that—"

Nate interrupted, "Sorry man, I really am. I didn't plan on it."

"You never do," Jack said testily.

"Listen, I ran into a little trouble, that's all." Nate turned to close the door to the truck.

Jack looked at him and said, "What the hell happened to you? You've got blood on your shirt. You get into a fight or something?"

"Yeah, sort of," said Nate, trying to buy time.

"Did you win or lose? By the looks of you, you lost. Who'd you piss off, or who pissed you off?"

"No one pissed me off."

"OK, then where'd the blood come from?"

Nate, faking embarrassment, said, "My fight was with a rose bush … maybe two."

Jack started laughing. "What a klutz you are, Jesus, I thought you were really in trouble."

"Well, I was," Nate said defensively. "The lines at the post office were horrendous. I had to stand in line forever. I knew I was going to be late. It was almost one o'clock by the time I got out of there. I ran back to the truck, which I had to park a mile away, and ended up tripping on the goddamn sidewalk. I fell backward into this row of bushes, and the thorns didn't like it. I felt like such an asshole, but it took me a few minutes to pull the thorns out. What pissed me off is that all these people stopped and asked if I was OK. It was humiliating."

Jack was still laughing. "Oh God, that is *sooo* funny. I think I'm going to wet my pants. I can't wait to tell the guys down at the pub."

"Oh, come on, don't do that, man."

"Are you kidding me? This is too good a story. It needs to be told."

"You jerk," said Nate as he walked toward the house. "You're going to do what you want anyway."

"I'm so glad you accept that about me," Jack laughed.

"See you in a few minutes," said Nate.

Well, I think I pulled that one off. I hate lying to him, but he'd never believe me anyway. I don't want anyone to know about it. If this is a gift, I'm not sure I want it. I need to talk to my grandfather, maybe when I see him this weekend. God, I'm so confused. Just let me get through the day.

At the end of the day, after they had shut down the equipment, washed down the dust, and put most of the hand tools away, the two of them walked out to the yard to go their separate ways.

After some small talk, Nate said to Jack, "You know, I've been thinking about what you said."

"About what?"

"About getting some extra help. It's getting to be too much, and as much as I like meeting with the customers, it's not fair to you or to the business to spend so much time not working with the stone. It's not good for me either, to distance myself so much from the thing I do best."

"So, what are you saying?"

"I'm saying, I think we should get someone to work in the office, someone who's good with paperwork, balance sheets, and people. You said you could find someone fast. Can you?"

Jack, trying to hold back his enthusiasm, said, "Yeah, I know a couple of people that could do that. Let me ask around. It's a good idea, and I know it will be worth it."

"OK then. Let's go for it. Just let me know when you find someone. I'd like to meet with them before I hire."

"No problem. Most people would expect that."

"Good," said Nate, satisfied with the decision. As Jack was going to his truck, Nate said, "Hey, wait a minute."

"What?"

"There's one more thing. Something else I've been thinking about for some time."

"What's that?" Jack was curious now.

"Well, we've been working pretty hard over the last few months, and I think it has been going very well. *Very* well."

"Me too, so?"

"Well, Jack, I was wondering if you'd like to become a partner with me."

Jack was astounded. "A partner? You mean, a non-Bearing partner? What would your grandfather say about that?"

"He said it was up to me."

"Shit, man, I mean, I wasn't expecting this at all. I don't know what to say." He was clearly caught off guard. "Geez, that's a huge thing. I mean, I'm honored for sure, and believe it or not, I think I'm feeling a little humbled. It's an unfamiliar feeling to me."

"Look," said Nate, "the honor would be mine. We can talk more about it. We'll need to sit down and hash it all out with each other, and an attorney, but not today. Just think about it, that's all. Let me know as soon as you can."

"OK, thanks, Nate. My head is spinning right now. I think I need a beer."

"You probably do. Have one for me too."

"You got it." They shook hands.

"Later, Jack."

"Later," said Jack as he started his truck.

Jack was elated, so much so that he wasn't paying much attention to his driving. He almost ran a stop sign. He slammed on his brakes, the horns around him cursing at him. He waved an apology to the drivers around him. Cautiously crossing the intersection, he pulled over to the side of the road under a huge oak tree, his tires crunching the acorns on the ground. He just sat there for a while trying to calm down. He couldn't wait to tell Katie about the job and about Nate's offer to become a partner in the business. But he would need to keep it together. Katie was behind the bar that night, so he couldn't distract her any more than he usually did. He would also have to count his beers. Getting himself wasted tonight would not be in his best interest. He wanted Katie to believe him and not blow him off as the drunken Irishman.

After Jack had left, Nate decided he would spend some time in the studio. He hadn't been in there recently and wanted to reflect on what was happening to him. He sat on his stool in the middle of the room, turning himself around every now and then to stare at the works he had created. He locked onto the unfinished headstone for his father's grave. It still was in its rough form. The next step would be to use the bushing tools for shaping the harder stones, such as granite and marble. It would have been easier for him to use rasps and rifflers on a softer stone, but Nate never looked for the easy way out. He chose marble for a reason. The result would be enduring, just like his father's spirit. Nate wasn't up to working on it that evening. It was not something that could be forced, despite his desire to finish it soon. The creativity and energy needed to come from within him, and right now that space was occupied by something larger than life.

Nate went back into the house and into the kitchen. He had to eat something, even though his stomach was not interested. He threw together a tuna sandwich. With it he had some chips, as was his ritual, and a glass of milk. Once he started eating, he realized just how hungry he was and took his time to enjoy it. The sun had set. Instinctively he went out to the back of the house to perform a fire ceremony. He was acutely aware that something of great significance was happening, though he still struggled to understand why he was chosen. *Why not my grandfather? He's such a holy man. Or my father*, whose quiet humility seemed to Nate to be a prerequisite for being special in the eyes of God. Nate didn't feel worthy enough or strong enough to accept this gift. He was grateful yet fearful of what was to come.

When the embers died, Nate decided to go back inside to his room. He needed more time to still his mind and open it to any message he might receive. In time, he was able to let go of the thoughts in his head until there was a sense of nothingness. His grandfather often remarked, 'Nothing doesn't become nothing. It becomes something else.' Of course, he was speaking about stone, but Nate now saw the deeper meaning. Something else would emerge as a result of emptying himself to the higher realm.

In his trance state, Nate felt a surge of warmth throughout his body. It was comforting, as if he were being held. The energy entered him, and he allowed it to embrace him. It was life-giving, and he felt himself being filled and renewed by it. As he experienced it, the vision reappeared—the same three figures, same crystal being given to him. He accepted it, as he had before, and thanked them for it. He then dared to ask them, "Why me?" He listened intently for an answer. Walking forward toward him, the angel spoke. "It is you because you are willing to accept it. You do not have to. You chose it. Choice is given to all people. It is their free will. You can see pain in others and always wished that you could take it away from them. Now you can." Then the vision faded away.

Nate came to and got reoriented to his room. The smell of the sage lingered, and he was conscious of the sacred space that surrounded him. He still felt the energy flowing through his body and didn't want it to stop. He didn't want to lose the connection to the source of this experience. In time, it subsided as Nate lay his head on his pillow. He was at peace and wanted to stay that way forever. But that was not to happen.

He wouldn't tell Haley about this. Nor would he talk about his encounter of yesterday. The only person he could talk to would be his grandfather. But how would he approach him? How would he explain all of this when he didn't understand it himself? It was early in the week, and he wasn't due to visit his grandfather until the weekend. He didn't want to panic. But the things that had happened to him were so unbelievable. Were they just coincidental? He was so confused, despite the vision.

Jack showed up to work earlier than usual. Nate heard the familiar sound of his engine pulling into the yard. Nate went out to meet him. He had had his coffee and felt ready to get started. Jack had a bounce to his steps and was grinning ear to ear. He had been able to talk to Katie last night. They had talked for a long time, Jack telling her about the conversation he had with Nate that day. Kate was ecstatic and could barely contain herself. This was all too good to be true. But it was true, and she was easily convinced that it was meant to be. Jack approached Nate. Nate knew what was coming next. He usually did.

"Mornin', Jack."

"Hey, Nate."

Jack didn't hesitate to get into it. He was too pumped up, and he usually was up-front with his comments or opinions anyway. He tried to be nonchalant as he took a sip of coffee, and then asked Nate, "Were you serious about what you said yesterday?"

Teasing him, Nate said, "About what?"

"You know about what. Were you pulling my chain, or did you really mean that you wanted me to become a partner in the business?"

"I was serious. Aren't I usually?"

"Yeah, right. So, I talked to Katie last night. 'No brainer,' she said. She was so excited for me, and herself, too."

"Why for herself?" Nate asked with a fake curiosity.

"Well, for one thing, we've been talking a lot about our future, and, uh, possibly getting married."

"You're kidding. You? Married?"

"Yeah, me, believe it or not."

"Hard to believe."

"So, the prospect of me becoming a partner with you kind of blew her mind. She knows how successful we've been and knows that financially we'll be OK."

"I think you're right about that."

"So, I'm going to take you up on it."

"Fantastic!" Nate said, smiling and pumping his fist. "Yesss! I was hoping you would say that!"

"One other thing," Jack said, a little concerned that he was asking for too much.

"What?"

"I think I've found someone to help in the office."

Smiling, knowing what was coming, Nate asked "And who might that be?"

"Katie, man. She wants out of her job. It's getting old for her. You know? She wants to have a day job so, well, so we can spend more time together."

Nate, pulling him along, said, "Katie? She's a bartender, a great one at that, but we need someone who's good with people *and* who knows something about running a business."

"Then she's our girl!" Jack proclaimed. "You don't know this, but she has essentially been running the bar for quite some time. She goes in a couple hours before her shift and pretty much does the inventory and ordering of the booze. She's been helping her boss with the paperwork too. She's good with computers and knows how to set up balance sheets and schedules shifts for the other employees. She doesn't know everything, but we figure she can learn what she doesn't know. She's a quick study."

"So far so good," said Nate. "I didn't know that about her. But there's one problem."

"Yeah?" said Jack, preparing to be disappointed.

"I'm not sure how it would work out, the two of you being so close to each other. That can be pretty distracting. And what if you're fighting about something? Like, if you're not speaking to one another, won't that be hard to deal with if you're working together?"

"I work with *you*, don't I?"

"Touché," said Nate. "Well, if she's as good as you say, then maybe we could give it a try. Like, maybe a three-month trial, something like that."

"She'd go for that. I know she would."

"When could she start?"

"Well. If we can limp along for another three weeks or so, she could probably start then. Her boss has been great to her for a long time. She doesn't want to just walk out on him. You understand?"

"Yeah. That's not a bad thing. It would give me some time to at least get a little more organized. I wouldn't want her to start in chaos. Besides, I admire her loyalty. It's the right thing to do."

"So," asked Jack with more optimism, "is it a go?"

"It's a go," Nate replied as he watched Jack's reaction.

"Oh, man! This is going to be *so* awesome. *Awesome!*" he emphasized. "Just awesome! I can't wait to tell her!"

"You know where the phone is."

Jack, beelining to the storefront, stopped, and turned to Nate. "You won't regret this, Nate! I guarantee it!"

Nate waved him off and went over to the yard to begin his work.

Chapter 37

Jack was so happy. Nate had never seen him this way unless he had a few drinks in him. Jack was usually pretty jovial, the court jester. Nate knew it was a cover-up, and for the most part it worked. But this was different. It was genuine and Nate couldn't have been happier for him. It was Thursday evening. Nate and Haley were having dinner together. They didn't go to their favorite restaurant, even though he felt the place had the best food in town. Instead, deferring to Haley's whining, they went to a local Chinese buffet. Maybe this would be better anyway. After all, a part of him was Chinese. Every now and then he felt he should honor that, even though it was mostly the food that kept him connected to this part of his ancestry. Then again, his eyes kind of gave it away, as did some of his spiritual rituals. He just never thought much about it.

They went in and took a booth near the windows. The waitress came over, and with her quiet accent asked if they wanted something to drink. They ordered a pot of tea, while a young man set them up and poured them some water. The place was busy, even though it was somewhat after the dinner hour. Its location, right on the main thoroughfare, and the reasonable prices made it a popular place. Nate did like that he didn't have to pay an arm and a leg and that he could eat as much as he wanted. He usually went back to the buffet a couple of times at least. It always baffled Haley how he could eat so much and stay in shape despite it. In some ways it annoyed her that he could get away with it, especially since she seemed to gain weight just by looking at food.

After Nate and Haley filled their plates, they reviewed their week. Haley's job continued to put her under a lot of pressure, but not because of her workload. That was overwhelming, yes, but more of the stress came from the feeling that her bosses were excluding her. She continued to think that something sinister was going on. Nate, as usual, coached her to try and mind her own business and stay focused on her work. Whatever was going on probably had nothing to do with her. She always listened to Nate and felt reassured by him.

When Nate came back from his second round at the buffet, he shifted gears to lighten things up. He told her all about the decisions he had made over the past couple of days, how happy Jack was as well as Katie. Haley had met Katie several times. They had double-dated on a couple of occasions. Haley loved Katie's sense of humor and vivaciousness. She felt that she and Jack made a perfect couple, even though, like Nate, she found it hard to believe that Jack could settle down into a serious relationship. With the two of them working in the same place, with essentially the same hours, it seemed as though they were planning a future together. Haley even went out on a limb and bet Nate that Jack and Katie would end up married before the end of the year.

Nate had a hunch that Haley was hoping for the same thing to happen for them. He wasn't ready to make a commitment. Other things were happening to him, and he didn't know what to do about it. He didn't talk about it, the one secret he couldn't share. He didn't tell her about the incidents he experienced over the past week. He didn't want to give her anything else to worry about. Thus, he avoided the subject, steering the conversation toward plans for the weekend.

After dinner, they decided to do some window shopping not far from the restaurant. There was a quaint neighborhood nearby that had many small shops. Most of them were trendy and expensive. They strolled into a boutique for women. Haley loved to look at the dresses and shoes, and especially the accessories. Her mother had tended to stay away from window shopping. She'd say, *I ain't got no lookin' money.* It was true for Haley too, and she knew she was strong enough not to spend her money frivolously.

After browsing around, Nate took Haley home around ten o'clock. The next day was a workday, and as she often said, "I need my beauty sleep." Nate figured she always had enough sleep because she was always beautiful. Walking down the street that night, he noticed that some people were not endowed with features that made them particularly attractive on the outside. He knew he was lucky, and that's all it was. But he couldn't help thinking, *Well, maybe they just don't get enough sleep.*

Returning home, he went through the house and into the studio. He continued to look at the headstone he was creating for his father, but then fixed his eyes on a block of raw, unpolished, Blue Pearl granite imported from Norway. It had been left over from a swanky project at a local mansion. The owners of the mansion were not well-liked. Essentially, they were snobs flaunting their fortune. The stone was extraordinarily expensive and was used to create a fountain on the rise of their front lawn for all to see. Attitude aside, it truly was remarkable.

Nate was able to pick out stones from the discarded granite left from the construction. The crew knew him well enough to know that he was always looking for remnant stone. This one was about one cubic foot. It was a special stone. He didn't quite know what he wanted to do with it but knew that inspiration would come to him. "What seems to be dead is renewable," according to his grandfather, who also added, "Everything that comes apart releases something."

At some point the stone would come apart. At some point the stone would speak to him and bring him the creative energy needed to make it something else, something new. He looked at it for some time, turning it, examining the grains, looking for faults and cracks. Sooner or later, he would know what to do, but not tonight. He was tired and needed to go to bed.

It was Friday. He was more anxious than usual. Tomorrow he would go to see his grandfather. He would tell him about the events of the past couple of weeks and kept wondering what his grandfather might say. As preoccupied as he was, he focused on his work. Every now and then he would take a break, and so would Jack. He'd come over and ramble on about all his ideas for growing the business to compete with the larger outfits, how they could better market themselves, increase profits, etc. Nate let him talk and talk and talk, even though he had no interest in expanding. Jack's enthusiasm reassured Nate that he had made the right decision. Jack would give it his all.

Around noontime, Nate decided he would do his bank business that day instead of on Saturday. He wanted to get to his grandfather's place the next morning earlier than he normally did. He told Jack that he needed to do so, and instead of getting his usual exasperated attitude from Jack, he was surprised that Jack said, "OK. Take your time, man. I've got it covered here."

Geez, thought Nate, *this business has become personal to Jack.* He promised himself that he would see the attorney next week to work out the details for reincorporating the business into a partnership. Hopefully, within the month, they would be able to finalize the contract. Nate felt that there would be few problems in terms of the split. Historically he and Jack had like minds when it came to business. He couldn't necessarily say the same for their personal lifestyles, but Jack had promise, especially with Katie in the picture.

Even though noontime was the worst time to go to the bank, like the post office, it had to be done. If he waited until later, he might not make it in time before it closed. That had happened too many times before. He also knew that there wouldn't be anywhere close to park. He hated that, and often wondered why he went to that branch. But his grandfather and father both used the main branch, and everybody knew him there. Old habits die hard. He also hated going to different grocery stores, even if the prices were better. At his store, he knew where everything was. He could get in and out of there fast. He hated grocery shopping, and the sooner he could get it over with the better.

It was a particularly hot day. As expected, he had to park several blocks away, circling around several times until he saw someone pulling away. After parking, he took his envelope full of deposit money and walked to the bank. After endorsing a pile of checks, he stood at the end of the shortest line there.

When he left the bank he walked back to his truck. He felt the sweltering heat more as the air filled with humidity. His shirt was starting to stick to him, sweat beading on his forehead. He couldn't wait to get into the truck and pump up the air conditioning. On his way back, he passed a schoolyard that he usually didn't pay attention to. It sounded like most schoolyards. Even though it was summer, kids were playing on the equipment or playing basketball, the favored sport in the city. There wasn't room for anything else. Nate couldn't imagine playing it today. He'd probably die of heatstroke or a heart attack. Not that he was old, but he no longer felt the invincibility of his adolescent years.

Passing by the fence and half looking at the kids, he noticed a group of them standing in a circle closer to the school building. He could barely make out what they were saying, but it sounded like, "Fight, fight, fight!" He stopped for a minute to get a better listen. Someone was being taunted.

"You think you're so fucking smart. You're always showing us up, you fat little bastard!"

"Yeah, you piece of shit. I'm sick and tired of hearing my parents say, why aren't *you* more like Sam! He gets good grades, and he doesn't even have a father!" Nate could hear them all egging on the fight.

"Beat the shit out of him, Julio!"

"Yeah," said another kid. "Kick him where the sun don't shine!"

Nate could hear the one called Sam crying, begging them to stop. He must be on the ground, thought Nate, because the others were looking down. Nate couldn't see what was happening and was feeling bad for the poor kid. Sam was crunched over on the ground. He was scared to death that they would kill him. The blows were vicious, and he kept saying, "I didn't do anything! I didn't do anything! Why are you doing this to me?"

Then his voice sounded smaller and smaller and farther away. They all stopped dead. Lying on the ground was a man they never saw before. He was bleeding from his head. Then they looked over to the fence, and there on the other side was Sam, crying his eyes out. They heard him say, "Why do you hate me so much? I didn't do anything to you!"

Then the man got up and wiped off blood that was dripping down his forehead with his shirtsleeve. He looked at all of them and asked the same question. "Why do you hate him so much? What did he do to you?"

They all backed off, a couple of them looking like they could cry themselves, and all looking scared. One of them summoned up the courage to say, "He didn't do nothin' to us, man." From another, "No, man, I don't know why I did this. I didn't mean it to go this far."

Then another, braver kid asked, "Where did you come from, man?"

The others in agreement said, "Yeah, tell us, man. You're freakin' us out! It's like you came from outer space or somethin' … and how did Sam end up over there?"

Nate stood tall among them. He looked down at them and simply asked, "What would you feel like if this happened to you?" Then he walked away and went out to the other side of the fence where Sam was sitting, crying, and shaking. Nate knelt and held him in his arms. The boy cried even harder. "Where do you live?" The boy pointed down one of the side streets. "Let me take you home. You're safe now. They will never do this to you again."

Sniffling, the boy took Nate's hand and started to walk him home to his mother. Reaching his house, his mother opened the door. His mother saw him and began to cry. "Not again, Sammie, oh you poor child." She bent down and took him in her arms.

Still sniffling, he said to his mom, "It's OK, Mom. Superman rescued me," as he sheepishly looked over at Nate.

His mother could not thank Nate enough for helping her son. She invited him in for a cold drink and offered to tend to the cut on his head. Nate said, "No thank you, ma'am, I'm fine. Gotta get back to work, you know? Glad to help."

As she cried, she said, "Thank you so much. God bless you. You're a wonderful man."

With that, Nate turned and went down the steps and made for his truck. He was shaking, though he hoped he didn't show it. *This cannot be me*, he thought. He was confused but convinced that this was all more than a coincidence. Something had happened to him. He couldn't wait to get back to work. Moreover, he couldn't wait to see his grandfather.

Chapter 38

That night, Nate and Haley went to see a movie. Nate suggested it because he didn't want to spend much time talking. His head was spinning, and despite the trust he had in Haley, he didn't want to explain something that was changing his life, something that even he had a hard time believing. He didn't know quite how to handle it. His grandfather would.

Saturday morning came quickly. Nate slept well, undisturbed by dreams or nightmares. Before going to bed, he sat in front of his altar and released the day and himself to God. He asked for guidance and courage. He asked for a peaceful night's sleep. His prayer was answered. He slept well and was ready to go visit his grandfather. After a hearty breakfast, he took off in his truck and made his way out of town. He rode in silence and prayed all the way there. He was excited, but at the same time afraid. He was hoping that his grandfather would be able to tell him what he was supposed to do with this gift, and why he had it to begin with. He needed to know.

He arrived about midmorning. As he pulled his truck up to the cabin his grandfather stepped out to greet him, mug of coffee in hand. He must have heard him coming. Nate got out, went up to the porch, and shook his grandfather's hand.

"How you been, old man?"

"Fine. Nice weather this week."

"It's been hot as hell," Nate said. "What are you talking about?"

"It's never that hot up here, always a cool breeze."

Nate knew this to be true. There was no need for air conditioning up in the mountains. All his grandfather had to do was open the windows and doors, and the breeze would float through the house.

"You're lucky for that," Nate said.

"I am lucky about a lot of things. Want some coffee?"

"Sure."

They went inside into the kitchen. Nate sat down in his usual spot as his grandfather poured the coffee. He looked up at the ceiling and noticed a water stain on one of the beams.

"What's up with the ceiling?" Nate asked, pointing up to the spot.

His grandfather looked up and said, "Looks like another leak. I guess I'll have to fix it."

"No, I'll fix it. If not today, then soon. We haven't had a lot of rain, so I'm sure I'll get to it before much damage is done."

"Well, whoever gets to it first."

"You don't go up there without me here. You think you're younger than you are. Don't take risks if you don't have to. I'm back in your life and here to help."

"All right," said his grandfather, waving him off. That conversation was over.

"So," his grandfather said, feeling Nate's anxiety. "How has your week been?"

"Oh, God. It's been the weirdest week, and I need to tell you about it. I couldn't wait to get here. Something is happening to me. I don't know for sure what it all means. I'm confused, and frankly, scared to death. I haven't been able to talk to anyone about it. They'd never believe it."

His grandfather put up his hand and said, "Stop, slow down. Let us go into the living room and talk. You need an ear."

Nate followed his grandfather, who took his usual seat. Nate took his spot on the couch across from him, feeling uncomfortable and awkward. His grandfather saw this and suggested they center themselves. They started breathing deeply, falling into a rhythm. Nate felt himself relaxing, as he was now accustomed to, and let his mind be still. His grandfather then said in the quiet of the space, "Let us ask Great Spirit to guide us in this conversation."

With that, he lit the sage, blessed Nate, the room, and himself, and sat back down as the smoke from the bowl rose to the ceiling. Nate felt at peace and was much calmer. After a short while his grandfather spoke. "Now, Nate. Tell me about what happened to you this week." Naturally, his grandfather already knew about it. A few nights ago, he had a dream similar to this situation. He would just listen.

Nate told him about the man in the park, the boy in the apartment, and the boy in the playground. He told him that it seemed like what happened was out of his control. He said that every time it happened, he'd get hurt, but never seriously, and he always recovered quickly. Other people involved were confused, but so was he. At the end, the result was always good. People were being helped. But he never intended for this to happen and didn't understand how or why it did.

His grandfather didn't speak right away. He never did. Nate was used to this but still found it hard to be patient. He waited expectantly, knowing that his grandfather's wisdom was worth waiting for. After what seemed to be endless silence, his grandfather spoke.

"Nate don't answer this question right away. I want you to invite the creator of all energy to inspire your response."

After a few minutes, Nate looked up at his grandfather. Then his grandfather asked, "So, what do *you* think this is all about?"

Nate slapped his hands on his knees, demonstrating his frustration and exasperation, but he didn't act on it and said nothing. He struggled to sit back and get himself focused again. He knew what to do, having made it a discipline in his life. He concentrated on his breathing until his mind was clear and waited for the words to come and tell his truth. His grandfather sat and lit his pipe. He knew the answer but was forcing Nate to trust his own thoughts and to stop second-guessing himself.

Calmer now, he looked up at his grandfather and said, "I have been given a gift." His grandfather nodded.

"I have been given a gift to absorb the pain of others in order to protect them."

His grandfather nodded again and gently said, "Go on."

"I am being used to unblock the anger that causes people to hurt others."

"Yes, Nate, so far, you are right."

"But there is one thing I don't understand."

"What's that?"

"In the vision that keeps appearing, the three figures who I guess are Father Time, Mother Earth, and Michael the Archangel, are all handing me a crystal, always saying, 'This is your gift.' But, Grandfather, I have no such crystal. I know you do, but you haven't given it to me."

"That's because you don't need it."

"But then, why? Why do they give it to me?"

"What did I teach you about the crystal?" asked his grandfather, encouraging him to figure it out.

"You taught me that it is powerful, enough so that its energy can heal people, society, and even the earth. That it can reveal unstable or blocked energy, and as a result, clears the way for positive, healing energy. That's all I know."

"Then you know enough," his grandfather responded, satisfied that Nate understood.

"But Grandfather. I'm sorry," shaking his head. "Maybe I'm just stupid, but I still don't get it."

"Put it all together, Nate. Think about the vision. Think about the power of the crystal. Think about what has happened to you over the past week."

Nate thought and thought. Then it dawned on him. He looked at his grandfather with an astounded expression, confused, but not confused, uncertain, but not uncertain. It was so hard to believe that he didn't even want to say it out loud. He felt embarrassed because his answer seemed so grandiose. His grandfather knew that Nate had to say it in order to own this gift and the power within him. He then said, "So, it looks like you've found the answer."

Nate hesitated, "But I am having trouble fathoming it."

"So, tell me. What does it all mean?"

"I think it means, well, that I am like that crystal."

His grandfather smiled, nodded, took a puff on his pipe, and said with great pride, "Yes, Nate. That is your gift, and it lies within you. You have the ability to take in the suffering of others, and in doing so, something good happens."

"But Grandfather. This is so much responsibility, and I do get hurt every time."

"Yes, you do, but as you said, you recover quickly. You also have trained yourself to listen to the Great Spirit and to pay homage to the creator of all positive energy. You must continue to do this and trust that when you ask for guidance, it will be given to you. But there is one thing that you must always, always remember."

"What's that?"

"Always remember that your gift has the power to work through you in positive as well as negative ways."

"What do you mean?" asked Nate with confusion.

"You have the power to help people, but at the same time, you can also manipulate and destroy them. You must continue your dedication to help change things in a positive way."

"I can't imagine myself doing anything to hurt someone."

"I can't either, but there may be a time when you are challenged by it."

They sat in silence for a while, taking it all in. Nate was enormously grateful for being chosen to be this person. But he also needed to ask for courage because he was still afraid. He had to trust that he would be protected.

They had a quick lunch. His grandfather told him that he was going to take a nap. He would be going into the sacred space of his room and would probably be there for a while. Nate said, "And while you're doing that, I'm going to take a walk. I'll check out the roof too."

"OK," said his grandfather. "Tell the creek I said hello."

Nate smiled. His grandfather was showing off. Although it wouldn't be too hard to guess that Nate would be going down to his favorite spot. He closed the screen door, and went out to the back as he had done so many times before. He made his way down to the creek. As usual, above he saw his old friend the hawk. He sat down on the warm boulder. He let himself be absorbed in the sounds and smells around him. He felt like a part of it all. Truly, he was.

Chapter 39

That night he and Haley were double dating with Jack and Katie. It was usually a fun time, especially when Jack made the plans. On this night, Nate didn't want to do anything with anybody, even Haley. He would rather have spent time in the studio or in his room. But then again, it would be good for him to be around others, just to keep himself in balance. Besides, he would have plenty of time tomorrow. Haley was going to visit an old girlfriend out of town. It was a girls' day full of reminiscing and shopping. Not Nate's thing, and he wasn't invited anyway.

They met Jack and Katie at the county fair. It was that time of year, and Jack loved amusement parks. They agreed to meet at the dairy building. After some ice cream, they went over to the livestock building, spending a respectful amount of time looking at the cows and pigs and chickens. They had fun trying to figure out why one would get a blue ribbon over another.

Jack then said, "OK, I've had enough of this." Feigning a coughing fit, Jack said, "Ok, I've had enough. This place smells like chicken shit. I'm outa' here. Meet you outside." Soon afterward, they left and caught up with him.

They spent the rest of the evening working their way through the crowd, eating fair food, and going on the rides. Jack went on all of them. The thought of being spun around in a cyclone made the rest of them sick to their stomachs. *Jack's a crazy one all right*, Nate thought. *He'll do just about anything for a thrill.* Nate and Haley had the opportunity to talk to Katie for long periods that night as Jack did his thing. They grew fonder of her each moment and were happy for Jack and her. They did belong together.

They closed the fair down for the night. Jack suggested they go to the pub for a while. He didn't want the fun to stop. The rest of them, however, said enough was enough. He faked pouting, but he also knew that he and Katie wanted to spend the night together, so secretly he was glad to end it. All agreed that Jack was the champion of planning their dates. He held his arms up in victory, pounding his chest, shouting, "You are so right! I'm the man! I am the champion!" They cheered and applauded him. Eventually, when the laughter died, they made their way to the parking lot. On the way they talked about how much fun they had. Once there, they parted, and went their separate ways. Nate dropped Haley off at her place. Both were tired, so they simply kissed, hugged each other, and said their goodnight's.

The next morning, Nate allowed himself to sleep in. He was emotionally exhausted. As he lay there in bed, he decided that today would be spent working on the headstone for his father, meditating, and praying. He got up around eight, well beyond his usual five thirty. He showered, had a quick breakfast of oatmeal and a banana, cleaned up the kitchen, and then went out to the studio.

He went directly over to the headstone and knew what he needed to do next. He had smoothed it down enough with hand tools and now needed to polish it to bring out the beauty of the grain. He went over to the shelf that stored the sandpaper. Not the kind used by woodworkers, but the silicon carbide paper that was able to cut into stone. The polishing phase of stonework was the most tedious, especially when done by hand.

Nate put on his gloves and started to work with the coarse grit. He would apply water over the stone to remove the sheared off dust particles and get a better look at the grain. Turning the stone, he would do the same in another section. After the first go-around, he went to the next grit level and did the same. He spent hours on the project, making sure that the surface was evenly sanded. Eventually he quit, leaving the final polishing for another time. He was getting closer to finishing and planned on doing so in the next week or two.

It was dinnertime. Nate wasn't particularly hungry. Working with stone helped a great deal to quiet his mind, but as soon as he finished, his thoughts started churning again. He was going over and over everything that he and his grandfather had talked about. His stomach was churning too, but instead of making dinner he decided to spend some time in his room. He was hoping for some reassurance, but more, he was going to ask for more courage. He knew he needed to let go of his fear. He would eat something later.

Monday morning, he was ready to go and was in the yard before Jack showed up. Jack was full of energy, even before he finished his second cup of coffee. They talked about their Saturday night excursion and how he and Katie spent most of Sunday picnicking at a nearby falls. She had to work later in the day. Jack was looking forward to her having the same work schedule as his. She was to start next week. By that time, the legal filing would be completed, and the company would soon change names, from 'Bearing and Son, Inc.' to 'Bearing and O'Leary Stonework, Inc.' Nate had already asked Jack to find an auto detailer to repaint the signs on the trucks. Changing the bronze engraved inlay on the storefront would take more time, but Nate wasn't quite sure he wanted to do this. Too much of the family heritage was invested in it. Maybe he would have another plate made to place underneath the original. Jack would probably be fine with that.

He, like Jack, was eager for Katie to start. He wanted to spend more time in the shop with Jack, and he was confident that Katie could be as sensitive to the customers as he had been, if not more so. And honestly, the paperwork was getting to him, especially since the business was growing. Spending time sculpting in the evenings or being with Haley would be a welcome change from the many hours he put in after the workday on paperwork. He was convinced that he made the right decisions, not only for the sake of the business, but also for the sake of his own life.

It was a hot and humid day in mid-August. Sweat was pouring off him and Jack as they worked. They had to take more frequent breaks to drink water and to run it over their heads. Nate was amused when Jack said, "Aw, go soak your head." He did so with pleasure and told Jack to do the same.

In the meantime, Nate was frustrated. He hadn't gotten to the bank on Saturday and was relatively pissed that he would have to do it today instead. That would mean he'd have to shower and change into his business attire. Normally it took only a fast change of clothes and a face wash. Today there was no way he could get away with that. He was soaked with sweat. He also hated to tell Jack that he would need to cover for him again.

When he did so, Jack said, "Go do what you've got to do, man. We'll limp along until Katie starts, then she can be the one to do all of that. That's what she's been doing for the bar."

"Thanks, Jack. Man, I can't wait. I just hope I don't put too much on her. She'll want to quit in a month."

"Oh, you don't know Katie, but you will soon enough. She'll definitely let you know if she feels taken advantage of. But I don't think that is going to be a problem. You're both decent people and know how to work things out. She doesn't bitch and moan like I do, and you seem to put up with that pretty well."

Nate smiled as he prepared to leave the yard. "Yeah, I do put up with you pretty well, you temperamental Irish boy."

"Hey," Jack called after him. "She's Irish too!"

"Yeah, well, she's learned to control it!" Nate shouted back, laughing. And he kept on walking back to the house.

Chapter 40

Nate headed out to the bank. Even the air conditioning in the truck was struggling to keep its cool. Nate had it cranked up as far as it would go, but he was still sweating. Maybe if it were a longer ride, it would cool him off, but the bank was not all that far away. It was around noontime. Again. He didn't curse at himself as he usually did because he knew that the visit to his grandfather's was extraordinarily important. But he did hate taking the time away from the workday doing errands like this, especially at this time of day.

As usual, the parking situation was horrendous. He flashed back to the episodes he encountered on his jaunts to the bank and post office last week, though now he was convinced that there was a reason for them. He was secretly hoping that his day would be uneventful. He needed a break and more time to integrate this aspect of himself. He didn't feel ready to deal with anything else right now.

He got to the bank. Even the short walk soaked his shirt. He noticed that the same was true for most of the guys in line, but not necessarily the women. Their string straps and loose, flowing clothing made more sense to wear, but he had yet to see a man let go of conventional business casual. He could never envision it being otherwise. Women in general were smarter. They learned that they could wear pantsuits, especially in the colder weather, and be perfectly comfortable with it. Men dressed the same pretty much all year round. He couldn't see himself changing the mold either.

When he entered the bank, an eerie feeling descended upon him. His anxiety rose, and his stomach tightened up. He didn't know why. He just wanted to finish his business and get out of there. Once again, he found himself standing in line. Looking around, he spotted Haley four lines down from him. When she saw him, she was like a little girl, smiling, giggling, and waving every now and then. She would blow kisses at him. He returned a couple of them but wanted to remain stoic about it.

Suddenly, a man in a black sweatshirt and hood plowed through the doors and shot a single round into the ceiling. Pandemonium set in. Most of the people couldn't see what was going on. Nate's heart pounded. He kept his eyes focused on Haley. She shouldn't be here! His mind was racing. Damn it! She's never here during the week! Why today of all days? She probably didn't have time to make it to the bank on Saturday either. She had gone to visit her friend.

The gunman ordered everyone to get down. Most of them were already on the floor. The men in the place were all yelling out the same orders to protect the women and children who were there. The atmosphere reeked of fear and anger while the gunman menacingly swung the gun around and barked at the teller to fill the bag. Nate felt her fear, the fear of the others, and his own.

People were begging for mercy, and children were crying when the gunman said, "I don't want to hear a sound from anyone! Someone will die if you all don't just shut up!" Then he dragged Haley to her feet, saying, "Someone like you, you black beauty, you." And he pressed the gun into her forehead.

Nate's fear and rage erupted. He felt powerless as he watched Haley struggle with her terror. He was losing control, his anger overtaking his senses. He did not call on the Great Spirit to guide him. He was too attached to the situation. It was too personal. And his fear for Haley's safety overrode his ability to remain detached. His rage was nearly impossible to contain.

The police arrived. The masked man, feeling desperate, knew he was trapped. Instead of being able to flee, he was forced to hold his ground. In doing so, he tightened his grip on Haley, putting her in a stranglehold as he punched the gun barrel harder into her temple. He threatened to kill her if the police didn't work with him. Nate knew that the police had handled any number of hostage situations before, but he had no trust that they could save Haley.

Sweat poured from him as he lay on the floor. He was shaking in fear and anger. He needed to do something. The voice in his head was screaming, *Do Something! Do Something! You have the power! You can kill him! Be a hero! Be a hero!* But Nate knew it was not his time. It wasn't up to him. It wasn't the reason he was given the gift. *Be a hero! Be a hero!* He tried to push the thoughts out of his head. The more he tried, the louder it got. Finally, in his rage, he screamed out loud, "*Leave me!*" It did.

At that same moment, the man who seemed so in control of so many innocent people turned the gun on himself and fired into his own head. Instantaneously, another bullet ripped through the front window. People screamed in horror. As he died, he collapsed onto Haley. The others who lay close by on the floor had blood and brain splattered on them. Screaming out their terror and scrambling to their feet, they ran for the door as the police came rushing in.

While most people were fleeing the scene, a man who said he was a doctor went over to where the two bodies lay. As he knelt beside them, he knew at once that they both were dead and that there was nothing he could do. He wept in his powerlessness, slowly getting up as the police entered the building. They looked at him as he shook his head, knowing what it meant. Nate slowly approached the bodies and dropped to his knees. He didn't speak or move. In time, the paramedics gently pulled him up and walked him out to the ambulance waiting in front of the bank. As the sirens cleared the way, Nate, lying on the stretcher, was oblivious to the reality around him. His mind was floating in nothingness.

The media was fast to respond. There were two shots fired, though people swore they heard only one. The autopsies found that the bullets were from different caliber guns. One was from the robber's gun, the other was from a rifle fired by a sharpshooter from the SWAT team. He had lined his site up at the man's head and waited for the clear shot. He had it and squeezed the trigger at the exact same moment the gunman turned the gun on himself, jolting Haley's head into the line of fire. It all happened in milliseconds. It was a tragic accident.

The next day Nate realized that he was in a hospital. He heard the overhead speakers paging doctors, calling out codes, clearing the codes. He felt the IV in his hand and saw that he was connected to a bag of fluid hanging over him. The door was open, and the noise of heels racing along the hallway, beds rolling, and elevator bells ringing gave him that surreal feeling. He wasn't sure why he was there.

As he turned his head over toward the open door, in came his grandfather, Jack, and Katie. They all looked somber yet relieved to see him awake. They had been standing vigil, praying that he was not lost forever.

As they approached the bed, Jack was the first to speak. "Hey, Nate, how are you feeling?" They waited for his response. Still bewildered, Nate replied, "I'm OK, I think. I don't know why I'm here, but there must be a reason."

Then he looked at each of them and then around the room. Someone was missing. Maybe she was at work, though he didn't even know what day it was. Maybe she just stepped away to get something to eat. He had to ask, "So where's Haley?"

"You don't know?" asked Jack. He looked at Katie and Nate's grandfather as if to say, 'I can't tell him.'

"Do you know why you're here?" asked Katie with obvious concern.

Nate saw her eyes filling up and realized that something was wrong. He stared at them. As he continued to scan their faces, he then knew that something horrible had happened to Haley. Feeling frantic he demanded to know. "What's wrong? What happened to Haley?"

His grandfather spoke. "Nate, there was a man at the bank, and Haley ..."

Nate sprang upright. Suddenly he remembered what had happened. "Oh God, I was there. Oh God." He looked up at his grandfather as tears started to flood his eyes. Barely able to speak, he said, "She's dead, isn't she? Is she dead?"

His grandfather nodded. Katie nodded as she started to cry. Her heart broke seeing Nate cry. Jack was also fighting back tears. Losing Haley was hard enough. Watching his best friend crumble was even harder.

"I remember it ... I remember it!" His gut split open and out poured unbearable grief.

He turned away from them, his body crushed under the weight of his pain. He scrunched himself up, as if he were trying to hold himself together. The sound of his agony filled the halls. A nurse came in and saw the visitors standing next to him, the old man's hand on the back of the patient's shoulder. Their grief-stricken faces were streaked with tears. She looked at them, sadly nodded, and said, "If he needs something, let me know." The three of them nodded at her, letting her know that they heard her. The nurse quietly closed the door behind her as she left the room.

Nate turned his face into the pillow. *"Why?"* he screamed. "Why did *she* have to die? Oh, God, *why* did you take her from me?"

Pounding the pillow with his fist, he cried, "Why did you let her die? She never did anything to anyone! Why? Oh, God, *why?*"

His grandfather remained silent as he helped Nate empty himself. Jack held Katie as she cried into his shoulder, his tears dropping onto her head. After a long while, a nurse tapped lightly on the door. In her hand she had a small cup with a pill in it, saying to the three of them, "This should help him calm down."

Nate saw her and heard her. "I don't want any fucking pill!" Then he started to vomit. His grandfather went to the other side of the bed to face Nate.

"Take it, Nate. Your body is exhausted. You need to rest, and you aren't able to do that on your own."

Wiping the vomit off his mouth and nose, Nate grabbed the pill and shoved it in his mouth as the nurse gave him a swallow of water. "You happy now, old man?" he said as he glared into his grandfather's eyes. "Maybe I should just pray about it. Maybe I should focus on my fucking breathing!" he said through his sobbing. His grandfather said nothing, standing by as his grandson wept until he could weep no more.

Nate finally fell asleep. His friends were thoroughly exhausted as well. Nate's grandfather encouraged them to go home and get some sleep. Reluctantly they left, reassured that his grandfather would not leave him alone. His grandfather stayed, sitting in a cushioned chair next to Nate's bed. He was awake all night, praying and meditating, invoking all above him to surround Nate and cover him with their love and protection.

Chapter 41

Nate was discharged from the hospital the next day. He still felt the aftereffects of the sedative he was given and refused to take a prescription for more. Instead, he left with his grandfather, who brought him out to his place in the woods. Jack had packed a bag for him. After the funeral he agreed to go back to his grandfather's cabin since Jack insisted that he do so. Jack and Katie, who went back to work at the business, assured him over and over again that they could keep things going for as long as he needed. They prayed that he would come out of this and not close the business or himself as he did after his father died.

Nate appreciated the silence. His grandfather watched him closely, heard his cries as his grief poured into the night, and saw his bitterness as he struggled to understand. They ate in silence, sat in silence, and grieved together in silence. His grandfather felt Nate's pain as if it were his own, but he didn't take it away. Nate had to walk through it.

Nate kept going over and over the scene at the bank. His grief and guilt overwhelmed him. He should have done something. He could have done something, but no, he had to choose. He was enraged at God for allowing this to happen. He avoided temptation, and instead of being rewarded for it, he lost the person that meant the world to him. He couldn't understand what God wanted from him. It appeared he couldn't hang on to anything. Everything he wanted was given to him, only to be taken away. It was a cosmic joke. Nate wasn't laughing.

After a couple of days, he decided to go outside for some fresh air. It was early September. Stepping off the porch, he stood and looked around. The trees were just beginning to change color, but it was barely noticeable unless you looked for a long time. The air was changing, crisper at night and the early morning. But it was later in the morning that Nate ventured out, and the sun still warmed the day.

Nate didn't know quite what to do with himself. Time seemed to stop, allowing him to be still. He wandered around and reluctantly turned to the back of the cabin. He saw the fire pit and saw that it had been recently used. Very recently. The embers were still smoldering. His grandfather, who knows why, must have had a ceremony last night. Nate didn't spend much time thinking about it.

He was drawn to the creek but didn't want to go there. He knew it would draw him out. He had already cried so much. He was exhausted and defeated. He felt crushed by the will of God, the Great Spirit. He felt abandoned. He felt alone. Listening to his gut telling him to go down to the creek, he felt fear. It was something that he didn't want to do. He decided to go there anyway. There was nothing more to lose.

He slipped as he made his way down the path and swore out loud. It was just another thing that fed his humiliation. "It figures," he said out loud to himself. "Just when I think I'm getting back on my feet I slip on the goddamn pine needles." He stood still for a moment and looked at the familiar trail, resolving to pay more attention to where he was going.

He went to his rock and sat down. The sun was shooting through the trees and had already warmed his seat. The creek babbled along, saying nothing. Insects were still buzzing around, making the best of what was left of summer. He caught an occasional monarch moving through but not staying around. It was as though it knew that soon it would have to leave before winter set in. *Maybe it's going to Belize*, thought Nate. He still remembered the stories his father told him. Maybe someday he would go there to join the butterflies and the hummingbirds.

As he looked around, he started to feel his grief. There were still too many things he was trying to figure out. Too many unanswered questions. He started to think about Haley. He missed her so much. He didn't know what he was going to do without her. His gut rose into his throat, choking him as he tried to hold back. He couldn't, and the tears started to flow. At first, they were silent, so that the trees wouldn't hear him. The tears flooded his eyes like the rush of the water. Soon the wind blew, covering the sound of his grieving. And he let it go. His agony pierced the silence and frightened the birds around him. He fell to the earth and buried his head in his hands. The wind heard his cries and carried them over the world.

He begged God for mercy, as people often do. Hoping that, by some miracle, reality wasn't true. He asked for forgiveness, though none was needed. He wept to his God and felt consolation knowing that Haley's soul had risen to the place where it was born. In time, his tears subsided. He felt the energy of the Great Spirit within him. He knew that he was loved, and knowing that, he was ready to return to his grandfather's cabin. He would find wisdom there. He would find truth.

As he was leaving, moving toward the path, he heard something in the woods. He stopped to listen. It sounded like a mewing, a pathetic mewing. He went to the sound. As he got close, he heard the struggle of a suffering animal. Then he stopped. It was a young doe, frightened but unable to escape. She didn't move as Nate approached ever so slowly. He didn't want to frighten her more. The closer he got, the more she struggled to run. She was caught in some roots and she couldn't move. Nate saw that her right foreleg was bleeding. He started to gently talk to her, trying to reassure her that he wouldn't hurt her. She didn't trust him, but there was nothing she could do about it. Her fate was in his hands.

Coming up to her, Nate could see that she was shaking in her terror. He reached out his hand to touch her, and she flinched. He drew back and waited, and then he reached out again. He told her that everything would be OK, that he would help her. She let him touch her, and he put his hand on her back, slowly stroking her, gently comforting her. He looked at the wound. It was a serious gash, but her leg wasn't broken. He nonetheless felt her fear and her pain. It resonated with his. He put his hands on her and cried with her. She knew he meant her no harm. He wished that she didn't have to suffer and felt his own helplessness. He couldn't leave her this way, so he stayed, rubbing her neck and her back, letting her know she was not alone.

It wasn't long before she was able to extract her leg from the roots that captured her. She backed off, shook away her weakness and stood in front of him. She stood upright, her fear dissipating. She backed away, nodding her head as she withdrew. Nate looked at her face, and then at her leg. It wasn't bleeding anymore—there didn't seem to be any wound at all. He nodded at her, as if to give her permission to leave. With that, she ran off into the woods, kicking up the dirt under her heels. Nate stood in awe and knew.

That night he created a fire and invited his grandfather to join him. His grandfather followed Nate as he circled the fire, bowing to the south, bowing to the west, bowing to the north, and then to the east. He thanked the spirit of God, above and below. As the fire extinguished itself, Nate and his grandfather sat in silence. His grandfather looked at Nate and nodded. Nate smiled and nodded back. Nothing more was said.

Review Requested:

We'd like to know if you enjoyed the book.
Please consider leaving a review on the platform
from which you purchased the book.

CPSIA information can be obtained
at www.ICGtesting.com
Printed in the USA
LVHW110413200721
693166LV00003B/405